Anne Goring was born in Manchester. She and her husband, a school master, lived in Singapore for six years and travelled in Malaya and Hong Kong. They are now settled in Devon. Anne Goring's writing includes short stories, serials, and full-length novels. In her spare time she enjoys reading and oil-painting, when she is not afloat in her cabin cruiser.

Also in Troubadour paperback

THE FLAME AND THE FLOWER by Kathleen Woodiwiss
THE WOLF AND THE DOVE by Kathleen Woodiwiss
VOTE FOR A SILK GOWN by Jay Allerton
THE SEVENTEENTH STAIR by Barbara Paul
FALLS THE SHADOW by Regina Ross
POLMARRAN TOWER by Charlotte Massey
THE FLAME OF THE BORGIAS by Jean Briggs
THE BLADE OF CASTLEMAYNE by Anthony Esler
RENDEZVOUS WITH DANGER by Margaret Pemberton
A CROWN IN DARKNESS by Margaret Mullally
THE LADY OF WILDERSLEY by Josephine Edgar
NO MARKS FOR TRYING by Stella Allen
MOORHAVEN by Daoma Winston
THE QUEEN BEE by Phylida Barstow
LOVE'S TENDER FURY by Jennifer Wilde
SHADOWS IN THE FIRE by Eva Dane
THE MYSTERY OF SALIGO BAY by Margaret Pemberton

Anne Goring

Morwenna

Edited by Lesley Saxby

Futura Publications Limited
A Troubadour Book

A Troubadour Book

First Published in Great Britain in 1976
by Macdonald & Jane's Publishers Ltd.

First Futura Publications edition 1977

ISBN 0 8600 7460 9
Printed in Great Britain by
Hazell Watson & Viney Ltd
Aylesbury, Bucks

Futura Publications Limited
110 Warner Road,
Camberwell, London SE5

CHAPTER ONE

I know now that my father cared for me. For many years I held only the memory of his bitterness; a childish remembrance of his despair, of his blue eyes staring at me in reproach from a face gaunt and hollowed with neglect and sickness. For by my very existence I had killed that which he held most dear . . . my mother, Kitty. As I roamed the poor, bare hovel or played with the one toy I possessed, the wooden doll he had carved for me in a kinder moment, that remorseless, haunted gaze would follow me. Sometimes the pain was too much and he would groan aloud, the drink-slurred words falling upon my ears like a knell, 'Kitty . . . Kitty . . . why did you leave me? I am a man lost . . . '

I would run to his knee and look up at him, laying my hand on his scarred, blackened one.

'But I am here, Father,' I would say eagerly. 'And Mrs Pike will be calling presently. She has promised us a pasty for supper.'

But he would push my hands away and turn his face from me and grope again for the bottle by his side.

Yet, in the end, he proved his love for me was not entirely dead. For he gave his life to save me and though life to him was a sad and lonely thing, he would not have wished the agony of its ending. It took me many years to realize this, but when I was very young I was full of suppressed sadness when I thought of it and this sometimes made me morose and sharp when I wished not to be.

It was Maxwell Thurlow who killed him. Maxwell, on his

grey horse with its thundering hooves, sending chickens and dogs flying as it tore down the village street.

Our cottage stood beyond the village, separated and unvisited by any of the villagers beyond the kind Mrs Pike. It seemed no hardship to me then. I was a child to whom solitariness came naturally. I played my games of make-believe, sometimes for hours in the cottage alone, and as I got beyond babyhood I learned to cook and tend the garden. Mrs Pike brought me vegetable plants from the Big House and a broken spade, with which I dug the rough soil. I found great pleasure in watching the plants grow and keeping the birds from eating them and the village cats from scratching them up. From these simple tasks I find pleasure still. But then, the cabbages and potatoes I grew helped to eke out the poor fare which was all we could afford on my father's erratic wages.

I was out of doors that dusky afternoon of a late October day, a day of dampness and mist, the sky low and quilted with cloud. Dead leaves lay in thick, sodden swathes in every rut of the road and the hedgerows were laced with dew-hung spiders' webs.

I had been picking blackberries, gorging as many as I put in the bowl. I must have looked a sorry waif in my tattered dress and dirty bare feet, my face and hands stained by the juice of the berries and my black hair in elf locks about my shoulders. Yet in my funny way I was content out there in the quiet afternoon with only the piping of a robin for company and the rustling of wild creatures in the long grasses.

I had thought to stew a dish of blackberries for my father's supper. There was little else to eat beyond stale bread and hard cheese, for my father had found no work of late. Who would take on a carpenter who half the time was drunk and the other half surly and silent? Times were bad enough and there were plenty of sober, reliable men eager and willing. It seemed as though once again we should have to rely on Mr

Thurlow, who, out of some idea of charity or pity, did not press for the rent and had found work for my father over the years. This casual employment, mending a fence or repairing a byre, along with Mrs Pike's constant generosity, were the buffers against us and the workhouse, a word that fell coldly even upon my unthinking ears.

But Mrs Pike, of late, had been kept busy at the Big House where she helped in the kitchens when there were guests. Although I missed Mrs Pike greatly, I knew that when she came to visit us again I should hear wonderful tales of the happenings at the Big House and all about the gowns the ladies had worn and, best of all, maybe there would be something special and delicious to eat – a left-over from one of the dinners. I longed for ham, thick, pink and luscious, and wandering back along the lane towards home I could almost feel my teeth sinking into that savoury pinkness.

Perhaps such imaginations made me careless, perhaps I was just tired after a day out of doors . . . whatever it was, as I came to where our cottage lay, tumbledown and neglected, a little back from the lane and deeply overhung by high elms, I caught my foot in a rut and, in saving myself, dropped the bowl. The blackberries flew everywhere and I remember how cross I was as I went on my knees to gather them up. Now they would be all dirty and muddy.

As I knelt there I heard my father coughing, and looked up to see him standing in the doorway. He was unshaven and unwashed and his face was dark with the weight of his thoughts. I felt, at that moment, a deep sensation of pity that was mingled with worry. He looked as careworn as the house, and the cold he had caught some weeks ago, when he had walked all the way from Macclesfield in a storm after a fruitless search for work, had settled on his chest. The cough was stubborn and though he had rubbed his chest with goose-grease and taken some black mixture Mrs Pike had sworn by, it got no better and the bouts of coughing left him weak and spiritless. It augured badly for the winter, for the country hereabouts is open and hilly and the winters bleak and cold.

'What are you doing, girl?' he called querulously. 'Time you were indoors!'

I sighed. Whatever I said would not please him when his mood was black as it had been for these several days past. He had finished all the drink in the house, even to the crock of ale he kept to wash down his supper. There was no money left to buy afresh and pride would not let him go to the inn and ask for gin on credit. There was nothing to deaden his thoughts and his temper was touchy.

'I shall only be a few minutes,' I said, hastily groping among the fallen leaves. In my absorption I did not hear the hoofbeats, muffled as they were by the hedges and the dry-stone walls that bordered the lane. But Father heard them and called out.

I half rose, in time to see the grey horse, huge and snorting and mud-spattered, bearing down upon me. Surprise and shock held me to the spot, then I was grabbed around the waist and flung across the lane. I thudded down on the ground, the breath driven out of my body. The horse snorted and whinnied, I heard my father groan and a strange voice cry out an oath, but I could not move to see what had happened. It seemed a long time before a rough but not unkind hand lifted me and set me on my feet. I felt limp and weak and gasped for breath.

'You are not injured, I think,' a voice observed. 'Merely winded.' He gave me a little shake, as he might a puppy. 'Child, for your father's sake you must recover. This is your father, is it not?'

I looked up into his face. It was a face I had seen once or twice before from a respectful distance – the young master, as Mrs Pike called him, Mr Maxwell. I saw the jutting hawk's nose, the young and hard lines of his face and the curly dark hair that, however well groomed, always hung in an unruly tangle about his ears. I saw the long eyes staring imperiously into my own and I knew that, despite his coolness, he was afraid.

My eyes travelled beyond him to where his horse danced nervously away from the crumpled bundle on the ground.

'He is not dead, child,' he assured me, 'but I need help to lift him inside. Run and find a couple of stout men, and hurry.'

I did not need to be told. I flew like the wind down the lane. Never had it seemed so long a distance to the few cottages clustered round the church and the inn. A couple of women were gossiping on the green and turned puzzled, scornful eyes upon me when I ran up to them.

'My father!' I gasped out. 'An accident . . . need help.'

One of the women, the publican's wife, a long-faced shrew of a woman said, 'What makes you think *you've* any right to come asking help of good honest folk?'

'Please,' I begged. 'He is badly hurt.'

'Hurt, is he?' the other said with a laugh. 'Then let him tend to himself, as he always has done.' She drew her skirts deliberately away from my reaching hands.

I was almost in tears. 'But Mr Maxwell needs help to lift him!' I cried.

I had said the magic words. I saw their attention sharpen.

'Mr Maxwell?'

I poured out what had happened and they exchanged glances. 'I would do nothing for *him*,' the publican's wife said, 'but if Mr Maxwell has sent her I suppose we'd better do his bidding.'

It seemed an age, but in no time at all they had called a man who was scything weeds in the churchyard and enlisted a few men from the inn. I ran ahead of them back to where my father lay in the lane.

Maxwell had covered him with his cloak. I saw the ominous stain that had soaked through the good grey cloth. My father's breathing was rough and irregular.

Maxwell caught at my arm as I went to throw myself on the inert figure.

'Leave him,' he said sharply, then in a gentler tone: 'It is better if he is not touched too much, not until I can get a doctor here.'

'A doctor?' I cried. 'For Father? Then you lied to me! He is to die.' There was no doctor in our village and it meant sending away for him. People only did that in the direst circumstances; normally they made do with home-made cures and potions.

'I did not mean to lie,' he said, and there was a troubled edge to his voice, 'but he is worse than I realized at first. I thought Stamper had caught him a glancing blow, but I fear he must have trampled him.'

'You lied! You told me he would not die and now he will!' I was frantic with terror. I hammered my fists against his chest but he held me off easily, his big hand trapping my two small wrists together.

'A little wild cat, eh?' he said. His eyes were pitying. 'Have you no mother, child?'

'My mother is dead,' I said, surly now.

'And your name?'

'Morwenna Tregarth.' I hated this man who held me so tightly and would not let me go to my father.

He lifted his eyebrows. 'Tregarth, eh? That has a foreign ring to it.'

'It's Cornish,' I said. I shook back my hair, lifting my chin. 'My father always told me that I should be proud to be Cornish. Cornwall is not really part of England. It is cut off by a wide river and the Cornish are descended from great kings and queens who ruled all of England when the English were still wild men living in caves.'

I was repeating parrot-fashion what my father had told

me, yet I could see in my mind's eye that lovely, mysterious place that was Cornwall. A land of fairy castles and enchantments; a land of brooding cliffs lapped by seas of rich, dark blue.

Maxwell's mouth twitched. 'And you, I suppose, are the beautiful princess who will one day claim her royal throne.'

Temper gave me strength to tear my wrists from his grasp. I hated him to laugh at me, yet his laughter lasted no more than a few seconds, for the men from the village arrived.

They carried my father into the house and laid him on his pallet in the back room. Concerned as I was, I noticed the ill-disguised flare of Maxwell's nostrils as he stared round at the poverty of the cottage and no doubt caught the smell of it.

Before he left he drew me away from the knot of the villagers who, now they were inside the cottage for the first time and under the eagle eye of the young master, were fussing around my father, and pressed some coins into my hand.

'Here,' he said. 'Your father will need good nourishment when he recovers. I will send the doctor straight away.' He was anxious to be off, nervous almost. Perhaps the closeness of poverty distressed him.

I heard the clatter of hooves and stared down at the money. There was enough here to keep the two of us in food for weeks, but the money lay cold upon my palm. I vowed that I would take it now and use it for my father, but some day I should pay Mr Maxwell Thurlow back. I hated him, and would never, never take charity from him.

My father died after a long night and day. The doctor came and shook his head, spoke of broken ribs and a pierced lung. 'There may, too, be other internal injuries,' he murmured to Mrs Pike, who ushered him out and left me in the candlelight by the bedside.

Dear Mrs Pike. I hardly knew what I should have done without her. She came hurrying from the Big House as soon as she heard the news. She soon shooed the nosy villagers away and brought me food and made me drink warmed milk when I turned away from the slices of thick ham I had dreamed of so eagerly earlier in the day. From that day to this the sight of ham always makes me feel ill.

My father regained his senses only once. That was on the evening of the following day. He opened his eyes, looked at me and smiled. It was a very sweet smile, full of warmth and gentleness. That must have been the way he'd smiled at my mother but, until he was almost dying, he never bestowed it on me.

'Morwenna?' he said, in a strange, whispery voice.

'Yes, Father?' I said, holding tightly to his hand. 'I am here.'

'Morwenna,' he breathed again. 'So like . . . so like your mother . . . so beautiful . . . ' His eyelids drooped then flickered open. They looked at me strangely. 'Forgive me, Kitty,' he said.

'Father!' I cried. 'Don't leave me! What shall I do without you?'

But it was too late. The breath fluttered in his throat and died away. And even though Mrs Pike came up and laid her kind arms about me, I felt quite, quite alone.

Thanks to the generosity of Mr Thurlow, my father had a decent burial. The parson, a lanky, pale personage with a monotonous voice, said a few words over him, and Mrs Pike pushed me forward to drop into the hole the bunch of wild flowers I'd gathered that morning. It was a quiet place at the end of the graveyard, but at least it was not a pauper's grave. Though my father despised the clergy and had never allowed me to set foot in the church, I somehow felt that the funeral service in that windswept churchyard gave me some status in the eyes of the villagers who had assembled there whispering among themselves. More, I think, about the presence of Mr Thurlow and the conspicuous absence of his eldest son, than of me. For by now I knew that Maxwell had fled from the cottage on the day my father died because he was in fear of his life.

Mrs Pike had related all this to me as we sat before a stick fire in the cottage. She had wanted me to go back to the lodge and stay with her until the funeral was over and my future decided, but I knew Mr Pike for a dour, hard man, unused to children, who would not take kindly to an urchin under his feet.

'Father will not harm me,' I said shortly to her protests that I could not stay alone with only a man in a coffin for company. 'I will not leave him.'

She saw that I meant it and argued no more. 'You're a strange child, to be sure,' she said, shaking her head. 'Scarcely ten years old and with ways of a grown woman.'

I did not feel grown at all. The hard-clenched knot of fear and misery I concealed well. I did not even cry. I had realized on my father's death that to be alone and a child was to be vulnerable. I thought it best to hide my feelings from everyone, even dear Mrs Pike. That way I could be hurt no more.

'You see, Morwenna,' she whispered as though someone might be listening, 'hearsay has it that Mr Maxwell is in trouble again. That was why he came through the village like he did. They say Mrs Morton's Fanny was almost sent flying and her fate might have been poor Mr Tregarth's had she not been quicker. Riding like a devil out of hell, they said.'

'He was,' I said shortly. 'And if you ask me, he *is* the devil himself.'

'Tch. Tch, Morwenna,' Mrs Pike reproved me. 'They say he was gambling at a house on the way to Buxton and accused someone of cheating; whereupon this other gentleman ups and accuses Mr Maxwell of flirting with his wife.' She looked nervously around the shadowy room as though it could conceal an eavesdropper. 'It came to a duel,' she went on eventually. 'They met at dawn, with pistols, and Mr Maxwell was the winner.'

I stared stonily into the fire.

'So he killed two men on one day,' I said.

'Oh, this man didn't die,' she hastened to say, 'but he was wounded and much enraged. He has threatened to have Mr Maxwell's life, even though the duel was fought fairly, with witnesses. So you see, Morwenna, that was why he was in such a hurry.'

'And so killed my father.'

'An accident, Morwenna,' she insisted.

'True,' I said. 'It is as much my fault as his. If I had not dropped my bowl of blackberries . . .' My voice broke, though I did not cry. I would not let myself.

'You poor, poor bairn,' Mrs Pike said, lapsing into her strange North Country accent that had long since been overlain by the flat Cheshire one. 'What is to become of you? If I could take you in, hinny, I would. But Albert would never allow it.'

I thought of how different they were, Mr and Mrs Pike; she so round and kind and generous, he so hard and straight. It puzzled me how they had ever come to marry, though Mrs Pike had told me that she'd been glad to get away from the service of a harsh mistress and had married the first man who'd asked her. They had never had children and she comforted herself by doting on other people's. She always had a pocket of sweets to hand out to any child she saw, and a child in tears racked her. I must have been a godsend to her, a poor helpless two-day-old baby.

It was she who had found the wet nurse to see me through the first sickly months of my life and who had ensured afterwards that my father did not neglect to feed me. Oddly enough, my father had never objected to her quiet presence in the cottage, perhaps because, though she lived near the village, in the lodge of the Big House where her husband was lodgekeeper and groundsman, she did not belong to it. She was looked upon as a 'foreigner' like my mother and father, which was why she had befriended my mother when they had first come here.

'Slim as a willow wand she was, and pretty as the day, with her big eyes and black hair, but she was not strong and had been used to life in a good family. Life as a carpenter's wife, with little money coming in, was hard on her. Yet they were happy: so much in love that you could feel it in the very air that surrounded them . . . '

And my father had told me how like her I was. On his deathbed. I had never known that before. I knew from peeping in the scrap of broken mirror I kept that my eyes were dark blue, like my father's, and I had assumed that my other features resembled his. I thought I was ugly with my thin, pointed face, browned by the sun, and dark, straight brows. Yet Mrs Pike insisted my mother was beautiful. Should I, too, one day grow to be pretty?

'So what will happen to Mr Maxwell?' I asked aloud.

'There is talk of him being sent abroad to the Colonies, to friends of Mr Thurlow's, until the fuss dies down. But how true it is I cannot say.'

As the minister intoned the final prayers and the shovels full of earth dropped with a wet clunk on the coffin, I realized that Maxwell must have already fled the country – or at least gone from the village, for surely he would have had the common decency to attend the funeral of the man he had ridden down with his fine horse.

I could not bear to see the clay covering up my father like that. I turned sharply away from the sight. I wanted to run home, away from the curious eyes that surrounded me, away even from Mrs Pike. I took two blind steps and came up against an unyielding object.

'Do not hurry away, child.' The voice was like Maxwell's in intonation, but lighter, gentler.

'I was going home, sir,' I muttered.

'But you cannot go back to the cottage now.'

I tilted my head the better to see him. He was not as tall as his son, though his high hat made him seem so. He was dressed in black and his gloved hand rested lightly on an ebony cane with a silver handle. His face looked sallow in the morning light and there were pouches under his light grey eyes as though he had slept badly. But it was a friendly face, nevertheless, the mouth smiling under its sweeping moustaches and short beard.

'But I must go back,' I said, bewildered. 'There is nowhere else until I can find employment.'

'Employment, indeed.' The smile twitched and died. 'And where were you thinking of finding employment? What is it you can do?'

'I can cook a little, sir,' I said, 'and Mrs Pike has taught me to darn and patch. And I know how to grow cabbages . . . ' My voice trailed away. My list of accomplishments was miserable.

'Cabbages, indeed,' he said, fixing his steady gaze upon my face.

I shifted from one foot to the other in the too-tight boots that Mrs Pike had procured from the Big House. Miss Jessica was my age but far daintier. Her cast-off boots were an agony to wear and I longed to kick them off and plunge my feet into the damp grass.

Unexpectedly, Mr Thurlow drew out a handkerchief and blew his nose loudly. Then he cleared his throat, and when he looked at me again I saw that he was not laughing at all. He did not speak to me again.

He said curtly to Mrs Pike, 'Fetch her things and bring her up to the house this afternoon,' and he turned on his heels and strode away.

'I do believe the master's taken a fancy to you,' Mrs Pike said as we hurried back to the cottage. 'Perhaps he'll let you work in the kitchen, Cook could do with a bit more help. You're on the skinny side, but you're quick and learn easy . . .'

She had my future planned by the time we were home, and though I was in some ways glad that Mr Thurlow was taking an interest in me, I had a great reluctance to go to the Big House to work. I should never forgive Maxwell Thurlow for what he had done and my resentment spilled over and took in all the Thurlows, however well-meaning.

It took little enough time to gather my belongings. The cottage, now that I was to leave it, looked doubly welcoming, an old friend that would soon be abandoned and forgotten. While Mrs Pike bundled together my one other petticoat and my everyday dress and patched pinafore, I went to the back room where father's pallet lay stripped and bare. I went straight to the roughly-fashioned chest that was the only furniture, took the burned-down candle in its tin holder from the top and carefully opened the lid.

I knew exactly what the chest contained, for my father had shown me many times. The contents were very precious to him, for they were all that he had left that had belonged to my mother, and though everything else of value in the cottage had been sold when the need for drink was too strong to be ignored, he could never have parted with these few treasures.

I lifted out the cotton-wrapped bundle and, kneeling on the floor, opened it gently. With reverent fingers I touched the little hoard. There were two lengths of finely-made lace, yellowed with age; a pair of kid gloves, as creamy soft as buttermilk; a pendant made of twisted yellow wire with tiny red glass beads, and a small leather-bound book with gold lettering on the spine. This latter I picked out, letting my fingers slide over the smooth, warm surface. It had always held a particular fascination for me, this prayer book. I didn't know why.

I opened it and turned to the fly leaf to where the indecipherable spidery scrawls in faded brown ink ran across the page. I peered down at it as though willing my eyes to make meaning of the words. I had asked my father what was written there but though with difficulty he could spell out words, he always turned over that page quickly and became uncommunicative.

'What have you there, Morwenna?' Mrs Pike had come up behind me on silent feet and now her bright, quick eyes took in my treasures.

'They were my mother's,' I said, covering them over quickly. For some strange reason I did not want even Mrs Pike to see them. These were mine now, all I had left to link me with the first ten years of my life and the mother I had never known. To let other curious fingers touch them was sacrilege.

She looked hurt for a moment, then her natural understanding took over.

'Aye,' she said gravely. 'They will be dear to you, hinny. Wrap them well now and hurry. Mr Pike will be wanting his dinner.'

She gathered up the bundle she'd made and I held tightly to my treasures. I cast a last glance around, at the worn cooking pot on the cold hearth, at the rough sticks of furniture and the chipped basins we'd eaten from. Then I darted quickly to a dark corner and picked up my one other memento.

Mrs Pike smiled. 'You're getting too old for dolls, hinny.'

Nevertheless, I hugged wooden, battered Tiggy to my chest, along with my other treasures, all the way to the Big House.

The Big House had a proper name. It was called Ashridge Hall, although no one in the village ever referred to it as such. I had peered in through the gates and glimpsed it through the laced branches of the beech trees that lined the drive, and I had many times wandered around the circumference of the high boundary wall that surrounded the grounds. Sometimes I had climbed a tree or a rise of higher ground in order to look over the wall at the sweeping green park or at the expanse of glasshouses where, Mrs Pike told me, strange, exotic fruits and flowers grew.

But never in my life had I expected to be invited to go through the gates and up to the Hall. I had on rare occasions visited Mrs Pike at the small stone lodge with its crooked chimney. But my visits had been brief for I knew Mr Pike did not like me there.

Now we went in at the small side gate, for the large gates were opened only to admit carriages or horses. Mrs Pike bustled me into the lodge and made me sit quietly in the corner while she prepared Mr Pike's dinner, and when her husband came in, she beckoned me to the table.

Mr Pike frowned at me but said nothing as Mrs Pike poured out her tale of Mr Thurlow taking an interest in me, and how I was to present myself at the house that afternoon. But I could see he accepted my presence with ill grace, and when he finished and went out to the scullery to wash I heard his complaining voice. I supped at my soup with a poor appetite, half-listening to the grumbling and Mrs Pike's short answers. But one phrase he used quickened my ears. It was a phrase I had caught once before, when people had been whispering about me and did not wish me to overhear.

Then Mrs Pike came back and I forgot about it as she said, 'Hurry, hinny. Go and wash your face and I will plait your hair. You must look your best for Mr Thurlow.'

Half an hour later we walked up the drive. It seemed a very long way, though it took no more than a few moments before we came to where the drive split in two and formed a wide circle around a lawn that sprouted a tall statue of a half-dressed woman. She seemed to scowl down at me from her great height, watching me with her blank eyes as though to remind me I had no place here.

We did not follow the circular sweep of the drive to the porticoed front door, but went through an arch in a high wall that led to the kitchen garden and the servants' entrance.

My feet were dragging now, both with the discomfort of my cramped toes and a reluctance to go inside. In the cheerless October light, the grey stone walls of the house looked cold and uninviting. I had the oddest feeling that once I went inside Ashridge Hall I should never again be free to leave it. It loomed above me like a prison must to a criminal condemned to a long sentence. I hung back as Mrs Pike went in.

'Come along, Morwenna,' she said briskly, holding the door for me. 'Don't dawdle now, Mr Thurlow will be waiting.'

And because there was nowhere else I could go, I followed her.

Mrs Pike took me into a bright, warm room. I glimpsed a long, scrubbed table, a vast, black range with a crisp fire burning and, it seemed, hundreds of polished pans set on shelves. The room was full of people – or so it appeared to my unaccustomed eyes.

At first, hanging back behind Mrs Pike's ample skirts, I was not noticed.

A voice, the cook's, called: 'Oh, I'm glad to see you, Alice. Everything's gone wrong this morning and I'm fair worn out. You'll be staying, I hope, and not gadding off looking after some other poor devil in trouble. Honestly, Alice, your kind heart's taken advantage of – '

The voice broke off and another one, younger, asked in amazement, 'Who've you brought, Mrs Pike? It isn't the

Tregarth child, surely to heaven!'

Mrs Pike stood aside and pulled me forward. I stood there, wanting very much to run away and hide, but holding my head up instead and staring back as boldly as I dared.

A circle of pink, surprised faces surrounded me. Later I could give the faces names: the cook Mrs Hunt, Emmy and Hetty the parlourmaids, Nellie the kitchenmaid, and little Jack who cleaned the boots and fetched in coal.

Mrs Pike went into the story she had already related to her husband. Hetty and Emmy 'ooohed' and 'aahed' in all the right places, but Mrs Hunt merely sniffed.

'If the master thinks to get me help, he could find me something better than that.' Her small gimlet eyes in her plump face looked me over as they might an unsatisfactory joint of meat. 'Proper scraggy little thing, isn't she? Looks as though a hard day's work would kill her right off.'

'She's wiry enough,' Mrs Pike said calmly, 'and to my knowledge hardly ails at all.'

'Well, I suppose she must be hardy to have survived at all with that drunken scum of a father.'

I found my tongue then. 'He wasn't drunken scum!' I yelled. The noise of my own voice frightened me. It sounded so loud in that room. 'He was a good father!'

'Indeed!' Mrs Hunt's face flushed with indignation. 'I'll thank you to keep your voice down in my kitchen.'

'I hate your kitchen!' I shrieked. 'I hate this house!'

'Really, the cheek of it!'

Mrs Hunt raised her hand as though to box my ears, when someone behind her said coolly, 'What is all this shouting, Mrs Hunt? I could hear it outside in the corridor.'

She was a small woman dressed in black, a lace cap set upon her iron-grey hair. She spoke so quietly, yet the effect was electric. The two maids began to busy themselves and little Nellie positively melted away through a doorway into the adjoining scullery. Even Mrs Hunt looked a little flustered.

'I'm sorry about the noise, Mrs Bradshaw,' she said, 'but it's this . . . this child Mrs Pike has brought in.'

'She called my father drunken scum,' I said sullenly.

Mrs Bradshaw pursed her lips and regarded me. In that moment I wished I had never opened my mouth, such was the chill of her gaze.

Presently she said, 'You are Morwenna Tregarth?'

I nodded.

'You will answer, always, "Yes, Mrs Bradshaw" or "No, Mrs Bradshaw" when I ask a question,' she said in that level, clear voice. 'Now, I will ask you again. Are you Morwenna Tregarth?'

I did not wish to answer but something compelled me to say reluctantly, 'Yes, Mrs Bradshaw.'

'Then you will come with me.'

She turned on her heel, but despite her command I now clung to Mrs Pike's skirt. I dreaded to go forward with this frightening woman, into an unknown house without the one person I could call my friend. But even Mrs Pike deserted me then. She unfastened my clinging fingers.

'Go with the housekeeper,' she whispered. 'You'll be all right,' and she gave me a little push.

We went down endless corridors and across a wide, square hall with an elegant staircase winging upwards to a gallery, down another, grander corridor, then Mrs Bradshaw stopped and tapped lightly at a door, opened it and went inside.

There was a smell of cigar smoke and my hobbled feet sank into a deep red carpet. But it was not the carpet that took my eye, nor the big leather armchairs, nor the wide desk littered with papers, it was the walls, or at least what the walls were covered with. Books. Hundreds of them, rising shelf upon shelf to the ceiling. I had never thought to see so many in my life.

I did not hear Mrs Bradshaw leave the room, and only

when Mr Thurlow spoke did I realize he was sitting in one of the armchairs.

'Come over here, Morwenna,' he said.

I dutifully crossed the expanse of carpet and stood in front of him. He looked me up and down, but not the horrid way Mrs Hunt had done. I felt no resentment, indeed I let my attention wander back again to the bookshelves.

'You seem taken by my library,' he said, amused.

'Library, sir?'

'That is what a collection of books is called.'

'You have a great many, sir,' I ventured.

He nodded. 'I have spent my lifetime acquiring books. I may tell you, Morwenna, there is not one book on these shelves I have not read, and there are few gentlemen can boast of that.' He seemed greatly gratified by my interest in his library. I rolled the new word around my head; it had a pleasant sound. 'But now, Morwenna, to business.'

He rose from his chair and began to stride across the carpet backwards and forwards as he spoke.

'It is great grief to me that my son was the instrument of your father's death, even though it was by accident.'

'He was riding too fast,' I broke in. 'We had no warning.'

Mr Thurlow frowned, his hand tugging at his small beard. Without his hat I could see that his hair was not at all like Maxwell's but pale brown and thinly dressed across his scalp.

'He is a headstrong boy,' he said. 'A wild lad, yet I think not badly intentioned and there was cause enough for his flight, even though I would not condone it.' He sighed, adding half to himself: 'Too late he realizes his folly, but now he must suffer for it, as I must do penance for having him leave me . . . and it seems that the innocent must suffer with us too.'

I was unsure of his meaning or whether, indeed, he was talking to me at all, so I remained silent.

He paced the carpet several times before, abruptly, he halted before the low fire burning in the wide hearth. With his back to it he suddenly said, in a harsher tone: 'Your father was a very unhappy man, Morwenna.'

'He was, sir,' I said, surprised. 'The villagers said he was wicked because he drank too much, but he only did that to forget his misery.'

'I remember when he was not like that,' Mr Thurlow said, unexpectedly, 'when he came here looking for work. An eager young man he was then, a hard worker, anxious to make a home for your mother. They had travelled then a long way from their home county and your mother was weary with it all, yet she never lost her smile or that lovely glow that drew everyone to her. I was intrigued, too, because they seemed such an ill-matched couple. He, though a willing worker and devoted to her, was rough and uneducated and she was a woman of breeding. It was so obviously a love match and I, having knowledge of how splendid a marriage can be when both partners are . . . suited to one another, gave your father work on the new stables I was having built, out of sympathy.'

He paused, then added curtly: 'It was for the memory of those happier days that I allowed myself to be lenient with him over the matter of the rent, and tried to help him with work when he was sober enough to attend to it. For I know how much he suffered when your mother died . . . and he did not have the advantages that I had to cope with tragedy.'

He seemed almost to have forgotten my presence as his mind cast back into the past. Had I not known something of his history, all this might not have made sense, but Mrs Pike had told me often enough how devoted Mr Thurlow had been to his first wife, Maxwell's mother, a wild, proud, beautiful woman, who had been thrown from her horse and killed when Maxwell was six years old.

'Well, Morwenna,' he said more briskly, 'now we have to

decide your future.'

I stared down at the toes of the hated boots. The fright that had overcome me when I first entered the house, and which had been lulled somewhat in this pleasant, strange room, now flooded back. I dreaded to hear the words that would send me to work in the kitchen with Mrs Hunt, who had spoken so nastily to me and whom I disliked on sight.

'I believe,' he went on, 'I can find a place for you somewhere in my household. You seem a sharp enough child and have already learned to face up to the realities of life, even if you are unschooled in other ways. The only other alternative is a foundling home and, from what I hear, many of those whose motto is charity scarcely live up to the word.'

Something in my dejected stance halted him.

'But do not look so frightened, Morwenna,' he said gently, 'I would not let you go to one of those places. After all, I must hold myself partly responsible for your situation now. Had I been more strict with my son, less tolerant of his wilfulness, your father might still be alive. But what is past is done with; we must not dwell on it.'

He put his hand under my chin and raised it so that I was forced to look at him.

'I want to help you, child. Because you are poor and very young and alone, life will not be easy for you. But I should like you to have some trade or occupation at your fingertips as that will ease your path when you are older.' He smiled benevolently. 'Now tell me, Morwenna, what would you most like to do?'

I was still holding my bundle of treasures. I could feel the hard edges of the prayer book pressing through my thin dress into my ribs.

The words spilled out as of their own volition. I spoke them not knowing that the audacity of them would strike Mr Thurlow's fancy, that by that one short sentence I bound myself to Ashridge Hall for life.

'Please, sir,' I said, 'I should like to learn to read.'

And that was how, in 1842, I came to live at the Big House.

CHAPTER TWO

'Morwenna! Morwenna! Where are you hiding yourself?' Jessica's voice came to me faintly. I sighed and laid down my pen. I should get no peace until she had found me and bubbled out whatever news she considered so urgent that it would not wait until I had finished my work for the morning.

Not that she considered what I did to be of any importance.

'You have no need to do it at all, Morwenna,' she would pout, when she wanted me to partner her in a hand of cards or accompany her on some errand. 'Burying yourself in here with all Papa's dull old books, just because he once happened to mention that his library needed cataloguing! You took a casual remark too seriously.'

'Your papa is very pleased that I am doing it,' I would answer. 'And don't forget I owe him a great deal. This is one small way that I can repay him.'

'Morwenna, you are so solemn sometimes. I can quite see why Papa thought I should mend my scatterbrained ways if you were my constant companion.' She would laugh deliciously because nothing displeased Jessica for long. 'I declare you grow more like our governess each day. Just wait, you will end by being a dry old spinster like Miss Webster, destined to teach other people's horrid children.'

'You admit, then, that you are horrid?'

'You know quite well what I mean,' she would say in mock exasperation. 'Young gentlemen like a cheerful countenance and a light-hearted manner. Mamma has told us many times. You will only put them off with your grave looks.'

'Then there will be that many more to adore you, Jessica dear,' I would say lightly, swallowing down the retort that came so clearly into my mind – that the mammas of the young gentlemen likely to come to this house would not be at all pleased for them to fall in love with a young woman of my parentage. 'Besides, Miss Webster is not a dried-up old spinster. She is a clever woman.'

I stood up and stretched my arms wide, noticing for the first time since I had entered the library how lovely the day had grown. I went to the window. The sky was cloudless, and sunlight flooded the lawns and terraces that led to the oval pond where the two stone cherub boys held conch shells aloft, dappling the water with a fine silver spray. I loved those two cherubs as much as I disliked the severe stone goddess by the front door. Often in my early days at Ashridge Hall, when I was heartsick and frightened, I had run to the pond and hidden under the bending fronds of the willow tree. From there, hidden as I was from all human eyes and protected by the tree's branches, I had talked to the cherubs as though they were real baby angels. And though they never moved or acknowledged my presence, I thought sometimes that their smiles were gentler and their chubby hands wished to reach out to me, and I was comforted.

It was a long time since I had felt the need to confide in them, but now the scent of the yellow roses wafting from the open window gave me a yearning to be out in the air.

Jessica's voice had faded away. No doubt she had gone up to my room, for I had told her earlier that I would be spending the morning sewing, but I had soon tired of that. I was a poor hand with the needle. Try as I might, stitches grew irregular and seams like a meandering river. As Mrs Thurlow so often sweetly pointed out, the more delicate, feminine arts were not for me. I was as clumsy on the pianoforte as I was with the needle, and though I longed to be able to sketch and paint all the beauty of nature around me, my water-colours were mere daubs compared with Jessica's delicate creations.

'Morwenna is quite clever in other ways,' Mrs Thurlow would say to her friends. 'Miss Webster has a high opinion of her intellectual qualities.' It was odd how she made that sound vaguely distasteful. Not that I cared. As long as I could bury myself in books, I could forget all the slights Mrs Thurlow heaped upon me and the condescension of her friends. There was so much to learn, so much knowledge about other places, other people, the world in which we lived, its history . . .

I went swiftly through the quiet house, across the galleried entrance hall with its portraits of earlier Thurlows staring down at me from the panelled walls and through the garden door of the music room. This way I could slip through the Yew Walk unobserved from the house.

The air brushed like warmed silk against my face as I went between the high, dark-green walls of yew. Jessica would be delighted now that the weather was settling at last. May had been so cold and stormy that she had grown quite dispirited, despite my assurances that there was plenty of time for a change in the weather.

'It will spoil everything if it rains,' she had wailed. 'We shall not be able to have the Chinese lanterns in the gardens nor open the big doors of the drawing-room and have dancing on the terrace.'

'Whatever the weather, you will enjoy every moment,' I had assured her, 'so don't get into a fret about things you cannot alter.'

It was to be a grand party. Mrs Thurlow had been in a flurry of excitement for weeks and Mr Thurlow, when he was at home, closeted himself for longer and longer hours in his library in order to escape the fuss. Invitations had been sent out, menus planned, music arranged, decorations discussed, rooms aired for those guests who would be staying, and in ten days' time Jessica would be launched into society on the occasion of her eighteenth birthday.

By contrast, my own eighteenth birthday had slipped quietly by two months ago. There had been gifts from the family, of course: a beaded purse from Jessica, a bottle of lavender water from Mrs Thurlow and a gold sovereign from Mr Thurlow – all gifts most suitable for a young woman in my situation.

I walked from the shade of the yews and across the lawn, my soft slippers making imprints on grass that was still dewy. I lifted the skirts of my plain brown dress and sank down on to the stone rim of the pond, dabbling my fingers in the water to bring the tame, fat goldfish hurrying to me.

I knew I should not envy Jessica, but I did. It was wrong, because I had so much to be grateful for. Mr Thurlow was a dear, kind man and through his charity I had received a decent education and the upbringing of a gentlewoman. I was fond of Jessica, to whom I had been a playmate, schoolfriend and confidante through our growing years. In Miss Webster, our governess, I had found a kindred spirit. Yet others in the household did not look on me so kindly. The domestic staff were either openly hostile, like Mrs Hunt, the cook, or watched me with sly eyes, like the housemaids, as though to say, 'There she goes with her airs and graces, but *we* know where she came from.'

Mrs Thurlow, of course, had never quite forgiven me for my first horrendous appearance in her private sitting-room. She had been gossiping cosily with the ladies who were staying as guests at that time, when Mr Thurlow, excited by this novel idea that had seized him, had broken in upon her, dragging me with him.

'My dear,' he had exclaimed, 'this is Morwenna, and I have decided it is our duty to educate her.'

I remember the short, astounded silence when all those

elegant, silk-and-satin clad ladies had frozen their glances upon me in that overheated, overscented room. I wished for nothing more than that the floor would open and swallow me.

Amid an outburst of whispers Mrs Thurlow rose slowly to her feet. In that moment she was magnificently cool.

'Why, Henry,' she said, 'you quite astonish me with your generosity.' She turned to her friends, quelling the rippling whispers with a calm glance. 'I tell him often,' she remarked conversationally, 'that he is kind-hearted to the point of foolishness. But it is an admirable trait in a man, is it not?'

And the ladies had been bound to agree that it was.

Mr Thurlow had then announced that I was to be clothed in decent garments immediately and be taken into the care of the governess, and would his dear Winifred make the necessary arrangements?

'Of course,' said Mrs. Thurlow. 'I will send for Miss Webster this instant.'

It was only later, Mrs Pike whispered to me afterwards, that Mr and Mrs Thurlow had had a fierce and bitter quarrel about my presence in the Hall, their angry voices upraised in the drawing-room, while the housemaids hovered wide-eyed outside. But Mr Thurlow had remained adamant, despite Mrs Thurlow's demands that I should be despatched to the workhouse forthwith and that I was no fit companion for a delicately reared child. Besides which I would be a constant reminder to everyone of Maxwell's hasty flight from the country.

When she saw that Mr Thurlow would not be moved, she put a brave face on it to her friends and in private made sure I did not forget that I was in the Hall on sufferance. However, as the years went by and I proved amenable and willing, she grew accustomed to my presence. She was also much mollified by the fact that I was not pretty and had few social graces. By contrast, Jessica appeared more delightful than ever, and the charming talents she possessed for singing and playing the pianoforte and for needlework shone more brightly against my odd predilection for books and reading. Mrs Thurlow saw to it that I was dressed always in dull, sober colours so that the delicate pastel shades that went so well with Jessica's blonde colouring always showed to advantage when we were together.

'Those pale colours do nothing for Morwenna,' she exclaimed tartly to Mrs Ackroyd, the dressmaker, who had once or twice suggested that perhaps the pale blue muslin or the lemon silk might suit Miss Tregarth for summer. 'No. Morwenna has far too sallow a complexion. You need a pretty rose and white colouring to carry pastels well.'

A little breeze blew the flying drops from the cherubs' conch shells across my face. I lifted my fingers from the water and laid them on the warm stone of the pond's rim. The cherubs smiled at me as though begging me to tell them why I was troubled.

Though I was too old for such nonsense I said aloud, 'I have much to be thankful for, but there is a restlessness in me which is hard to explain or understand. I feel . . . insecure . . . unsettled . . . and I wish I knew what the future held for me . . .'

They had come often into my mind in recent weeks, these slithery little thoughts. I could not help comparing Jessica's situation with my own. She would soon be plunged into the social round of local society. It was her right, her heritage. It was quite likely that by summer's end she would have found herself a rich and personable husband.

And where should I look to find a marriage partner? Certainly not among the young men Jessica would be meeting. Who would have eyes for a dowdy and fortuneless orphan? Where then? The village? I shuddered at the thought. They had disliked me when I was the poor child of a drunkard, and now they hated me because I had been plucked from poverty and set above them.

No. I could not see that I would ever marry. So what would happen to me? Would I be allowed to stay at Ashridge Hall? Or remain a companion to Jessica when she married, as she surely would? Or would I end as a governess like Miss Webster, looking after the spoiled children of the rich?

I sighed and the cherubs smiled and did not answer. It was as I thought: their magic was all gone now, they could offer no comfort or help.

'There you are, Morwenna!'

I had been so absorbed in my thoughts that she had come upon me unnoticed.

'I have searched high and low for you,' Jessica cried, flinging herself down beside me in a flurry of lavender flounces. 'I have the most exciting news to tell you!'

Her face was aglow, her eyes sparkling. She really was an attractive little creature with her pale curls, her rosy, smiling mouth and cornflower blue eyes. I smiled at her fondly.

'It must be urgent to bring you out without your parasol. Your mamma will not be pleased if you have a sunburnt nose for your party.'

'Then I shall blame it entirely on you,' she said with asperity, 'for making me rush out of doors to find you. Now do *listen*, Morwenna, for I swear you will be as thrilled as I when you hear what I have to say.'

She wafted a sheet of paper under my nose.

'Can you not guess? It is the thing I most longed for all this time.' Then, unable to contain herself any longer, she rushed on: 'It is Maxwell. He is coming home and hopes to be here in time for my birthday.' She danced to her feet and did a little pirouette on the grass. 'And there is more!'

'More?' I said faintly.

'He is engaged to be married and is returning to England with his bride-to-be, a Miss Isabel Pritchard!' She sighed ecstatically. 'I could not have wished for a better birthday gift.'

'I am delighted for you, Jessica,' I said quietly, staring down at the fish moving so tranquilly among the still, brown weeds.

'It is such a romantic attachment,' Jessica went on. 'They only met on the ship on which they were travelling from Singapore to England; and now they are touring the Continent as Miss Pritchard has never been out of the East Indies since she was a child. Her papa is with them, of course. He is a rich merchant and Maxwell is bringing them both to Ashridge Hall in order to meet the family.'

Something startled the fish and they suddenly threshed at the water with their tails, diving away under the lily pads in a flurry. The movement gave a sinister quality to the weeds that eddied about in the disturbed water, long, brown tendrils groping like thin, boneless fingers. The sight gave me a curious sense of unease, and despite the warm sun I felt a sudden chill.

'Maxwell says Miss Pritchard is very beautiful.' Jessica's head was bent over the letter and she had not noticed how I shivered. 'See, here is what he writes: *"She has hair the colour of a new-minted penny, a glorious burnished copper, and despite her years in the East, the palest alabaster complexion."* Is that not an elegant turn of phrase, Morwenna? I think Maxwell must be deeply in love with her.'

'I am sure he is,' I said. 'And I am glad for your papa's sake that Maxwell is coming home.'

'There is a letter for Papa, too. I am longing for him to return from Manchester and to see the expression on his face when he hears the news. He has been urging Maxwell to come home for so long now. Why, it is almost eight years since we have seen him . . . how I loved him when I was a little girl. He was such a tease, yet so kind when I took a tumble or was in a pet about something . . . 'She broke off suddenly, her eyes flicking wide and her small teeth catching at her lower lip. 'Oh, Morwenna,' she whispered, 'I – I quite forgot . . . about what happened. About your father.' She put out her hand and laid it sympathetically on my arm. 'Will Maxwell's homecoming bring back a lot of unhappy memories to you?'

I was touched by her perception, for Jessica did not usually think too deeply about anything.

I smiled and said as calmly as I could, 'That is all in the past, Jessica. I shall feel nothing but pleasure when the family is reunited once more.'

Jessica gave me an enthusiastic hug, all dimples again now that this small cloud had been removed from her horizon.

'How sensible you are, Morwenna,' she said, 'and I am sure you will like Maxwell when you get to know him.' She laughed happily. 'He was a wild one, true, when he was younger, but I think it was more from high spirits than from wickedness. Mamma did not approve of Maxwell at all and told him so often. I sometimes think he was deliberately reckless in order to provoke her.'

'Eight years is a long time,' I said. 'He will have changed, no doubt.'

'I expect so,' Jessica said, almost wistfully. 'But I do hope he has not taken his role as a prosperous businessman too seriously and become as dull and pompous as some of Papa's acquaintances.'

'He made his fortune only after many hardships,' I said lightly. 'He will have exciting tales to tell you.'

'Of course he will.' She laughed. 'And twenty-seven is not *so* elderly, is it, Morwenna? He surely will not have grown too staid.'

'Surely not,' I agreed, standing up and shaking out my skirts. 'I believe Mrs Ackroyd is expecting us for a fitting before luncheon. We had better not keep her waiting.'

Jessica chattered on as we walked decorously back to the house, which lay tranquil under the pale arch of the sky, the sun mellowing the harsh grey stone of its walls. A large and elegant house. I wondered if it would look small now to Maxwell Thurlow, who had seen Indian palaces and Chinese temples and had dined with Sultans and statesmen. It seemed a trifle ironic that he had been sent abroad almost as a punishment, yet had fallen on his feet quite miraculously.

He had gone to America at first, to stay with friends of Mr Thurlow, but his restlessness had carried him farther. He had not stayed with them long but gone to seek his fortune in the Far West, prospecting for gold. He had found nothing and had then worked his passage on a ship sailing for Australia. From there he had travelled to Java and had met there a dealer in silks and spices who had taken a liking to him. Maxwell had thrown in his lot with this man, the business had flourished and diversified and now he was a partner in a well-found firm with outlets throughout the East Indies.

And soon he was to return. I was repelled by the thought. For all my reassurances to Jessica, the old bitterness had been re-awakened and I wondered, too, if it would bring with it the nightmares that had haunted me during the early months I had spent at Ashridge Hall. The wild hooves, the sweating, mud-spattered horse, the groans of the felled man, my own stunned helplessness, had woven the fabric of my dreams, so that I had woken sobbing and afraid. The nightmare, of recent years, had occurred only when I was worried or upset, but the remembrance of that dreadful October afternoon still lingered in the far corners of my mind.

It seemed cool in the house, and dark. We walked up the curved flight of stairs from the hall and at the top I paused, my eyes involuntarily meeting the steady, dark gaze of Thérèse Thurlow. From the sombre background of the painting, the smooth oval of her face gleamed in soft ivory flesh tints. How handsome she was, and how Mr Thurlow must have loved the sensuous curve of her mouth, the tumbling, careless black tresses of her hair, the haughty tilt of her chin. The portrait was a formal one but the artist had managed to convey a sense of devil-may-care arrogance, a certain exotic foreignness that must have clung to this half-Spanish, half-Irish beauty in real life.

And those eyes, long and dark and faintly mocking, I had seen them in another face. They had looked down at me from Maxwell Thurlow's great height. I wondered how she felt now that her son was returning to Ashridge Hall and bringing with him a soon-to-be bride. Then as Jessica and I walked along the gallery to our rooms, I smiled to myself for indulging in such fancies. Thérèse Thurlow was long in her grave. Even so, I often felt that she watched the comings and goings that went on around her, like an amused spectator at the theatre.

'There you are, Jessica. It really is too bad of you to keep me waiting.'

Mrs Thurlow was already ensconced in a gilt chair in Jessica's large pleasant room, while Mrs Ackroyd hovered timidly by, her mouth full of pins and her arms full of white silk material.

'I am so sorry, Mamma,' Jessica apologized. 'I quite forgot the time. I was busy telling Morwenna the wonderful news about Maxwell.'

'Indeed!' said Mrs Thurlow sharply. 'For myself, I have far too much to think about without having these last-minute surprises sprung upon me. I think it is quite thoughtless of Maxwell to give us so little warning. Why, it is barely a week to your birthday.' She set her mouth in a tight line. 'Morwenna, help Jessica with her dress!'

Obediently I assisted Jessica out of the lavender muslin, thinking to myself that Mrs Thurlow desired Maxwell's return as little as I did. From all accounts she had always resented Maxwell, whom she had called a spoilt brat from the first. But perhaps the resentment went deeper than that, for Maxwell must have been a constant reminder to her of Mr Thurlow's first, idyllic marriage and the less comfortable situation of his second.

Superficially, Mr and Mrs Thurlow maintained a respectful and polite manner towards each other, yet one could not live in the house for long without becoming aware of undertones of friction. Perhaps Mr Thurlow had sought as his second wife a comfortable, pleasant companion on whom he could rely to run his household efficiently, give him more children and be an ornament on social occasions. Perhaps Mrs Thurlow, so much younger, perhaps a little like Jessica in her romantic expectations, had looked for some semblance of the passion she had read about in the novels she perused so eagerly: a passion Mr Thurlow could not give her as it had all been given to Thérèse.

In any event, they had both been disappointed in the marriage. There was no meeting of intellects, no large family to engross them both. Mrs Thurlow had suffered greatly through the birth of Jessica and, being a strong-willed woman, had determined not to suffer again for the sake of a man who more and more removed himself from her to the comfort and seclusion of his study and library, or plunged himself actively into the business of making money among the cotton mills and factories of Manchester. Mrs Thurlow denied Mr Thurlow her bed and turned all her attention to Jessica.

I laid Jessica's muslin gown on the bed where there was a tumbled array of half-finished skirts and bodices and lengths of material. Among all this lay a dress made up in a colour I would have delighted in, had I any choice in the matter. It lay in a scarlet swathe across the white coverlet, a rich, deep red that turned almost to flame where the sunlight caught it. It was the same tantalizing, living colour as the glass beads in my mother's pendant.

I turned away. My dress was to be of a muted mouse-grey that I had disliked on sight, but Mrs Thurlow had pronounced it perfectly suitable when Mrs Ackroyd had brought the swatches of silk for us to make our choice. I had seen the crimson then and fingered it lovingly, but I was surprised to see now that Mrs Thurlow had chosen such a bold colour for Jessica.

'Do stand still, Jessica,' Mrs Thurlow commanded. 'How can I see the fit at the waist if you fidget so?'

Mrs Ackroyd's nimble fingers darted at the material with pins, smoothed and pulled the silk. Mrs Thurlow nodded, allowing herself a slight, satisfied smile.

'That will do very well, Mrs Ackroyd.'

'I think so, ma'am,' Mrs Ackroyd agreed, standing back to view the finished effect.

Jessica peered at herself with delight in the long mirror. 'I could imagine myself a princess in this gown,' she exclaimed. 'What do you think, Morwenna?'

'A princess, indeed,' I said wholeheartedly. 'You will have every young man at the ball vying for your favours.'

She looked adorable. The dress was white, threaded with rose-pink velvet ribbon and embroidered at the low, frilled neckline with tiny seed pearls. As I looked at her I again felt that unworthy stab of envy. Jessica's future was as straightforward and assured as any young lady who had a rich father and a doting mother. Mine was uncertain, shadowy and dependent on other people's whims.

'Now off with it,' said Mrs Thurlow, 'and try the two morning dresses. The blue, I think, needs a lace trim at the neck. It is very plain . . . '

Jessica was whisked in and out of the garments that were to set the seal upon her successful entry into society, Mrs Ackroyd fussing round her like a small hen. For all her insipid appearance and the near-sighted stare of her pale eyes behind the round spectacles, she was clever at her trade and much patronized by the local gentry.

'Wait until Papa sees me in all this finery,' Jessica cried. 'And Miss Webster. Do you think she will travel back with Papa today?'

'I dearly hope so,' Mrs Thurlow said tartly. 'It was inconsiderate of her to rush off and leave us when she knew how much there was to do to prepare for the ball.'

'Her brother could not help being ill, Mamma,' Jessica said, emerging flushed from the embrace of a tight taffeta bodice. 'There was no one else he could call upon to help him run his household.'

'Let us hope it is nothing catching he has suffered from,' Mrs Thurlow said, unappeased. 'I hear the cholera has broken out in some parts of Manchester. It would be beyond bearing if she brought some dreadful disease back with her.'

'It was a chill that turned to a congestion of the lungs, I believe,' I said quietly. 'And I am sure she will be back with us soon, now that Mr Webster is recovering.'

'I do not at all like the idea of Henry calling at the house.' Mrs Thurlow frowned. 'He said he had business in the area and it would be no trouble to see if Miss Webster was ready to return. But these slums are such vile places, full of thieves and persons of a low kind. Indeed, I would have thought Mr Webster could have found a more suitable living so that his motherless children could be decently raised.'

'I understand he chose the district particularly,' I said. 'Miss Webster says that he feels a calling to work among the poor and he is very well thought of by the people there.' I paused and some little devil of mischief made me add: 'After all, it is these poor unfortunate people who keep us all in comfort here at Ashridge Hall. We should be thankful that clergymen like Mr Webster see to their welfare.'

'I cannot think what you mean, Morwenna,' Mrs Thurlow said, with ice in her voice.

'It is quite simple. The mills and manufactories, in which

Mr Thurlow has so wisely and profitably invested, would grind to a halt if all the people who worked in them went away. It is these honest, decent folk who are forced to live in overcrowded slums because they cannot afford to live anywhere else. And it is they who enable the mill owners to make profits and – ' I held up Jessica's ball gown – 'so buy their daughters pretty dresses.'

'Morwenna!' Mrs Thurlow was visibly shocked. 'Such a disgraceful idea! I hope you do not entertain any more notions like that. I suppose it is due to all these books you read.'

'It is the truth,' I said, perhaps with more heat than was wise. 'It is not so long ago that spinning and weaving was done by the people at home in their villages. But now machines do that work much faster and much better. All the people had to move from their villages and come into the town to find employment. So it is that the city grows and spreads and becomes overcrowded and disease-ridden in places where the poor congregate. Miss Webster says . . .'

'Ah,' Mrs Thurlow said, pursing her lips and nodding. Her eyes were needle-sharp. 'Now I understand. It is Miss Webster who puts all these – these – ideas into your head . . . '

'Oh, no,' I cried, realizing too late that I had said too much. 'I have discovered this for myself, through my reading. I only meant to say that Miss Webster knew in her childhood so many places that were open countryside that are now laid waste by factories and squalid slums . . . '

Mrs Thurlow held up her hand and my protest died on my lips.

'I have heard quite enough,' she said coldly. 'I can understand with your – background – your need to champion those who, through misfortune or laziness, are less well off than we are. Very creditable, no doubt. But while you are under my roof I will not have you talking in this bold and headstrong way. It displeases me greatly.'

'Oh, I have a pin caught in my hair,' Jessica wailed from the suffocating folds of her gown. 'Help me, Morwenna, do, and save all your solemn talk for when Miss Webster returns.'

'If this is the kind of conversation which is normal in the schoolroom,' Mrs Thurlow said, quick to catch Jessica's innocent remark, 'it is perhaps as well that Miss Webster will not be with us much longer.'

It was my turn to be shocked, and I was glad Jessica had not heard this horrid piece of news. When Mrs Thurlow saw my face, a small, triumphant smile creased her plump cheeks.

'You could not think, surely, that you need a governess any longer? You are both grown girls and there is nothing left for Miss Webster to do.'

'But where will she go?' I asked.

'She will no doubt get a good position elsewhere,' Mrs Thurlow said vaguely. 'I cannot trouble myself over trivialities, I have far too much on my mind at present.'

I untangled the pin from Jessica's fine hair with fingers that shook. I was right to have felt uneasy about the future and I had the strange suspicion that this was just the first sign of changes to come.

With Miss Webster gone, I should be without the person who had cared for me most through the miseries of my adjustment to life at Ashridge Hall. She had set herself to fill the gap in my life left by my father and Mrs Pike. She had watched over me, kindly but firmly, and had taken care never to show favouritism in the schoolroom when I began to show an aptitude for learning. But when the nightmares came in the dark hours it was she who crept from the room next to mine and held me until I stopped sobbing. I both respected and loved her, and it was unbearable that she should now be dismissed on the whim of a petulant woman.

For whim I believed it to be, and no doubt my own hasty words had given Mrs Thurlow the excuse she needed. Mrs Thurlow did not like Miss Webster. It was probably pique as much as anything else because Mr Thurlow tended to side, amiably, with Miss Webster over any disciplinary matter and regarded her favourably because, like me, she was bookish. Many an evening they would hold a discussion on some book they had been reading while Mrs Thurlow plied her tapestry frame with an air of martyrdom.

Miss Webster herself had never mentioned leaving. Perhaps she thought herself secure here until Jessica married and no longer required a chaperon. This house had been her home for longer than it had been mine; it would be a hard blow for her to have to leave it.

'I think they will all do very well,' Mrs Thurlow said, pushing her bulk up from the gilt chair 'The extra lace on the blue, Mrs Ackroyd, is all the alteration required.'

'Very good, ma'am,' Mrs Ackroyd said meekly, then added:'There is the matter of Miss Morwenna's gown.'

'Oh, yes,' said Mrs Thurlow harshly, 'and I am most displeased about that, Mrs Ackroyd. Most displeased.'

'I cannot think how it happened,' Mrs Ackroyd fluttered. 'I was so very sure you had told me . . . see, I wrote it down quite specifically . . . here in my notebook . . . ' She held up the small book. Mrs Thurlow did not glance at it.

'Then you made a mistake,' she said. 'I would never have ordered such a vulgar colour. Most unsuitable for a young girl, and the material is far too expensive for a gown that will be used so little.'

I stared from one to the other, bewildered.

Mrs Thurlow swept to the door. 'The material cannot be wasted now,' she snapped, 'so I suppose she must wear it and look a silly sight . . . Hurry now, Jessica. Come to my room and I will let you try on those pearl clips that might go well with the blue.'

The door closed behind her. Mrs Ackroyd busied herself, deliberately avoiding my eye until Jessica had danced off after her mother and we were alone.

'Now, Miss Morwenna,' she said calmly, 'you had best try on your gown, though I think it will need a little alteration.'

From the bed she picked up the rich red silk and held it out to me. I felt my mouth drop open.

'It cannot be . . . ' I whispered. It was uncanny. I had told no one of my longing for the crimson silk, yet here was Mrs Ackroyd giving it to me to try on.

'Don't you like it?' Mrs Ackroyd asked, seeing my hesitation.

'Like it! It's beautiful.'

A self-satisfied smile crept on to Mrs Ackroyd's lips. 'I knew you were admiring it when I brought the samples. I thought then how the colour would suit you.'

'Then you . . . you did it on purpose!'

Mrs Ackroyd blinked at me innocently from behind her round spectacles.

'I made a mistake, miss. I could have sworn Mrs Thurlow chose this material, though she says it was the grey. But in all the confusion, what with Miss Jessica changing her mind and Mrs Thurlow fussing as she does – well, I must have noted it down wrongly.'

I could get no more out of her. But as she was hooking me into the dress she paused and peeped over my shoulder into the glass and said to my reflection, 'I make dresses for many ladies because it is my living. I do what pleases them, even though I do not always agree with what they choose. I dress plain ladies and pretty ladies and it is all the same to me. Yet sometimes, when I fit a pink satin on a figure grown fat with idleness or with all my skill try to make some rich and ugly woman appear better than she is, I long for real beauty of face and figure to lend grace to what I make. It is rarely come across.'

I laughed aloud at what she implied. 'But you cannot think that I am worthy of your skill. I am too tall and too skinny and my face will never be my fortune!'

'Miss Jessica is pretty,' she said obscurely, 'as Mrs Thurlow was once. But it is a prettiness that soon fades; like a rose that opens in the morning and is overblown by sunset. Once Miss Jessica's youth has gone, it will take her charms. But you, miss . . . '

'I have no charms now, so I cannot get any worse,' I said, amused. 'Is that it?'

'You have been told so often you have no looks that you believe it. I have heard it said many times in the years I have been coming to this house. "Morwenna is such a gawky child. She has no grace. Her hair is too straight and coarse to hold a curl. Her hands are so clumsy and big." Well, there's none so blind as those as don't want to see what's under their noses.'

'You talk in riddles,' I chided.

'It is no riddle,' she said frankly. 'You have qualities that are – less showy. You are not skinny, as you put it, but slender and fine-boned. Mark my words, if you live to be eighty they will still be saying that you are a fine-looking woman.'

'Then I hope I live to hear it.'

She shook her head at my flippancy and stood quietly back to let me ponder on the image that faced me in the mirror. It was certainly different from the usual picture I had of the drab charity child.

The dress was perfection. The bodice was cleverly cut so that the narrowness of my waist and the swell of my bosom were both emphasized and it clung like a second skin. The skirt fell away in two deep flounces, but apart from that it was plain to the point of severity. The beauty lay all in the cut of the gown and the glorious colour of the shot silk that changed and shimmered with every breath. It was a colour that lent warmth to my usually pale skin and somehow enriched the darkness of my hair.

Mrs Ackroyd reached up and loosened the tight knot into which I normally screwed my oh-so-straight locks.

'You should wear your hair pulled forward a little, so that it covers your ears and frames your face . . . so.'

'It improves me,' I admitted, adding nervously: 'Do you think the bodice is cut a little low?'

'It is exactly right on you,' Mrs Ackroyd said. 'You have a shapely figure, do not be ashamed of it.'

The more I viewed myself the more I liked what I saw and I felt quite upset when Mrs Ackroyd began to unhook me.

'Best take it off in case Mrs Thurlow comes back and catches sight of you. Or else – ' She broke off with the return of her usual timid look, as though she had said too much.

I was puzzled at her haste, but as I slipped out of the folds of heavy silk and back into my old brown cotton and saw the radiant girl in the glass become once again the everyday, self-effacing Morwenna, I caught the drift of her fears. Mrs Thurlow could not have imagined how the gown would suit me, nor how dramatically changed I appeared in it. She would certainly not appreciate having the quiet creature, who by her drab appearance and solemn ways made such a splendid foil for her daughter's charms, suddenly becoming noticeable. Once she realized I looked so well in the dress she would never allow me to wear it, however she hated the waste.

But I wanted to go to the ball. Suddenly I was filled with excitement and anticipation. An hour ago I had looked forward to the event merely as a spectator who would sit quietly in a corner and watch the glitter and show pass by. In a gown such as Mrs Ackroyd had made for me I should surely become something more than a mere onlooker . . .

'Shall I help you to carry the dresses to your room?' I asked quickly.

'That would be most kind, miss.'

We gathered up the garments, both of us moving rapidly – almost like small children who might be caught any moment in a misdeed. It seemed imperative that we escape, and I found myself holding my breath and putting my feet down quietly as we hurried downstairs to the small room that had been set aside for Mrs Ackroyd and two of her apprentices.

I put the dresses down on the long table and turned to Mrs Ackroyd. 'I scarcely know how to thank you,' I said in a low voice.

'Thank me, Miss Morwenna?' she said innocently. 'To be sure, I made a mistake that turned out for the best, and I am glad of that for your sake.'

'I am grateful all the same, that you made such a mistake.'

'I wish Mrs Thurlow could be so generous,' she said shortly, but there was a twinkle in the eyes behind the round spectacles as she added: 'I will send the dress to your room when the hem is finished.' Then she busied herself looking over the work the two girls sitting by the window had completed in her absence.

I closed the door quietly and went back up the stairs to my own bedroom, not a large, airy one like Jessica's but cramped and oddly shaped. At some time in the past this room had been partitioned off from the larger one where Miss Webster slept, and it had been a comfort to me more than once to know that she was close to me. Small as it was, I loved this room: I felt secure here – it was a little part of Ashridge Hall that was mine.

I sat on the narrow bed and opened the top drawer of the chest that stood next to it. I groped beneath the darned stockings and brought out a chipped marquetry box Mrs Thurlow had once discarded. I opened it. Dear little Tiggy, my beloved wooden doll, lay on top. I took her out and placed her on my pillow, where she had lain for many long nights until I had grown old enough to be able to sleep without her. I took out the soft kid gloves that were now too small to fit my hand, the lace, and then the prayer book. It fell open as I held it and the familiar bold writing stared up at me:

To Catherine Gweniver Pendine on the
occasion of her sixteenth birthday from
her loving father, Oliver Pendine.
Treroc.
Cornwall

My grandfather had written those words and I had pored over them when they had finally made sense to me and become something more than indecipherable scribbles. What had he been like, this man who had loved a daughter, given her presents, then finally cut her off completely from his life? I had felt nothing but anger for him at first, but with the passing years had come understanding.

I had only the tales Mrs Pike told me, the barest bones of the story about the young girl at the house with its grounds running to the sea and of the poor carpenter who had come to the house seeking work: of the passion that had fired them, over-riding all sense and reason: of the snatched moments away from the sharp eye of the strict father, of the consequences that had forced them to run far away from those who would have pointed the finger of scorn and that had still ended in tragedy.

I remembered, as I sat there, my own voice piping out into the quiet of the schoolroom when something one of the maids had said, and the memory of Mr Pike's sullen grumbling at my presence in his house, came back to me.

'Please, Miss Webster,' I said, 'what is a bastard child?'

Miss Webster's hands froze in the act of turning a page of her book.

Jessica sighed over her copybook, unheeding. 'These sums will not come right,' she announced. Miss Webster, uncharacteristically, said briskly, 'Then leave them for a moment, dear. Run to my room and fetch me a handkerchief from the drawer in my dresser. I quite seem to have mislaid mine.'

Jessica had escaped gladly from the dreaded chore of arithmetic, and Miss Webster called me over to where she sat at the high desk.

'What makes you ask that question, Morwenna?'

'It is what I have heard other people call me,' I said. 'What does it mean?'

Her fingers rested on the open book. The sun came through the window behind her, dazzling my eyes so that it was difficult to see her face.

'It is a coarse expression,' she said gently. 'I do not want to hear you use it again. But I will tell you what it means, though when you grow older and understand more fully, you may be hurt by it.'

'Hurt?' I said puzzled. 'How can it do that?'

'Because cruel people may taunt you with it and may force you to feel shame. But it is not your fault, my dear, only that of your parents who were forced by circumstances . . . but, no matter.' She paused, as though seeking for words. 'You see, Morwenna, your parents did not marry. I do not know the full story, though rumour has it that your father . . . he was already married when he met your mother.' She put out her hand and laid it against my cheek. 'You must always remember this, when anyone treats you unjustly, that you are a child of love. A love child is another name for that other ugly one. Think of that when you meet proud, scornful people who despise you . . . '

I closed the prayer book and laid it aside. I was glad it had been Miss Webster who had told me what I was. We had never spoken of it again, yet the knowledge of it was always in my heart, and the mingled shame and sadness, too, when I came fully to realize what she had implied.

But I wanted to think no more of the past. My eager hands delved into the box again and I drew out the pendant. Sunlight sparked and flashed off the red glass as I took it to the light and examined it. The beads lay across my palm suspended from the twisted gilt wire like tiny droplets of blood: It did not seem too cheap or showy and it would match perfectly the silk of my dress.

I was still bemused by Mrs Ackroyd's scheming, for, despite her denials, I knew she had planned to make me the dress from the moment I set eyes on the glowing silk. It was a daring thing to have done, for Mrs Thurlow had a malicious temper when she was crossed and would have been furious had she suspected intrigue.

As I held the pendant and thought of the beautiful gown, I vowed to myself that for Mrs Ackroyd's sake I would wear it proudly to the ball. By rights I had no place there at all. Gawky Morwenna Tregarth, love-child of pauper parents, what business had I mingling with the rich and grand? Fate had woven a tangled web, indeed, to bring me here. I wondered what other devious entanglements she had yet in store.

Miss Webster returned with Mr Thurlow in the late afternoon. Jessica and I were in the music room when we heard the rattle of hooves and wheels. Jessica broke off the cheerful air she had been practising and went to the hall on flying feet. I followed in time to see Mrs Bradshaw taking Miss Webster's bag and Mr Thurlow laughingly holding at bay an excited Jessica, who was pouring out her news all topsy turvy.

'Now take a deep breath, Jessica,' Mr Thurlow chuckled, 'and begin this wild tale again. In fact, it might be better if you waited until Miss Webster and I have refreshed ourselves. It has been a trying journey. The heat in the city is insufferable and the train journey was both tiresome and dirty.'

'Oh, no, Papa,' Jessica cried. 'I cannot wait that long . . . ' And she began again on her garbled story.

'Maxwell home?' Miss Webster said sharply, glancing at me. 'Is this true, Morwenna?'

'It is,' I said calmly. 'He hopes to be here for Jessica's birthday, along with his fiancée and her papa.' I smiled at her. 'But you will learn all about that in the greatest detail from Jessica. I have heard nothing else the whole day.'

She seemed reassured by my calmness.

'It is good to see you again, my dear, and it is a blessing to be back.' She glanced round the panelled hall with its weighty portraits of Mr Thurlow's forebears. From the open doorway came a warmly scented draught of air and she breathed deeply. 'After the closeness of the city, you cannot imagine how fresh the countryside is.'

'I am so pleased to have you home,' I said, pushing aside the awful knowledge that Mrs Thurlow would soon be dismissing her. There was time enough later to give her that news.

'How is your brother?' Mrs Bradshaw asked, helping her off with her cloak. I had thought Mrs Bradshaw very forbidding at first, but it was just her manner. She ruled the household as an officer might run a regiment, with discipline but scrupulous fairness. She and Miss Webster had much in common and a close friendship had grown between them.

'Charles is much, much better,' Miss Webster said. 'There are many kind people in the neighbourhood who have promised to help in the house and with the children until he is properly recovered. I thought it safe to leave him, especially as Mr Thurlow so kindly offered to escort me back to Ashridge Hall and to call again next week to see how Charles makes progress.' Her eyes went to Mr Thurlow, now with good humour allowing himself to be led away into the drawing-room by his daughter. 'He is such a kind man. He knew I would be worried, for though Charles is well enough to write he would tend to paint a brighter picture for my sake. Mr Thurlow will give me a more honest opinion of how Charles fares.'

'That is good news by all accounts,' Mrs Bradshaw said. 'But you look tired – it must have been a trying time for you.'

She did look weary. There were shadows under her hazel eyes, and the dark green of her dress served only to accentuate the pallor of her face. A plain face with a high, bony nose, yet the intelligence in the clear eyes and the sensitivity of the mouth lifted it out of the ordinary. She had seemed very old to me when I had first come here, as any adult does to a child, and I had grown so accustomed to her appearance that I never thought of her age. But seeing her after an interval of two weeks was like seeing her afresh. She seemed, in her weariness, younger than before, more vulnerable. I realized with surprise that she was not many years beyond thirty.

'Morwenna shall escort you to your room,' Mrs Bradshaw announced firmly, 'and I shall bring you a tray of tea myself. Then you must rest an hour before dinner.'

'That sounds delightful,' Miss Webster murmured, submitting gratefully as I took her bag and led the way upstairs.

'Lavender and well-polished furniture,' she said as she went into her room, 'the whole house smells of it. I fear my brother's house is not so sweet. There is a foul tannery nearby and even the street where he lives is not wholesome.' She sighed as she unloosened the strings of her bonnet and sank on to a chair. 'He is a good man and a dedicated one; his life is bound up in trying to help the poor in every way he can. But his health is suffering and it is not surprising. Those squalid streets . . . you could not know how awful they are.' She forced a smile. 'But no matter. I am away from it all and will soon recover my good spirits again. I have felt very depressed these last days.'

'When you are tired, it brings on depression,' I said cheerfully. 'Tomorrow, when you are rested, you will feel much brighter.'

'That is what Mr Thurlow said.' She took off her bonnet and smoothed down her hair. 'Though I would never have troubled him with my small worries, he noticed how downcast I was. He is most observant for a gentleman – and, for a man in his position, very willing to listen and learn. He had a long talk with my brother yesterday and showed a great interest in his work, especially in the school he runs. My brother says that it is only through education that the poor will better their lot, and Mr Thurlow agreed with him entirely. Poor Charles was so surprised. He is accustomed to abuse from factory owners when he tries to enlist their aid.'

She stood up and went to her dressing-table, her hands resting lightly on its top. She stared at herself for a few moments silently in the mirror, then turned abruptly away. With her back to me she said slowly, 'I almost married once. Have I ever told you that, Morwenna?'

'No,' I said.

'You sound quite amazed,' she said. 'Is it so strange that your strict, plain governess should have the natural feelings of a woman?'

'You are not strict,' I burst out, 'nor so plain . . . '

She gave a laugh that had a bitter sound. 'He . . . this man I loved . . . thought me personable enough. I would have married him and been the mother of his children and been doubtless in straitened circumstances. But happy, Morwenna. Happy.'

'And are you not happy here, then?'

She ignored the question and went on as though half to herself. 'My father did not think the match suitable. My suitor went away. And when my father died, there was no money to speak of and my brother could not afford to keep me. So I became a governess. First in a miserable household where I stayed only because I could not afford to lose the post. Then, mercifully, I came here. For nine years I have lived in this house and have thought myself lucky. But now I wonder . . . '

'Miss Webster,' I said softly, 'why do you tell me this?'

She turned round quickly and faced me. Her eyes were brilliant, whether with unshed tears or with a fierce contained anger I could not tell.

'Take your happiness, child, when it is offered to you. I was too meek, too pliant, too dutiful a daughter.' She looked at me strangely for a moment. 'You are very different from the girl I was. You have an inner strength that will serve you well. God knows, you will need it. It is not an easy world for a woman alone. A man fares much better. He has the authority to make his way independently, but a woman must be submissive and docile and have no will or mind of her own.'

A tap at the door cut her short. She started, blinked, and the fire washed out of her face, leaving her grey and drained. Her voice was steady enough as she called, 'Come in,' and murmured some pleasantry to Mrs Bradshaw, but her hand shook as she took the cup of tea as though she was still torn with some inward emotion. I felt that, had we not been interrupted, she would have told me the reason for her strange outburst. It was so unlike her. It was as though I had been permitted to glimpse, just for a few moments, the heart of the woman who lived under the cool, contained mask of the governess. I felt troubled by it. She was deeply unhappy and I was helpless in the face of it because I knew neither the cause nor the remedy.

Miss Webster did not come down to dinner. She sent to say she felt unwell and would retire early. As if not to be outdone, Mrs Thurlow declared herself to have a headache and went to her room after picking at her meal, so that Williams, her maid, could pamper her. Jessica coaxed her papa to the music room to hear the new songs she had learned, but I could not settle to any quiet occupation. The restlessness I had felt earlier in the day was stronger than ever. The news of Maxwell's homecoming, the secret of the new dress, Miss Webster's strange emotional state, all these combined to disquiet me. I could not shake off the peculiar sensation of approaching change, a feeling that strengthened as the sun dipped behind the trees and the long summer dusk settled like a blue haze across the lawns and flower-beds and the tree-lined rides of the gardens.

The house became gloomy and oppressive and, even though the maids were about their nightly task of lighting the lamps and candles, I felt as though the walls were leaning in on me, heavy and brooding.

I needed air . . . space . . . diversion, something to shake me from this silly mood. I thought of Mrs Pike and suddenly I wanted to talk to her, to listen to her cheerful gossip, to sit in the lodge and be fussed over and given elderberry wine and home-made biscuits. Mr Pike would be at the inn with his cronies at this hour. Mrs Thurlow was safely in her room and could not forbid me to go, for she did not approve of being on too friendly terms with the servants.

I fetched a shawl and hurried from the house into the still and beautiful evening. The land was dark now but the skv was washed with light and colour. To the west the horizon was barred with gold and vermilion; higher, the sky paled to a clear translucent green which deepened to a rich blue overhead. A thrush piped out his strong, clear call from the topmost branch of an old lilac bush, and faintly I could hear Jessica singing. It had a melancholy ring to it across the deserted garden.

My footsteps crunched in the gravel and I hugged my shawl about my shoulders as I skirted the grassy circle where the haughty stone goddess stared before her with blank eyes. The drive lay deep in the shadow of the great beeches that had been planted by Mr Thurlow's great-grandfather when he had built the house. As I walked underneath them I felt as though I had plunged into the mouth of a black tunnel, dank and chilly and smelling of dew-wet grass.

Involuntarily I quickened my steps, anxious to see the welcoming light from Mrs Pike's kitchen. Then I heard something that, in a weird and awful way, reversed time for me. I was no longer the quiet and studious Miss Morwenna of Ashridge Hall, but a child again; half-wild, barefoot, stooping over the tumbled bowl of blackberries in the ruts of a country lane.

Invisible, part of the black shadows and heading straight for me, was a horse.

I stood there, frozen into immobility, as though I were a sapling that had taken root in the gravel. Terrified, I listened to the thundering hooves pounding up the black tunnel towards me.

Blindly I stared into the darkness. I could see nothing. The pounding hoofbeats mingled with the thumping of my heart. The noise filled my head with a nightmare intensity. Any moment now the grey horse would be upon us and I would feel the blow as my father thrust me into safety. Then I should turn and see him lying there, stricken down for ever.

I wanted to call out, but my voice was thick in my throat as suddenly I focused on the horse that tore itself from the shadows. I caught the glint of metal, the mad eyes of the horse, and recognized the white face of the rider as he struggled with the rearing, whinnying mount.

Then I was falling, falling away into the shadows, slipping from reality into merciful oblivion . . .

CHAPTER THREE

There was a girl standing by my bed, dark-haired, dark-eyed, in an old-fashioned blue gown. She looked sad even though she smiled and held out her hand to me, and I thought how beautiful she was. She was small and slender and though she was young there was the heaviness of pain and suffering in her shadowed eyes. She reminded me of someone but my head ached and I could not think who.

'Who are you?' I whispered.

She shook her head sadly and did not answer. And as I watched, her features seemed to blur and thicken, the blue gown faded and I was looking at Mrs Pike's homely face.

'Bless us, she's awake!' she said. 'It's me, hinny – Mrs Pike. Fancy you not recognizing me.' She spoke to someone behind her. 'She must have knocked her head as she fell. It's mazed her.'

'Not you,' I murmured, 'not you. The other – the girl . . ' My voice trailed off. It was too much effort to speak. I closed my eyes again. I wished the girl in the blue gown would return; I felt strangely comforted by her presence.

I did not want to move, but my head was lifted and a glass put to my lips. I choked as the fiery spirit caught my throat and burned into my stomach. Then I was properly awake and staring round in bewilderment. I was in the comfortable kitchen of the lodge, lying on the sofa. I could not remember how I had come here.

'The brandy has brought the colour to her face,' Mrs Pike was saying. 'It's fortunate I keep a little by me.' Then to me, kindly: 'Are you feeling more yourself?'

'Yes,' I faltered. 'Yes . . . I am. But what . . . ?'

'Lie quietly,' Mrs Pike said firmly. 'You took a bit of a tumble, fainted from fright, no doubt – .'

'She had need to be frightened! Appearing out of the darkness like a wraith and startling my horse!' A man's voice, deep-toned, angry. 'I was damned near thrown.'

It all flooded back then – the black tunnel under the beeches, the horse thundering towards me . . . I felt a deep and convulsive shudder go through my body. Despite the brandy I was cold; cold as the thick, white frost that covered the grass in winter.

Slowly I forced myself to lift my head and look across the room to where he stood, a tall figure, stooped slightly to avoid the low-beamed ceiling. Amber lamplight, caught at a ruffle of white silk against olive-brown skin, glinted on a carved green stone set in a gold ring on one hard hand that drummed impatiently on the mantelshelf, putting in jeopardy Mrs Pike's precious china ornaments. All this I took in before I dared to examine his face.

When I did, I knew I had been right to be afraid out there in the darkness.

Long black eyes stared at me with ill-concealed irritation. An older face than I remembered; sun-flushed skin taut over the bones of cheek and jaw and jutting hawk's nose.

My cold lips formed a name. 'Maxwell Thurlow,' but he did not see as he took two long strides across the kitchen and spoke curtly to Mrs Pike.

'She is well enough. I must be on my way.' He raised an eyebrow. 'I thought to surprise them at the Hall and I am impatient to see my father again, but it seems that fate is littering my path with obstacles. The railway journey suffered every conceivable delay and on the very doorstep a foolish servant girl practically throws herself under the feet of the hack I borrowed at the station.'

'Oh, sir, she is . . . ' Mrs Pike opened her mouth to reveal my identity, but I shook my head warningly at her. She looked puzzled, but to my relief turned to Maxwell and beamed at him. 'It is good indeed to see you. Welcome back to Ashridge Hall. Mr Thurlow will be a happy man this night.'

His expression softened to a half smile. 'Thank you. Mrs Pike, is it not?'

'Fancy you remembering, sir, after all these years!'

'There is little I have forgotten about this place,' he said shortly. 'Both the pleasant . . . and the unpleasant.'

But he had forgotten me, as well he might. He had seen me only once and then I had been a ragged urchin. Perhaps it was the memory of that which had made me caution Mrs Pike. I was dishevelled now, and distraught. I wanted no questions and curious looks: I needed time to recover my composure. I had dreaded for years having to meet this man who had killed my father, this man whom I instinctively despised and hated. That it should have happened like this was an added humiliation.

'Good night to you,' he said to Mrs Pike, who bobbed a curtsy as she held the door open for him. I waited to hear the horse clatter away before I pushed myself upright on the sofa.

'Now, now, rest a while.' Mrs Pike bustled back to me. 'You cannot go until you've recovered properly.'

'But I must,' I said, scraping back the loose strands of hair that had fallen across my face. 'The whole house will be roused once Maxwell arrives and I shall be missed. You know Mrs Thurlow does not like me to come here and she is sure to ask where I have got to.'

'She'll find out soon enough anyway,' Mrs Pike said practically, 'once Mr Maxwell discovers who his "servant girl" really is. Besides, it was he who carried you here.'

I thought of myself lying limp and helpless in Maxwell

Thurlow's arms and found no pleasure in the picture.

I smoothed down the torn and dirtied skirt of my dress with a hand that trembled. 'You are right, of course.' I sighed. 'I fear I am more shaken than I imagined. I cannot seem to think logically. But I *was* coming here to see you, Mrs Pike. I had to get out of the Hall for a while. I felt . . . Oh, I do not know how I felt. It doesn't seem important any more . . .'

'You have had a bad shock,' Mrs Pike said gently. 'Seeing him again must have revived memories best forgotten.'

'It was the horse,' I whispered. 'In the darkness I was confused . . . it frightened me.'

'As well it might.' She laid a work-roughened hand on mine. 'Why did you not let me tell Mr Maxwell who you are? He would have understood your fear.'

'I want no understanding from him,' I said bitterly. 'Nor pity.'

She shook her head in surprise. 'You still brood then over what happened to your father? But it was an accident, hinny. I had thought you would have been reconciled to that after all this time.'

'Reconciled?' I repeated harshly. 'My father was a difficult man and unkind sometimes because of his own unhappiness. But he was all that I had, the only person bound to me with ties of blood. Maxwell Thurlow took him away from me and for that I shall never, never forgive him.'

Perhaps it was the brandy that made me talk so, and I was instantly sorry that I had allowed even kind Mrs Pike to see how deeply I felt. Such thoughts were better kept locked away. So when she had warmed some milk and stood over me while I drank it, I mocked myself lightly.

'It is no wonder he thought I was a servant, such a dowdy sight I look. This grey dress is the one I dislike most, so I am not sorry to see that it is ripped quite beyond repair.'

'It's a pity,' Mrs Pike said sternly, 'that Mr Thurlow does

not notice how you go about. But it is so like a man not to heed what his womenfolk are wearing. If he was more observant he would realize that Mrs Thurlow keeps you almost threadbare.'

I laughed. 'I would never reproach Mr Thurlow for the pettiness of his wife. He has given me something of far greater value than pretty dresses – a good education.'

'That's as maybe.' Mrs Pike sniffed. 'But you're not a child now. A lot of book-learning is not much use to a girl when she gets to a marriageable age. It's fine looks and fine clothes that attract admirers.'

'Then it is fortunate I am not looking for a husband,' I said, glad that I had diverted her attention. I finished the milk and handed her the mug. 'That has quite revived me. Thank you for your kindness, I am quite able to walk back to the Hall now.'

My brave words belied the weakness I felt in my legs as I hurried up the drive. Though the beech trees no longer looked sinister and the darkness was the usual, placid country dark, I could still sense the echo of the terror I had felt earlier.

I slipped indoors by the deserted music room and fled up the back stairs, catching, as I did so, the sound of excited voices and the rattle of footsteps on polished floors as though the servants were scurrying about.

I was safely in my room, candle alight, and out of my ruined dress, by the time the tap came on my door.

I called the maid to enter and she announced, breathlessly: 'Please, miss, Mr Thurlow said to come down to the drawing-room. Mr Maxwell Thurlow has arrived all unexpected.'

'Thank you,' I said calmly. 'Tell Mr Thurlow I will be down directly.'

But I did not hurry. I forced myself to dress slowly, wishing that I had something grander to put on than the drab fawn gown that was too tight on me, but which was the only garment suitable to wear, apart from the unlamented grey which had come to ruin in the gravel and the old cotton dresses I wore during the day. I would have liked to make an imposing entrance, looking formidable and grand and knowing myself to be beholden to nobody. But that was not possible. What I had I owed to Mr Thurlow's charity: I had lived with that knowledge long enough and learned to accept it. But to appear before the arrogant and headstrong Maxwell Thurlow in the role of the charity child was a different matter. It was hateful.

I pinched my pale cheeks to bring some colour back to them and wished, as I stared at my solemn face in the mirror, that he had stayed far away in the East Indies. 'You are being very childish,' I told my image firmly. 'It was bound to happen some day.'

But the thought gave me no comfort as I walked down the stairs under the bold, mocking gaze of Thérèse Thurlow and nerved myself to open the drawing-room doors.

For a moment they did not see me. I closed the doors quietly and leaned back against them, not wishing to disturb the pleasant domestic picture before me.

The room was the most elegant in the house; long and high-ceilinged, with tall windows set in shallow alcoves down one side and at the far end glass doors that folded back and gave on to a broad terrace. Yet it was not a formidable place. Mr Thurlow's parents and grandparents had furnished it for comfort as well as beauty. Stylish Hepplewhite sofas sat cheek by jowl with Adam chairs and pieces from more humble, local craftsmen. The oak floor was scattered with French carpets faded to palest rose, and on one of them, back to the white marble fireplace where the silver candelabra blazed with a dozen brilliant points of light, stood Maxwell Thurlow. He looked at ease now, all irritation gone as he smiled down into Jessica's bright face. She hung on his arm, chattering excitedly, while Mr Thurlow sat in his favourite high-backed chair, one hand gently tugging at his short, greying beard, but his eyes fixed on his son as though he could not drink enough of the sight of him. Even Mrs Thurlow was disposed to be pleasant, all simpers, despite her sharp words of earlier in the day. Mrs Bradshaw hovered behind a flustered maid who was handing round glasses of wine.

It was Mrs Thurlow who sighted me first.

'Ah, there you are, Morwenna. Where have you been hiding yourself? Emmy has been to your room three times and could not find you anywhere else in the house.' She spoke sweetly enough, but her mouth was pursed to a pink button of disapproval.

'I am sorry,' I said quietly. 'I went into the gardens for a little air. It was such a warm evening.'

'What an odd creature you are,' she scolded, 'wandering about in the dark on your own. But do not stand there gawking as though you had never been taught any manners.'

It seemed a long walk from the doors. I hoped I looked composed, though under Mrs Thurlow's gimlet stare I felt awkward and clumsy-footed. I was grateful when Mr Thurlow stood up and took my hand, smiling kindly.

'Morwenna, my dear,' he said, drawing me into the candle-lit circle, 'you met my son, Maxwell, once before in less happy circumstances.' He paused, choosing his words. 'That meeting was brief and had tragic consequences. But a deal of water has flowed beneath the bridge since then and I hope it has washed away all distressing memories.' He glanced from me to his son. 'I should like you both to forget all that has happened in the past. You are both changed and grown.' He pressed my hand gently and released it. 'Will you both now start afresh and be friends?'

I did not answer. How could I and not lie? I lifted my eyes to Maxwell's face. There was surprise there, fleetingly, and I expected any moment for him to reveal that we had already met. But surprise was replaced by cool, frank appraisal, the detached curiosity of a stranger. The dark eyes studied my face, then moved slowly, almost lazily, downwards in a minute scrutiny that ended at my toes. I stood stiffly, aware of the constraints of the dress that prevented me from taking a deep breath and of my bony wrists sticking uncomfortably from the tight cuffs of the too-short sleeves.

It felt like hours that I stood there, though it must have been a matter of seconds before he said quietly, 'So this is Morwenna.'

I sketched a curtsy in acknowledgement and he went on, amusement in his voice: 'You are not quite what I expected.' I knew he was thinking of our earlier encounter; the dishevelled little serving maid, startling his horse and foolishly going into a faint because of it. Mr Thurlow, of course, took him to mean our long-ago meeting.

'Yes, she looked very different when you saw her last,' he remarked.

'Indeed,' Maxwell agreed. 'A veritable ragamuffin, as I recall.' A smile quirked the corner of his mouth and narrowed his eyes, encouraging me to join in his little private joke. But I could not – would not – respond, and the amusement died from his face, leaving it austere and expressionless. His eyes never left mine and I wondered if he sensed a challenge.

Jessica saved me from having to answer.

'Of course they will be the dearest friends, Papa,' she exclaimed. 'Morwenna said to me only this morning that she bore no ill-will towards Maxwell.'

'In that case,' Maxwell said lazily, 'I see nothing to prevent our friendship.' Amber and gold lights swam in the wine as he held the glass aloft in his brown, hard fingers. 'I will drink to that, Morwenna,' he said. 'To our friendship.'

Was I the only one to detect the undertone of irony? Mr

Thurlow certainly did not. He looked gratified and called to the maid, 'Emmy, a glass of wine for Miss Morwenna.'

I took the glass, the stem cool to the touch as he went on. 'Now I shall propose a toast,' he said. 'We shall drink to this happy reunion. Maxwell, my son, welcome home.'

When we had drunk the wine we sat in the candlelight. There was no escape, but fortunately the family was so used to my quietness in company that my silence did not trouble them. Not that Jessica would have given me much chance to speak anyway. She bombarded Maxwell with questions. When was dear Miss Pritchard to arrive? Was she as beautiful as he had written? Why had she not travelled with him to Ashridge Hall?

'My dear Jessica,' Mrs Thurlow protested fondly, 'Maxwell will tell us everything in good time.'

Maxwell looked at his half-sister in the tolerant way he might have regarded an over-excitable puppy.

'She is very beautiful,' he said gravely, 'and we met scarcely three months ago, when she joined the ship, as I did, in Singapore. They were to disembark at Lisbon and travel the Continent in order to allow Isabel to see something of Europe's beautiful cities, and they asked me to join them.'

Jessica clasped her hands together. 'And was it in Venice that you . . . declared yourself?' she asked breathlessly. 'After you had fallen hopelessly in love on board ship?'

'I confess,' he said solemnly, 'that it was in Florence, one superb moonlit evening, that I begged her to be my wife. There were guitars playing a haunting tune below the balcony of the hotel and the scent of lemon blossom in the air.'

'Truly?' breathed Jessica, her eyes round. 'Oh, but that is just as I had imagined.' She turned to me. 'Did I not tell you, Morwenna, that it was a most romantical attachment?'

So appealed to, I had to answer. 'Indeed,' I said, 'you would have disappointed Jessica very gravely, Maxwell, had it not been otherwise.'

Maxwell's mouth twitched, and Jessica burst out, 'You are both teasing me!'

'It is the truth,' Maxwell said. 'I swear it.'

'But why have you not brought Miss Pritchard with you?' Jessica cried.

Maxwell drained his glass and set it absently on the mantel. 'Isabel, I fear, was a trifle wearied by our travels. Her father thought it best she should rest for a few days before travelling north.'

'She is ill?' Mr Thurlow said, with concern.

Maxwell's black brows drew down. 'I have been a little worried about her this last week. When we arrived at the house of her cousin in Sussex, a doctor was summoned, but he said she was merely overtired by the journey and by the change of climate. The temperatures on the Malay peninsula are high and it is constantly humid and enervating. The sudden change to the cool, brisk weather on the European continent must have been startling to one accustomed most of her life to the East Indies.'

'Oh, I hope she will soon recover.' Jessica sighed. 'I cannot wait to meet her.'

'She told me before I left she would make every endeavour to be here before your birthday,' Maxwell said, 'and she is a young lady who does not give such assurances lightly.'

'Were you terribly upset at leaving her?' Jessica asked. 'How could you bear to tear yourself away?'

'I did so in the knowledge that she was in capable hands and merely in need of cosseting and rest.' He smiled at his father over Jessica's bouncing curls. 'Truth to tell, once I set foot in England I was devilish impatient to return here.' He glanced round the room. 'I feared there would be many changes. but it is all just as I remembered it.'

'Only the people living here altered, eh?' Mr Thurlow laughed.

'You and . . . Mother, very little.' I noticed the slight

hesitation before he spoke of his stepmother. Was it a word that came uneasily to his lips now, as it had done long ago when his own beautiful mamma had been replaced? Mrs Thurlow did not notice. She preened slightly.

'Henry is a little greyer, of course, but he keeps his upright carriage,' – her small, plump hand patted the blonde curls peeping from under her elaborate lace cap – 'but I do confess that the women of my family do tend to look youthful to quite an advanced age.'

'But your age is not at all advanced,' Maxwell said. Again the undertone of irony, undetected by everyone else. 'You are as young as ever.'

'Why, Maxwell,' Mrs Thurlow bridled, 'I declare you have become quite courtly. Your sojourn in the East Indies has greatly altered you in that respect. I recollect you were not always so discreet in the way you talked.'

'To my cost,' he drawled. 'Now I have learned better.'

Yes, I thought grimly to myself, you have learned it pays to flatter and cajole rather than to antagonize people.

'But you have found me much changed, haven't you?' Jessica demanded, seeing the conversation slipping away from her.

'You were a little dumpling and a naughty one at that,' Maxwell teased, 'so any change is for the better.'

Jessica pouted. 'Then you do not think I am grown a shade prettier?'

'Well-bred young ladies should not dangle for compliments,' Maxwell said sternly. Then he relented and pinched her cheek. 'But I think you have grown into a charming minx and doubtless you will be breaking many hearts in the next year or two.'

Jessica giggled delightedly and Mrs Thurlow, pleased, said: 'You are so right. It is no secret that she already has admirers.' She leaned forward confidentially. 'Even young Lord Easthulme, who so tragically received the title when his father was killed in a shooting accident on the estate, has condescended to grace Jessica's birthday celebrations.'

'He is a foppish young man,' Jessica objected. 'I cannot think to like him too well.'

'Now, now, my dear,' Mrs Thurlow reproved her. 'We must show respect for him, a person of his quality. His family has held the title for well on three hundred years.'

How Mrs Thurlow would have liked to see Jessica become Lady Easthulme! I only hoped that Jessica had sense enough to resist being drawn into such an alliance. It was a line that had become unstable and eccentric. The late Lord Easthulme was reputed to have committed suicide because he thought he was being pursued by packs of wild dogs, and the current Viscount lived with his feeble-minded mother in a decaying half-timbered house three miles away. There was no money, yet there were many mammas in the district to whom that was no barrier. They saw young Lord Easthulme and his title as legitimate prey, and I had heard it whispered that he pandered to them and came eagerly to local social functions for the simple reason that at Easthulme House they could not afford a decent table. Anyone who wished to keep in his Lordship's good books ensured that the most tasty delicacies and appetizing dishes were spread before him.

The black eyes looked from Jessica to me, eyes that mocked as did his mother's from the gilded frame on the staircase. 'And Morwenna?' he said. 'Do you, too, have a train of admirers?'

Mrs Thurlow gave a high laugh, holding just the right nuances of surprise and disparagement. 'I'm afraid,' she said in her most sugary tones, 'that Morwenna does not try hard enough to acquire the qualities men so look for in a young girl.' She paused and added with a sigh: 'And though she has had every advantage, her looks go against her.'

I fixed my gaze on my hands clasped tightly in my lap as

Mr Thurlow in a kindly voice said, 'But she has a fine intelligence, and is busily engaged in restoring order to my library which I have allowed to become sadly muddled over the years. I should be sorry indeed if some young blade spirited her away before her task is finished.'

I smiled gratefully at him, fighting down the mingled vexation and discomfort Mrs Thurlow always managed to arouse in me.

'Ah yes, but men seeking a wife do not require her to be clever,' Mrs Thurlow declared. 'Beyond the dictates of normal polite conversation, of what use to her is a deal of knowledge gained from books? It will not help to make her a more dutiful and pleasing wife.' She appealed to Maxwell: 'Is that not so?'

'A man would be a fool to marry a woman who considered herself to be of superior intelligence to his own,' he answered. 'I do not see the domestic scene as a battleground for supremacy. A man should be master in his own house; a woman loving, tender, devoted to home and children . . . '

'And indubitably docile and submissive to her husband's wishes, however inconsiderate or foolish she may think them?' I could not help it, the words were out as soon as they shaped themselves. 'Is that what you believe?'

'Of course. It is the natural order of things.'

'It is natural for a man to have the authority to shape his own life, while it is natural for the woman to submit to the will of others? To be regarded as a chattel and an adornment and to be viewed as a frivolous creature with scarcely a coherent thought in her head?'

'I did not say I wished my wife to be frivolous or superficial.'

'But you implied it.'

His look had sharpened, there was an alertness about him that his languid stance against the mantel denied. His face seemed harder, the bony nose more prominent. There was something almost feline about him, the poised containment of a panther waiting to pounce. I thought, with an inward and instinctive tremor, that this could be a dangerous man to cross.

'I think not,' he said softly. 'You mistook my meaning.'

'Then you are a rare man indeed,' I rushed on, 'because this natural order of which you speak so knowledgeably encourages men to think themselves superior in every way, just as it delegates women to the inferior, dependent role. By that very token, even the most brilliant of women must consider herself less than the dullest-witted of men, purely because she is female.'

There was a short silence. I could almost feel the indignation flowing from Mrs Thurlow, Jessica's bewilderment and Mr Thurlow's quiet surprise at my outburst.

Maxwell merely stared. Then he threw back his head and laughed, white teeth gleaming in his olive-brown face.

'Well, well,' he chuckled. 'The kitten has claws, not to mention a headful of the oddest notions.'

'Naturally you would think my ideas strange,' I said. 'That is because you have not had the occasion to consider them.'

'And when I have; what shall I do then? Order my future wife to turn herself into a nag and a scold? Humble myself slavishly before her? Allow her to handle all my business affairs while I take control of the domestic staff or sit dandling babies in the nursery?'

Jessica giggled and I felt colour flooding into my face. That was not at all what I meant. His ridicule confused me, and my arguments, which I had mulled over often enough, sounded less convincing when expressed aloud to a disbelieving audience.

'Morwenna, you quite forget yourself,' Mrs Thurlow breathed through tight lips. 'I will not have such unseemly displays of rudeness. Apologize to Maxwell at once for being so forward with your opinions. Then I think it is time you retired to your room.'

'Do not banish her on my account,' Maxwell said lightly. 'I found the conversation most diverting.'

'Pray do not encourage her,' Mrs Thurlow snapped, adding quickly with a placatory smile when Maxwell's face darkened at her tone: 'She has shown a sadly argumentative streak of late, which is most unbecoming.' She shot me a venomous look. 'She must learn the value of control and how to defer gracefully to her elders and betters.'

She could have said outright, 'Morwenna must learn to know and keep her place.' That was her meaning, however she tempered her words.

I stood up and said quietly, fixing my eyes on the dusty tips of Maxwell's boots, 'I am sorry if I have caused any offence. I did not mean to do. And now, if I may be excused, I am feeling rather tired . . . '

'Of course, my dear,' Mr Thurlow said mildly. 'And, Jessica, I think it is past your bedtime.' Used to smoothing ruffled feathers, he knew how to tide over an awkward moment. He nodded affectionately at his daughter. 'We cannot have those pretty rosy cheeks looking wan tomorrow. And by morning, no doubt, you will have thought of a hundred more questions to ask Maxwell.'

'I want to hear all about your travels,' Jessica said eagerly. 'And about that time you encountered pirates in the China Seas and . . . '

'Tomorrow!' Maxwell interrupted with a laugh. 'Go to bed now, minx, and dream about the surprises the morning will bring.'

'Surprises?'

'A few trifles I have brought back with me. The trunk should be delivered from the station before noon.'

'Presents? For us?' Jessica ran to him and flung her arms about his neck when he nodded, smiling. 'You are such a tease, but a dear one. I shall *never* sleep now for wondering what delicious things you have brought.'

I followed her from the room with relief. As we climbed the stairs I listened absently to her chatter, glad that I did not have to answer beyond an occasional murmur of encouragement. I was absorbed in recounting the humiliation of the last minutes and appallingly conscious of the uneasy road that lay ahead. With Maxwell in the house, each family meeting, each meal, each trifling conversation held yawning pitfalls. I detested him. I could not help it: it was something burned into my mind and heart. Because of that it would take all my self-control not to rise to his taunting or to respond sharply even to his more agreeable remarks.

If I put a step wrong, Mrs Thurlow would seize on the opportunity to admonish me. But as long as I remained docile and quiet I should not draw attention to myself. I sighed as we reached the gallery and Jessica tripped off to her bedroom.

The role I was called upon to play grew harder with passing time. Once it had seemed little effort to set myself to please Mrs Thurlow and to amuse Jessica. There was always the compensation that I could forget everything in the delight of reading and studying. Now I found myself weary of it, like a moth that has changed and grown within its tight cocoon and seeks to rip the constricting shell apart and emerge a new creature.

And what sort of a creature should I turn out? I wondered, my sense of humour returning the further I got from the charged atmosphere of the drawing-room. No butterfly born merely to flit among the blossoms with no thought for the morrow, that was certain. I had not the temperament. But what was my metamorphosis to be?

I reached my room without discovering the answer, and such flippant thoughts were swept away when, in the quietness of the dim corridor, I heard an unusual sound.

I paused at my door, staring at the sliver of light fanning out from under the door of Miss Webster's room. She could not have heard my approach. The noisy, distressing sobbing had muffled my steps.

I stood there, irresolute. I wanted to run to her, to comfort and console her, but some instinct held me fast. Such abandoned weeping could only mean she thought herself alone; it would perhaps upset her more to know someone had overheard. If only I knew what had made her so unhappy while she had been in the city.

I took a step towards her door, but my skirt swept against a small table, setting the tall vase on it rocking. I caught at it and set it right, but the sound had been enough to disturb her. The crying was cut off as though she had stuffed a handkerchief to her mouth. I could almost sense her holding her breath, and I was sure then that she would not welcome an intrusion.

I went to my room, closing the door with a cloud click, moving about as noisily as I could so that she would not think I was listening. I got into bed and heard nothing through the thin partition wall until I was slipping away into sleep. Even then I could not be sure; the sound of crying could so easily have been part of my own dreams.

I had meant to get up early next morning, but I slept uneasily through the night and lay longer than I intended. When I drew back the curtain the sun was throwing long blue shadows from the trees across the thickly dewed lawns, and a gardener's boy was already at work in the flower-beds below the terrace.

I dressed hastily and when I arrived in the dining-room I was relieved to see only Miss Webster seated at the long table. She looked so composed it was hard to imagine she had been the originator of those primitive sounds of distress.

'Good morning, Morwenna,' she said brightly, as I helped

myself from the covered dishes on the sideboard and sat beside her. 'We are alone as usual, I see. I would have thought Jessica might have arisen early for once in honour of her brother's arrival.'

'Jessica is a lie-bed.' I laughed. 'Like her mamma. It would take more than the return of the prodigal son to drag her from her slumbers.'

Miss Webster frowned. 'Do not be disrespectful, Morwenna,' she said. 'Maxwell is no prodigal son, despite his earlier wildness. All that is past. He has proved his worth in recent years.' She paused, then added gently: 'Do not let past events cloud your judgement.'

'Have you met Maxwell yet?' I asked, looking at her through my lashes. Her face was pale and her eyes heavy, but she was quite calm.

She shook her head. 'He and his father went riding early, so Emmy informs me.' She neatly buttered a wafer of bread. 'But I expect he is much changed, is he not?'

'Let us hope he makes a habit of his morning rides,' I said shortly, 'then we shall not have to suffer his company at breakfast.'

'So you did not take to him?'

I speared a piece of grilled kidney with undue fierceness. 'No,' I said, 'and never shall. I will keep out of his way while he is here and I shall dance with joy the day he leaves.'

'If he does leave.'

I stared at her. 'What do you mean?'

'Perhaps he plans to return here for good,' she said calmly. 'You must prepare yourself for that. After all, this house is his inheritance. He has made a large fortune in the East and may prefer to remain now in England and become a gentleman of leisure, as he could well afford to.'

I was aghast at the prospect. Stupidly, I had not even considered that he could be back in England for good. I had assumed that this would be merely a holiday for him and in a few months he would go back to the East.

'But surely his wife will want to return to the East Indies,' I said. 'She has lived there most of her life and her father is a merchant there.'

'Wives,' said Miss Webster, 'do not stay with their papas when they marry. They go with their husbands. It is not beyond the bounds of possibility that they will live here. The house is large enough. A wing of it could easily be converted for the newly-weds.'

I put down my fork, my appetite suddenly diminished. 'That is conjecture,' I protested. 'And I cannot think Mrs Thurlow would be particularly agreeable to having another woman in the house to challenge her authority.'

'She would have little say in the matter. The choice is Maxwell's.' She patted my arm. 'But do not let us worry about it. Whatever we think or say, we cannot alter anything. We are very small cogs in this household and must accept with good grace what others decide.'

She spoke without a trace of the bitterness that had been so evident yesterday. I wondered if last night's tears had brought her a measure of relief from her troubles, whatever they were. She rose from her chair.

'I think Jessica will have no mind for French and music this morning, so I shall see if Mrs Bradshaw needs any assistance. I know she is to sort linen for the guest rooms today. If not, I shall be in my room writing letters, should I be wanted by Mrs Thurlow.' She smiled. 'We must take advantage of these few days of peace in the house. Next week it will be full of guests and there will be so much hustle and bustle we shall not have a moment to ourselves.'

She had gone from the room before I realized I had still not told her that Mrs Thurlow meant to dismiss her. I sighed aloud. I did not want to tell her, especially when she was already obviously burdened with worries. Perhaps, I reasoned, as I pushed back my chair, it would be kinder to let the blow when it came be swift and clean. I walked through the house and out into the gardens with the guilty knowledge still nagging at me. I did not think Mrs Thurlow's threat was an idle one, but perhaps she would yet change her mind. As I walked through the terraced flower garden, past the glass-houses where exotic fruit and flowers were nurtured in cloying heat, I decided I would say nothing to Miss Webster yet. I would wait to see how events worked out.

The dogs came to meet me as I went into the stableyard. Skip's long legs took the cobbles in great leaps as he hurled his black shaggy body ecstatically in my direction. Dancer followed more sedately, his uneven gait unable to compete. Tom, the stable boy, poked his head round the door of the tack room and grinned. 'They were getting real anxious, miss. Thought you'd forgotten them this morning.'

'As if I would!' I said.

I gave each dog the titbit they were expecting, then walked around the stables, stroking the soft thrusting noses of the horses, enjoying the gentle wickering of recognition with which they greeted me.

It had taken me a long time to get on such friendly terms with the horses. I was still uneasy and unsure on horseback and could only be persuaded into the saddle when it was absolutely necessary, though Jacob, the old groom, had taught me to ride with great patience. The fear I had of horses went far deeper than he could know or realize. Even so, I had a love for all animals and this had helped me to overcome my trepidation enough to approach the horses when they were safely behind the stable doors.

But it was really the dogs I had come for, as I did every morning. I called them and set off on the path that led through the carefully laid-out park with its scattered old trees.

They snuffled on ahead, Skip bounding back and forward, Dancer, nose to the ground, investigating every rabbit burrow and molehill. Dancer was the oldest, a grey-muzzled foxhound, his once bright tricolour coat faded. He had come to grief a few years back when the hunt, crossing Mr Thurlow's land, had negotiated a high wall and a ditch. Jessica and I had been watching the hunt from a high vantage point, and when the horses and hounds had passed we had seen one of the hounds still struggling in the ditch. We had gone down to him and, in his pain from a broken leg, he had snarled at us. But I had managed to soothe him enough to carry him away and later, when the Master had wanted to have him put down, I had begged Mr Thurlow to let me have the hound. So I had nursed him better, though his leg had healed crookedly, giving him an odd bouncing gait. Skip, I had rescued as a shivering scrap when he and the rest of his litter had been dumped in the village pond. He had managed to escape from the confining sack in which they had been placed, and I had carried him home, a dripping, half-dead bundle.

I would dearly have liked to have taken both dogs to live in the house but Mrs Thurlow would have none of it. So they lived comfortable lives around the stables in the care of Tom and paid for their keep by waging war on the rats in the outhouses. Skip loved everyone who would give him a friendly word. Dancer was a bad-tempered old hound, giving his affections meanly. The only persons he fawned upon were Tom and myself. He tolerated with suspicion people who had rightful business about the stableyard, but woe betide any stranger who put in an appearance. Jacob declared him to be a fine watch dog and for that reason alone put up with Dancer's peevishness.

We came to the stile and the dogs, knowing their routine, looked at me eagerly. In cold or wet days this was as far as we came, where the high stone wall around the park kept at bay the sheep that cropped the rough grass on the hilly common land beyond. When I began to climb the stile, both dogs gave yelps of excitement and flung themselves past me and over the wall.

There was a breeze as I climbed the hill. It was scented with the heavy, nutty perfume of gorse. The sun was warm, and when I got to the top I thankfully dropped to a jutting outcrop of grey stone and looked back the way I had come.

The house in its fine green park was serene in the sunlight. Beyond it I could see the road that led to the village and the golden spire of the church amid the clustering trees. At the bottom of the hill a lone rider moved towards the house. From this distance it was difficult to be sure but it looked like Mr Thurlow's chestnut gelding. If so, where was Maxwell?

It was Dancer who warned me. He had flopped down by my side, tongue lolling, and submitted gracefully to having his ears fondled. I felt him stiffen and heard the low growl in his throat as he turned his head. I looked too, but for a few moments nobody appeared. Then I heard it, the thump of hooves on turf.

'Why, good morning.' Maxwell came from the other side of the hill, his horse picking its way easily round the gorse bushes. He looked as surprised to see me as I was chagrined to see him. 'You are out early.'

'It is not so early,' I said coldly. 'I am out at this time every morning.'

'Walking that misshapen old hound and that disreputable hearthrug of a mongrel?' His tone was bantering and good-humoured, but I could not bear to have fun poked at my beloved dogs.

'They cannot help their appearance any more than a human being can help being born ugly.'

He raised his black brows. 'Do you suppose that fearful watchdog will allow me to descend from my horse?'

'If I tell him so.'

'Then please do.' But he gave me no time as he swung himself down smoothly from the saddle and looped the reins over a wind-twisted hawthorn. Dancer's lip lifted and he snarled louder, his muzzle pointing threateningly at Maxwell's polished boots. But, strangely, he made no other move as Maxwell approached.

'A fearsome looking beast.' Maxwell stared down at Dancer, then he bent down and held his hand to the nose of the elderly hound. I caught my breath. Dancer had been known to seize a man for far less, but the gesture seemed to take him by surprise. This ungloved, brown fist he sniffed carefully, ears flopping forward. Then, still grumbling, he replaced his head on his paws. I felt annoyed. Dancer should know better than to include Maxwell among those whom he tolerated.

'I like dogs,' Maxwell said, 'and I think they sense it. Most certainly they seem to know when people are afraid of them, and take advantage.'

'You, of course, have no fear,' I said cuttingly.

'No,' he said, 'not of dogs. Though I must admit that young ladies who regard me as though I were the very devil, with horns growing from my scalp, do tend to intimidate me.'

I glared at him. He was smiling.

'Meaning?'

'Meaning a certain Miss Morwenna Tregarth, who has made it quite clear that, however her benefactor would wish it, she intends to remain hostile to me.'

'And can you give me any reason why I should not?' I said fiercely.

'Only that hate is a sour creature to have as a companion.'

'Then what should I do? Simper and smile and treat you as though you were St Michael dropped down from heaven?'

'I am neither devil nor angel,' he said. 'I am merely human. Because of that, I have done much in my past I regret.'

'Regret will not make the dead alive again.'

'So you intend to hold your father's death against me for ever?'

'I shall never forget,' I said, looking away from him down to the village, and the mounded elms which hid the cottage where I had lived and the road where Maxwell had changed the course of my life eight years ago.

'I am sorry about that,' he said gravely. 'Sorry, too, that we had to meet again in such a dramatic fashion. The shock must have been great when I appeared out of the darkness last night – like an unwelcome ghost from the past.'

His understanding only fanned my anger. I did not wish him to be sympathetic and kind.

'You were riding far too fast. Riding wildly, as you did once before.'

He laughed. 'A gentle canter merely – that old hack was capable of nothing more. I fear your imagination supplied the wild galloping horse.'

Common sense told me that he was probably telling the truth. In the drive, in the dusk, my mind had jolted back to that other fearful autumn day and somehow the two events had become intermingled. I had had the illusion of thundering hooves, it had been enough to cause me to panic and faint. But pride would not let me admit it, not to Maxwell.

I said coolly, 'We doubtless have a very different idea of what we mean by speed.'

I saw from the sardonic twist to his smile that he thought me a foolish, contrary creature. I sat up the straighter on the stone, willing him to go away, but to my dismay he moved a step closer so that he stood above me like a tall, black shadow blocking out the sun.

There was no sarcasm in his voice when he said abruptly, 'I am glad I did not make things more difficult for you by blurting out the manner of our meeting. I fancy my stepmother would have found some means to have roasted you for it, even though it was purely an unfortunate mishap.' He paused, then: 'Does she treat you unkindly? I know to my cost that she can be deviously cruel to those she takes a dislike to.'

I said, pushing back the remembrance of all the slights I had suffered over the years, 'I have no cause for complaint. I have been treated well and given an education by your father.'

'And never for a moment been allowed to forget it, I'll be bound,' he said softly. 'My father is a kind man but he has his blind spots. For the sake of peace he chooses to remain oblivious to the more fraying aspects of domestic life. He knows that you are well-fed, correctly taught and clothed – after a fashion,' he added drily, so that I involuntarily looked down to see if my ankles were showing beneath the hem of my almost indecently short dress. 'Beyond that, he likes to assume that you have fitted smoothly and comfortably into his household and that his wife gives you the same consideration and care that he has done.'

It was so close to the truth that I bit my lip in vexation. It was galling to know that Maxwell had been in the house for so short a time and had summed up my position so accurately.

'If you had been an empty-headed girl,' he went on, 'thoughtless and uncaring, I should not bother to speak to you like this. But I could see that each barb my dear step-mamma fired at you last evening found its mark. I shall try to ensure that in future you are treated in a kindlier manner.'

It was the last thing I wanted. That Maxwell should set himself up as some sort of champion in order to protect me was a horrifying idea. I got up quickly from the stone and faced him.

'I thank you for your concern,' I said, controlling my voice with care, 'but I do not think you have any right to walk into my life and start interfering.'

'I only wish to make sure my stepmother does not carry

her malice too far. Perhaps a word in my father's ear . . .'

'No!' I cried. 'It would only aggravate Mrs Thurlow and make my situation worse. I beg you to leave everything as it is. I am perfectly capable of looking after myself.'

He made as if to argue, then closed his lips together as if he had thought better of it. I felt at a disadvantage as he towered over me. I was tall for a girl, but Maxwell overtopped me by a long way and his black stare was uncompromising and hard.

'Please do not interfere,' I said again, and I felt relief when he nodded curtly.

'Perhaps you are right,' he said. 'After all, in the coming months I shall be travelling and seldom in residence at the Hall. I should not be able to see that my stepmother does not too often put you at a disadvantage. Later on – well, we shall see.' Then he said something that washed away all relief and filled me with a sort of hopeless despair. 'Once I am married, I shall be bringing Isabel to live here permanently, and then maybe I shall be able to exert such influence as I have in your favour.'

He nodded at me, mounted his horse, and without a backward glance moved away down the hill, leaving me to contemplate a future that must now necessarily be shadowed by the man I most wished to avoid.

CHAPTER FOUR

Maxwell said, 'I hope my choice suits you. I'm afraid I am sadly out of touch with what is fashionable in England.'

'Why, everything is beautiful!' Jessica cried.

She sat on a low chair in the small parlour where the large travelling trunk had been placed. It was unlocked and its contents spilled over on to the carpets like the contents of a fairy-tale treasure chest. Peacock silks from Siam, bright soft shawls from Kashmir, Japanese fans made of painted paper and lacquered wood . . . Jessica was delving into the chest and bringing out fresh treasures each moment.

'Look, Mamma! This is the most exquisite blue brocade. And, Papa, this must be for you.' She held up a white silk waistcoat embroidered in green and gold. 'You will look perfectly noble in it. And what is this – another shawl? It has a very gaudy animal embroidered on it.' She gave a mock shiver. 'It is a dragon and very horrid he looks. I should be quite alarmed to wear it.'

'Yes, it is a little lurid,' said Mrs Thurlow, dismissing the dragon with a glance. 'It is not to my taste.' Her greedy fingers darted among the silks Jessica had handed to her. 'I prefer the Kashmir shawl.'

'You must divide the spoils however you please,' Maxwell said, smiling. Casually he bent and gathered up the cream shawl with its fierce dragon outlined in red and gold, then he strolled across to where I sat with Miss Webster and dropped it in my lap. 'I think,' he said quietly, 'that you might like this, Morwenna.' His smile was mocking. 'I seem to recall that you once told me that the Cornish were the ancient kings and princes of England. If there is truth in that, perhaps you have the most claim to this.'

'How could that be?' I said sharply. I touched the shawl. It was fine and light and a faint spicy odour of sandalwood came from its soft folds.

'Because the dragon has five toes and that means the shawl was destined for Imperial use. Or so the man who sold it to me informed me, and he seemed an honest dealer.'

'So this could have been made for a Chinese princess,' Miss Webster said, obviously intrigued. 'Think of that, Morwenna. It would be an honour to wear it.'

'I am no princess,' I said. 'I thank you, Maxwell, but this is far too grand for me.' A part of my mind coveted the delicate silk, admired the strong, fierce lines of the dragon that was embroidered with such artistry that it seemed ready to leap from the confines of the silk. But I did not wish to accept it from Maxwell. I held it out to him. 'I would never have the occasion to wear it,' I said coolly.

The smile left his face and his eyes went bleak and cold. He said, shortly, 'It is yours. Whether you choose to wear it or not is your affair.'

He turned his back and Miss Webster whispered in my ear, 'My dear girl, you should always accept a gift graciously and not look as though he had committed a mortal offence in offering it to you. Now you have displeased him, and look how generous he has been. Even the maids have not been forgotten; each has received a little memento.' She gestured at the presents laid out in her lap – the painted fan, the length of plum-coloured brocade. 'And I am genuinely moved by his generosity to me.'

He could well afford to be generous, I thought sourly. Nevertheless I smoothed my hands over the flaring head of the dragon, and that contrary part of me I so wished to subdue felt a quick flush of pleasure. The shawl of an Imperial princess for Morwenna Tregarth!

I felt, instinctively, that something so magnificent could only have been destined for a palace. I could wear it with my red beads and the scarlet dress and imagine myself for an hour, at the ball, a princess. I had long ago relinquished the idea that the Cornish people were all descended from kings. How foolishly my head had been stuffed with such notions when I had first come to Ashridge Hall. I had soon learned from my schoolbooks that Cornwall was merely a remote English county, peopled not by fabled princes but by tin miners and fisherfolk. Still, I had read the legends of King Arthur with more than a passing interest, and there had been secret pleasure in the fact that, though spelled differently from the books, my mother had borne the name of King Arthur's queen, Guinivere.

Maxwell still kept his back stiffly to me, and the thought came to me that it was strange he seemed to remember a brief conversation with an urchin child so well after all these years. Had the events of that dreadful afternoon become engraved upon his mind, as they had on mine?

'Do come and look, Morwenna.' Jessica was beckoning me over. 'Such pretty carved figurines. What are they made of, Maxwell?'

Reluctantly I went across to the trunk. Maxwell took up a small rounded figure of a man. 'This is of jade. It is what is known as a laughing Buddha. Perhaps, Father, it would look well on your desk.'

'Indeed, yes,' Mr Thurlow said with satisfaction. 'I should find that pleasant to look at while I was writing dull letters to my managers or lawyers.'

'And this I am very pleased to see!' Maxwell exclaimed, as Jessica handed him another figurine. 'Would you believe it – I searched high and low for my Kuan Yin before I left Singapore. My good servant must have packed it in here and forgotten where he had put it.'

'What did you call it?' Jessica asked.

'Kuan Yin. The Goddess of Mercy. She has been the constant companion of my travels in the East. She was given to me by an old man in gratitude for a service I rendered him.'

'It is very delicate,' Jessica said.

'The work of a craftsman in ivory,' Maxwell agreed. 'See how finely the robes are carved and how he has caught the smile that is mysterious and knowing and compassionate. The Chinese have many deities but the most honoured and best loved is the Goddess of Mercy. Many miracles are attributed to her, and it is believed that merely speaking her name with reverence is enough to avert an impending disaster.' His hard fingers, oddly gentle now, touched the graceful folds of the ivory gown. 'She has certainly protected me through storms on the China seas and brought me more luck in business ventures than I could have expected.'

Mrs Thurlow looked down her nose at it. 'Such heathenish ideas, Maxwell,' she rebuked. 'It smacks of idolatry.'

'Heathenish? Perhaps,' he said. 'It depends upon your viewpoint. I know that the Chinese consider themselves a superior and civilized race and regard the white man as a rough barbarian. Certainly,' he added coldly, 'we have little to be proud of in our behaviour towards them. For example, the so-called Opium War brought us great benefits in that we can trade freely now with China, but it was a treaty won by brute force.'

'I understand that there are great profits to be made in the supplying of opium to China,' Miss Webster remarked.

'Quite,' Maxwell agreed. 'And when the rulers saw so many of their people becoming weakened in body and mind by the use of the drug, that was when they decided to try and stop the traffic.' He shrugged. 'But what use were their pitiful weapons against the might of the British?' He paused. 'But I fear I bore you with my opinions. It is a subject on which I feel strongly. I have myself seen men worn down to feeble skeletons from excessive smoking of opium. The trade is a degrading one.'

'Were you involved in the war?' Jessica asked, wide-eyed, her butterfly mind picking out the one fact that might offer a little excitement. Discussions on anything of a serious nature bored her dreadfully.

'It was well over before I arrived in the East,' Maxwell said. 'As you should know if you attended properly to your schoolbooks.'

Jessica wrinkled her nose. 'I have no head for dull facts.'

'As Miss Webster knows to her costs.' Mr Thurlow laughed.

'Well, a war in some remote spot is hardly of interest to us here in rural Cheshire,' Mrs Thurlow said. There was a peevish note in her voice. Obviously she did not take kindly to the implied reproach in Maxwell's lecture, but surrounded as she was by proofs of his generosity, she could not say so outright. 'We have more immediate concerns – have we not? – for if we do not stir ourselves the afternoon will be quite gone and it will be far too late to drive to the river, as we had decided.'

Jessica, immediately diverted, jumped to her feet, tumbling the silk haphazardly into the trunk. 'Everyone must hurry,' she declared. 'The carriage is ordered and we shall take some refreshment with us. It will be just like old times.'

I had hoped to escape the outing and had found an unexpected ally in Miss Webster.

'I am sure you have so much to talk about of a private nature.' she had said quietly to Mr Thurlow, who had suggested the outing at luncheon. 'Morwenna and I will occupy ourselves most agreeably here.'

'Nonsense,' Mr Thurlow had said. 'You and Morwenna must come. The outing will do you good, Miss Webster, after all your troubles of the last weeks.' He would listen to no more arguments so Miss Webster had submitted, though rather less charitably than usual. I wondered why. She was normally eager for any jaunt into the countryside, especially when the weather was as fine as it was today.

Jessica had gone from the room, followed more sedately by her parents. Maxwell delayed and as I carefully folded the Chinese shawl and prepared to leave, he said, one hand gesturing towards the abandoned trunk: 'I should like you to have something else, Morwenna. A length of material for a dress.' His mouth twisted in a smile. 'I shall consult my stepmother, of course, and doubtless we can between us decide on something suitable.'

I knew he was thinking of our conversation on the hillside this morning, and the irrepressible thought crept into my mind that there would be a battle of wills when Maxwell suggested his idea to Mrs Thurlow. She would, without doubt, consider everything the trunk contained far too fine for me, and Maxwell would override all her arguments in his casual and overbearing way. I smiled at the thought of it and Maxwell, taking my smile for agreement, gave a curt nod in my direction before he left the room.

'You see, he is basically a most considerate man,' Miss Webster said. 'He has much of his father in him.'

I did not argue. Miss Webster, like everyone else, seemed to see only the charming, superficial Maxwell Thurlow. I saw, or thought I did, the arrogant, unfeeling inner man, the man who had ridden down my father. I did not like him and nothing anyone could say would ever change my mind.

A tributary of the River Bollin ran a little way from the house and the drive to the picnic place was a pleasant one. The road skirted the tilled fields of one of Mr Thurlow's tenant farmers before dipping down through woods carpeted with bluebells and the long spurs of new bracken. In the freckled shade of the trees the light was green and cool. It was almost like being plunged under water, and the lone rider who eased his mount over the ruts ahead could have been a strange submarine animal moving towards us.

'Why, it is Lord Easthulme,' Mrs Thurlow cried.

The man reined his horse alongside the carriage, acknowledged his introduction to Maxwell with brief courtesy, quickly dismissed Miss Webster and me with a disinterested glance before his pale eyes turned to Jessica. Lord Easthulme looked a better figure on a horse than he did on his own plump legs. He was not more than twenty-two or three years old but already he had a flabby look. The buttons of his riding coat were strained against the inexorable push of his stomach, though I had to admit that with his small neat features and soft, thinning fair hair he was not unpleasant to look at. But in another few years his fondness for food and drink would, I fancied, clothe his small frame in layers of gross flesh. He would not look so personable then.

'I have been to look over a horse I was thinking of buying,' he said, 'but it is a no-account beast.' He drew out a handkerchief and mopped his forehead. 'The heat is fierce today. But upon my soul, Miss Thurlow, you look as cool and fresh as a woodland nymph.'

'Indeed she does,' Mrs Thurlow agreed. I could see that she was more than delighted by this chance encounter and Jessica did look charming, if a trifle impatient, in a straw bonnet trimmed with pink ribbon. Her mother, seeing her anxiety to be off, said: 'Lord Easthulme, you must be quite weary with riding in this heat. We are driving to the river; perhaps you would care to join us for a glass of wine before you proceed further.'

Mr Thurlow, with perhaps a little less enthusiasm, pressed the invitation. Lord Easthulme promptly accepted.

We drove on a little way until we reached the stretch of open ground running down to the river. Here we alighted and went to the water's edge. Mrs Thurlow was soon settled in a chair in the shade of a clump of birch trees and rugs were spread for the rest of us. Maxwell opened the hamper we had brought and plunged the wine bottles and the stone jars of ginger ale to cool in the stream.

Lord Easthulme set himself out to be entertaining. He was a man with the facility for dramatizing trivial incidents into amusing anecdotes. In his rather loud nasal voice he told of a misunderstanding with his tailor, of a horse that had cast its shoe in a sudden snowfall, of an innkeeper who had tried to cheat him over a night's lodging. '. . . I told the fellow that he should mind his manners or I would duck him in his own horse-trough. The threat of water upon his person had a more admirable effect than that of a horsewhipping could have done. I fear the rogue had not washed for a twelvemonth . . .'

In all these anecdotes he showed himself in a most agreeable light. Human enough, I supposed. But though Mrs Thurlow and Jessica laughed and exclaimed at every baited pause, Mr Thurlow merely regarded him with a polite smile and Maxwell seemed totally unamused and busied himself intently on pouring the wine and ginger ale and handing round some of Cook's delicious patties.

'A rather overbearing young man,' Miss Webster whispered in my ear. 'I think our little outing is not turning out quite as poor Mr Thurlow would have liked.'

'If only he would stop talking,' I murmured, 'we should have a chance to listen to the birdsong and the sound of the river.'

'Perhaps we could go for a little stroll, you and I,' Miss Webster said. 'I should very much like to chance upon the kingfisher we glimpsed last time we were here . . . if we could slip quietly away without being noticed.'

But as we stood up and began to saunter along the river bank Mr Thurlow said, 'I shall stretch my legs, I think. Would you excuse me, my dear,' and Lord Easthulme said: 'Why, that sounds a fine notion. Perhaps Miss Thurlow would care to accompany us?' Then Mrs Thurlow, not to be outdone, declared herself to be in need of a little exercise, too.

Miss Webster shot me a wry look. 'Our kingfisher will fly away and hide unless his Lordship is suddenly stricken with lockjaw,' she said tartly, so that I had to turn my head away to hide my smile from the rest of the party.

We could not walk down the path more than two abreast and somehow, to my chagrin, after Miss Webster had paused to examine a clump of honeysuckle, I found myself walking with Maxwell. As Mr Thurlow had caught up with Miss Webster and apparently took the same deep interest in the honeysuckle, I had no option but to continue with him.

He did not seem disposed to talk, for which I was grateful, and strode ahead purposefully while the sound of Lord Easthulme's braying voice receded behind us. At the point where the path began to climb away from the river and the river itself became a small waterfall, we stopped. He leaned back against an overhang of mossy grey stone and stared moodily into the swirling water.

'He is a fortune hunter,' he said presently.

'Lord Easthulme? It is well known in the district that he wants a wealthy wife. There are also many mammas who would like a title for their daughters. Mrs Thurlow regards him as a catch.'

'Then I pity poor, unsuspecting Jessica. And if I have any say in the matter she shall not contemplate a marriage with him.'

'But you will not have any say, will you?' I said. I knew it was an impertinent remark but I wanted to goad him.

His mouth tightened. 'You think not?'

'She is only your half-sister,' I added. 'Surely it will be for Mrs Thurlow to decide; that is, if Lord Easthulme offers for her hand. There are other pretty and rich girls in the neighbourhood, you know.'

'Then I wish he would turn his attentions elsewhere.

There is bad blood in that family. I had the misfortune to meet his father once. He was a drunken lout who had gambled away a fortune in his time. A marriage there will bring only misery.'

'A son does not necessarily turn out to be like his father.'

'But the signs are already there. There is an air of decadence about the man.'

I found myself in reluctant agreement with Maxwell. Jessica, so heedless and easily led, could be guided into a marriage that would make her unhappy. I did not like Lord Easthulme with his pale, greedy eyes, and I secretly hoped that Maxwell would try and influence Mr and Mrs Thurlow. But I would not give him the satisfaction of knowing that.

'It occurs to me,' I said sweetly, 'that you are burning to put the whole household in order now that you are returned. First my affairs have come under your scrutiny, now Jessica's. Eight years' absence has given you a crusading zeal. But there will be many ruffled tempers at Ashridge Hall if you set yourself at odds with all its inhabitants. You cannot expect to leave a place for such a length of time, then return wanting to change everything that displeases you.'

'Doubtless,' he said with sarcasm, 'you will derive much pleasure from pointing out where I go wrong.'

I could not lie. 'Indeed I should,' I agreed calmly.

'Then perhaps I should appoint you as my conscience, to ensure that I do not tread on too many toes.' His eyes narrowed against the slanting sunlight. For a moment he seemed uncertain whether to be amused or angry at my temerity. Perhaps he was unused to girls who stood up to him.

'An appointment I should reject instantly,' I answered. 'I have no fancy to be your keeper.'

Amusement won. 'You should watch out for yourself, Princess,' he mocked. 'That barbed tongue of yours will lead people to assume you are as prickly and unapproachable as a porcupine, when all the time,' he added softly, hearing the sound of voices drawing near, 'there is a woman of warmth and sensibility hiding under the prickles.'

I turned away, oddly confused by his words. But I forgot my confusion instantly at the sight of the little tableau that was in the space of a few seconds acted out in front of my eyes.

Mr Thurlow and Miss Webster were strolling along the path. Miss Webster was carrying a small posy of honeysuckle and bluebells she had gathered and she seemed to be staring down at them with an unduly concentrated air; almost as though she was determined to find a focus for her eyes rather than look at Mr Thurlow, who was chatting away pleasantly, totally unaware of the strained look she had.

As they negotiated a sycamore sapling that leaned across the path, a branch caught at Miss Webster's hand so that some of the flowers were flung to the ground. Mr Thurlow bent to pick them up and as he handed them to her with a courtly bow, for a fraction of time their hands touched. The contact was so fleeting as to be hardly noticeable, but Miss Webster started as though she had been burned. She slowly raised her eyes to look at him. In the languorous warmth of the summer afternoon, the air drowsy with the sound of bees and tumbling water, their glances met. I saw her lips move: 'Thank you.' But the phrase had no meaning: it was her eyes that spoke. In that moment her homely face was beautiful, filled with inexpressible feeling.

The erect and severe governess in the dark dress and the spare, middle-aged man with the greying beard seemed, then, to become different people. Younger, innocent somehow, touched with a radiance not entirely born of the sunlight that dazzled my eyes and haloed their figures in a nimbus of gold.

Then it was over. Miss Webster turned away, her look

tight and withdrawn. Mr Thurlow, wearing a puzzled, almost dazed air, blinked and looked about him as though noticing where he was for the first time.

I could have imagined it. It could have been an illusion. But I knew it was not. With a sense of shock I realized exactly the implications of what I had just witnessed. Miss Webster's uncharacteristic behaviour since she had returned yesterday all became frighteningly clear.

I wondered how long she had lived with her secret. Surely not for all the years she had lived at Ashridge Hall! The burden would have been too much to bear. Perhaps there had been an imperceptible growth of love and only these last weeks, when she had been caring for her sick brother and Mr Thurlow had visited her in Manchester, had the bitter-sweet truth been revealed to her. Whatever the answer, it was only now, exhausted after her nursing duties, that she had allowed the mask to slip and show the pent-up emotions beneath.

I was overwhelmed with pity for her situation. At the same time, as I saw Lord Easthulme approaching with Mrs Thurlow and Jessica, I felt deeply afraid for her. Her situation was already precarious, though she did not yet know it. If Mrs Thurlow got the merest hint of Miss Webster's feelings, it would surely bring disaster.

I glanced at Maxwell. He, too, had been watching but his face was expressionless. Perhaps he noticed nothing amiss, but I knew enough of him now to realize that there was little that passed him by unobserved.

'Ah, there you all are,' Lord Easthulme cried with a high laugh. 'You have positively raced along. For myself, I find even the slowest pace far too energetic in this heat and I am already athirst for another glass of that cooling wine.'

'Then we shall return straight away,' Mrs Thurlow said gaily. She fanned herself. 'It is quite airless in the valley here.'

We began to retrace our steps along the path. For the first time I was glad of Lord Easthulme's flow of loud, trivial conversation. It covered the fact that four members of the party were silent – Miss Webster, Mr Thurlow, Maxwell, myself.

Though the sunlight was as pleasant and warm as before, I seemed to sense a shadow lying across us all.

The shadow, to my uneasy imagination, coloured the next few days. The household appeared subdued. Of course, it could have been the anti-climax. After the initial excitement of Maxwell's return there was a flat aftermath. The men closeted themselves in Mr Thurlow's library to discuss business, which meant I could not lose myself, as usual, in my self-appointed task of cataloguing the books. My one escape route was closed and I seemed to find myself constantly at the beck and call of Mrs Thurlow, who was tetchy because she and Maxwell had crossed swords over the matter of the dress length that was to be given to me. Maxwell had won the battle. They had finally agreed upon a length of Indian muslin in pale almond green with a border pattern of flowers. It was the least ornate of all the materials in the chest, yet it had obviously irritated Mrs Thurlow to have to give it to me. She made sure I understood how much she had sacrificed in parting with it, and gave Mrs Ackroyd instructions that it was to be made in the plainest possible style. 'Men have such impracticable ideas.' she declared. 'It is a material that will soil far too easily.'

I was torn between genuine pleasure at the prospect of a new dress to wear instead of shabby, outgrown cottons, and a dislike of receiving Maxwell's charity and Mrs Thurlow's condescension. My other gown, the one for the ball, now hung in my wardrobe protected from dust by an old sheet Mrs Ackroyd had pinned around it. I knew that the dust-cover was in the nature of a disguise, to keep its beauty from inquisitive eyes.

To the superficial observer, the household went about its way normally. Mrs Thurlow and Jessica made some afternoon visits. Miss Webster took Jessica and me through our lessons in French conversation and escorted us into the grounds to sketch the splendid roses. She had quite recovered her composure. The mask was securely back in place. Mr Thurlow was his usual quiet and courteous self, and if he did not discuss the book he was reading or some item of interest in the newspaper with Miss Webster, well, surely that was because he was fully occupied in bringing Maxwell up-to-date with his affairs. Yet I noticed how frequently his eyes were drawn to her when he thought he was unobserved; as we sang hymns in the family pew of the church on Sunday, or listened to Jessica singing and playing for us in the evenings. He looked troubled, almost morose, though the look was instantly gone if someone spoke to him or called his attention away.

I avoided Maxwell as much as I could. I made sure I did not oversleep again and was out with the dogs before anyone but the servants were about. I wanted no more meetings to spoil the beauty of those solitary summer mornings, and I was pleased when Mr Thurlow announced at luncheon on Monday that he was taking Maxwell with him to Manchester the following day.

Mr Thurlow was considering the purchase of a mill. 'It is an old building,' he had told us some weeks ago, 'and is somewhat dilapidated. But it has shown a profit in the past, and if I can persuade the owner to lower his selling price it will allow me a margin to set about modernizing it.' That was something he much enjoyed – buying a run-down business and turning it into an efficient and profitable proposition. 'I aim to make my workers satisfied,' he always said. 'Given good working conditions and a fair wage, there will always be men and women eager to give an honest day's labour.' It was for that reason that he insisted on his managers and overseers being upright men, for once he had put a business on its feet he did not concern himself with the chore of day-to-day running but merely kept a firm hand on the reins. To that end he spent several days each week in Manchester, staying at his club in King Street.

Miss Webster knew the mill. It was not far from where her brother lived and many of his parishioners worked there. 'It will be a blessing if Mr Thurlow does buy the place,' Miss Webster had confided privately to me. 'Charles has had a great deal of trouble with Mr Chorlton, the present owner. He has no belief in workers' rights and has opposed every effort made to improve their lot from the Factory Act to the Ten Hour Bill. But he is an elderly man and ailing. A succession of idle managers has allowed the mill to become sadly run down.' She shook her head. 'It will take a deal of capital to bring the mill back to a decent standard. I have heard that the whole building vibrates when all the machinery is going, as there are weaving looms packed on all floors, a purpose for which the mill was not intended. The workers have sometimes feared that the whole building was going to fall down, and my brother has appealed to Mr Chorlton on more than one occasion to call in an engineer to check on its safety.'

I, too, hoped that Mr Thurlow would buy the business but my motives were not so philanthropic. The taking on of a new venture like this always involved a great deal of hard work and kept Mr Thurlow very busy. With Maxwell here, he would be bound to help his father and, while he was engaged this way, then the household would see less of him, which would certainly be to my satisfaction.

But their visit to Manchester this week, with the birthday celebration in the offing, was to be brief. They would stay only one night and return Wednesday evening. I looked forward to the respite. I found Maxwell's presence a continual strain; it was like a probe constantly touching on a sensitive nerve. He had only to walk into the room where I was and I could feel myself tensing, every muscle and fibre of my being stretching taut and alert. Yet it was an odd thing that, even when he had left with Mr Thurlow, the sense of his presence seemed to linger in the house. At meal times I half-expected him to walk in at the door, apologizing for his lateness. I caught myself listening for the sound of his brisk footsteps ringing on the polished oak strip floor as we sat quietly sewing in the evening.

It came to me, as I laboriously worked at what would, hopefully, change from a piece of crumpled linen into a cushion cover, that so long as Maxwell and I lived under the same roof I would never know peace of mind. I was angry with myself, and sad and bitter, too. I felt that I should have more self-control, but where Maxwell was concerned, the wound was too deep. An old wound, true, but the scar would always be sensitive and no amount of reasoning or logic could heal it.

The letter for Maxwell arrived on Wednesday morning. It was sealed flamboyantly and addressed in a small, feminine hand.

'It must be from Miss Pritchard,' Jessica said, picking it up from the tray as we came indoors. 'Do you suppose it is to say when she will arrive?'

'Most likely,' I said calmly.

'It is very neat handwriting.' She held it to her nose. 'And smells delicious.'

'Put it down,' I said. 'Neither the letter nor its perfume is for your benefit.'

She was not deterred. She turned the letter over in her fingers. 'I wish Maxwell was here. I am so eager to know if she is well enough to come.'

'He will be back within a very few hours. Your curiosity

will not have to wait long to be satisfied.'

'But this very letter could be to inform us that she is to arrive today!'

'You make a drama out of everything,' I said, laughing. 'I am sure that Miss Pritchard will give us adequate warning of her arrival.'

But as it happened Jessica was right and I was wrong. We had barely finished luncheon when Mrs Bradshaw hurried in.

'There is a Mr Pritchard just arrived, ma'am,' she announced a little breathlessly. 'And a Miss Pritchard.'

'I knew it!' Jessica cried. 'There must have been a delay in the post.'

'Maybe so,' Mrs Thurlow said a little tartly, 'but they have come at rather an awkward time, with your father and Maxwell not here . . . Are their rooms prepared?'

'As you ordered, ma'am,' Mrs Bradshaw said. 'In the West Wing.'

'That is something, at any rate. Now do sit still, Jessica; it ill becomes you to display such impatience. Show them to the drawing-room, Mrs Bradshaw. I shall be along in a few moments.'

We waited while Mrs Thurlow nibbled a last strawberry tartlet and patted her lips daintily on her napkin before she rose and led the way to where the Pritchards waited.

It was Mr Pritchard who spoke, who expressed dismay that his daughter's letter had arrived only today, who apologized profusely for the inconveniece their unexpected arrival must cause and generally set himself to be charming, as introductions were made. But it was Isabel Pritchard who drew my eyes.

My first reaction was that she was too beautiful, too fragile-looking to be real. Her oval face was pale, with the thick, opaque pallor of a magnolia petal. Heavy lids weighed down with long, gold-tipped lashes gave the grey eyes a sleepy look that the faint blue shadows underneath emphasized. She had sunk into the chair as though her legs were too tired to carry her slight weight, and her hands lay limp in her lap. Yet despite her obvious exhaustion, not a curl of glossy copper hair, nor a ribbon, nor a frill on her crisp white dress was out of place. She reminded me of the elegant china doll that had once been Jessica's pride and joy.

At her feet crouched the oddest creature; a small, brown-skinned woman wrapped in strangely patterned robes. She was fanning her mistress with a paper fan, her small eyes in her wrinkled face watching us all with monkeyish sharpness as she quietly crooned some outlandish melody.

'. . . even though we made our journey in easy stages,' Mr Pritchard was saying, 'I'm afraid my daughter has suffered unbearably. She really has not fully recovered from her recent indisposition – '

'Oh, Papa, you make me sound such an invalid,' Isabel protested. Her voice was soft and languid. 'You must forgive me, Mrs Thurlow. I am merely a trifle tired and will soon recover when I have rested for an hour or two.'

Mr Pritchard, a dapper little man with sandy hair and bushy side whiskers, gazed at his daughter with devotion plain to see on his round red face. 'She may look a frail creature – ' he smiled – 'but she has an iron will when she has set her mind on a particular object. She was perfectly determined to get better in order to attend the forthcoming celebrations.'

'And I am glad you have come,' Jessica breathed. 'I have been longing to meet you – and you are every bit as beautiful as Maxwell told us, Miss Pritchard.'

'I am Isabel, my dear Jessica. Do not let us be so formal.' She was obviously pleased with her reception and responded sweetly by saying: 'I, too, have looked forward to meeting Maxwell's family, but he never told me he had such a *pretty* little sister.'

Jessica blushed and Mrs Thurlow said, 'When Maxwell left us, Jessica was only a child.'

'And I do believe that brothers are notoriously blind to the charms of their sisters.' Mr Pritchard chuckled. 'I could never quite understand why bold, strapping young men turned into tongue-tied, calf-eyed jellies in the presence of my own sister. Clara used to get quite cross with me, as I remember!'

Mrs Thurlow laughed, warming visibly to her guests, then exclaimed: 'But I am forgetting myself. Have you dined? Or perhaps you would like a little light refreshment – some tea, perhaps, or a glass of Madeira?'

'For myself, nothing,' Mr Pritchard said. 'We have already eaten. Isabel . . . ?' He looked questioningly at her.

She lifted a small, white-gloved hand, spreading the fingers wide, then letting it fall wearily again to her lap. 'A cool drink would be most welcome,' she said. 'Could it perhaps be brought to my room? I have need of a rest more than anything else.'

'Of course,' Mrs Thurlow said. 'Morwenna shall show you to your room and make sure you are quite comfortable there.' To me, rather more sharply, she added: 'Morwenna, give your arm to Miss Pritchard, you can see she is a trifle indisposed.'

I stepped forward to take her arm. As I did so, the foreign woman, with surprising litheness, stood up and placed herself squarely in front of the chair, blocking my way. A pair of eyes, as shiny and hard as wet pebbles, glared at me. She spat out some words in a strange language.

'Aminah!' That was the only word I heard clearly as Mr Pritchard embarked on a reprimand. The woman hunched her shoulders under the long, brightly patterned tunic and shuffled her broad bare feet that were encased in heelless slippers. The eyes still watched me with barely concealed malevolence.

'You must forgive Aminah,' Mr Pritchard said, turning to us apologetically. 'She has been with Isabel since she was a small child and has been faithful nurse and maid all these years. I'm afraid she thinks that gives her the right to be more bold than is acceptable in a servant. You see, she has never before been away from the Malay States. This journeying to strange countries is all very new and trying for her and has made her more than usually possessive of her mistress.'

Mrs Thurlow frowned. 'I hope,' she ventured nervously, 'that this – this person will not upset my own servants. They may not take kindly to a foreign woman especially one with such peculiar ways.'

'Aminah will be no trouble at all once we are settled,' Mr Pritchard assured her. 'She will sleep on a pallet in Isabel's room, as she always has done. If she is allowed the use of a stove, she will prepare all her own food. The servants need not be troubled at all by her.'

'I trust so,' Mrs Thurlow said, still apprehensive. 'I find her rather wild-looking and more than a shade frightening in appearance.'

Mr Pritchard laughed. 'If you had seen the way she has devoted herself to Isabel, how she cossets her and anticipates her every wish, you would not say that. It is more than likely that she is scared of you and this big, new house, and is bolstering up her own courage by a show of aggressiveness.'

Mrs Thurlow did not look convinced any more than I. Aminah might have been devoted to Isabel Pritchard, but it seemed that she scorned the rest of us.

Isabel rose to her feet and stood there, swaying with the effort. I stepped forward and tucked my hand under her elbow. She had gone so ill-looking, I thought she might faint. Aminah, showing concern and so ignoring me, supported Isabel on her other side.

'Had I better carry you upstairs, my dear?' Mr Pritchard

asked anxiously. 'You look quite overcome.'

'No, indeed,' Isabel said. Her voice was low but firm. 'The dizziness is passing.' She smiled wanly. 'You must not fuss over me, Papa. I have quite enough of that with Aminah. I shall be quite well when I have rested.'

We went slowly up the stairs, Aminah murmuring words of encouragement in her own tongue. There was an odd hesitancy about Isabel's walk, as though she had difficulty in moving her left leg from stair to stair. 'I'm afraid I have sat so long that my foot has gone to sleep,' she cried almost gaily as we reached the top. But I noticed the fine dew of perspiration on her short upper lip. The climb had been a tremendous effort for her.

When we came to her room she gave a huge sigh and sank immediately on to the pristine cover of the bed. 'How welcome this is,' she breathed, the heavy eyelids dropping over her eyes, the lids curving down and the lashes casting shadows on the thick, white skin of her cheek.

Aminah leaned over her, untying her bonnet, loosening the neck of her dress, removing her shoes. Isabel lay motionless all the while, looking more than ever like a small, fragile doll.

I watched her from the other side of the bed. I felt sorry for her helplessness, for the illness that must inevitably cloud what was to have been a happy reunion with Maxwell.

'Is there anything I can get for you?' I asked gently. 'Would you like me to stay? I could sit and read to you, if you wished.'

She did not open her eyes. 'It is kind of you,' she said in a whisper, 'but Aminah will cope perfectly well.'

As though she understood the English words, the little Malay woman smiled maliciously at me. Then she spoke out, loudly and incomprehensibly, ending with what sounded like *'Pergi! Pergi!'*

'No, no, Aminah,' Isabel said weakly, 'you must not talk

like that.' She lapsed back into what was presumably Malay before saying to me: 'I am sorry. She is not normally like this. She is a kind soul. It is almost as though this house has had a strange effect on her. She has been strange and uneasy ever since we entered the grounds.'

'It is no matter,' I said, passing it off lightly, though I was well aware of those penetrating wet-pebble eyes staring at me as if they would pierce me to the heart. 'I will leave you to rest and send Emmy up with some of Cook's refreshing lemonade . . . '

I got no further. I had reached over to straighten the pillow under Isabel's head and found my wrist caught in a hard, brown hand.

'Not touch!' Aminah hissed. 'Not touch, Missy!'

Then she added a phrase in Malay which had a sudden and startling effect on Isabel. The sleepy eyes opened wide and she pushed herself up on one elbow.

'That is a terrible thing to say,' she gasped.

I looked from one to the other. 'What – what was it? Do tell me what she said.' I kept my voice steady though the Malay woman's vehemence, the tight grasp of her fingers, had sent a cold spear of fright right through me.

'Oh, it is foolishness,' Isabel said. She laughed, but the laughter wobbled and her eyes were troubled. 'You see,' she began hesitantly, 'Aminah's family, her mother and grandmother, have all been wise women, with a gift of the second sight. Aminah has inherited that – or at least the other servants, who were superstitious and ignorant people, believed so. They held her in some awe. From time to time she sees – or believes she does – things that others do not.'

'Oh? And what does she see here, at Ashridge Hall?' I mocked, though truth to tell I felt a sudden coldness upon me as though I stood in a draught. 'We have no ghosts that I know of.'

Isabel shook her head and lay back, the rich coppery

waves of her hair startling against the whiteness of the pillow. I did not know why I thought of her then as a tragic figure, lying so pale and weary and beautiful in the quiet room. She had everything that I had not – wealth, position, security, but the sympathy I had felt earlier for her was now stronger than ever, which made what she said next so ridiculous, so outlandish.

'I am so sorry,' Isabel said flatly, 'but Aminah has taken against you in a most illogical manner. She says – ' the troubled grey eyes under their heavy lids lifted to mine sadly – 'she says that there is much unhappiness for me in this house. She says that you . . . you wish me harm.'

'But that is foolish!' I burst out. 'We hardly know each other. We have only just met.'

Isabel Pritchard moved her coppery head restlessly on the pillow and added in a flat, cold little voice: 'Nevertheless, Aminah insists that before long you will be wishing me in my grave . . . '

Her eyes closed again. I stared down at her, aghast and frightened by what I had heard. Then I turned on my heel and fled from the room.

CHAPTER FIVE

Mr Pritchard had said that Isabel had a strong will and she proved it by coming down to dinner. I was convinced that it was sheer will-power that kept her back so straight and her smile so pleasant as she turned from Mr Thurlow to Maxwell at the dinner table, talking to each in turn. Her face was blanched but her eyes were bright and feverish, and I noticed that the hand which raised the glass or toyed with spoon or fork trembled slightly.

Only once during the meal did the conversation take an awkward turn when, in a sudden silence, Mr Pritchard was heard to remark to Mrs Thurlow, 'Aminah is a wonder. She has brewed Isabel one of her mysterious concoctions and it has quite revived her.' Then, seeing all heads turn his way, he added to Isabel: 'Has it not, my dear?'

'Quite remarkably, Papa,' Isabel said quietly, and down the length of the table our glances met and fell away in quickly covered embarrassment.

I saw Mrs Thurlow's lips tighten at the mention of Aminah and she deftly changed the subject. I knew, because Miss Webster had whispered it to me before we had gone in to dinner, that the Malay woman had already caused trouble in the kitchen. 'Mrs Bradshaw said that she stalked into the kitchen bold as you please, took a saucepan and began boiling up some revolting herbal mixture over the range,' Miss Webster had said, amused. 'I should dearly love to have seen Cook's face! As it was, she took immediate umbrage and threatened to give in her notice if the woman was not removed on the instant.' Her hazel eyes twinkled. 'Aminah has caused something of a sensation among the domestic staff. They are saying she is a heathen and a witch and not fit to mingle with decent Christians. The scullery maid, a half-witted creature, had an hysterical fit, crying and screaming about the evil eye. Mrs Bradshaw scolded them all roundly. But she has had the good sense to give the woman the use of an old outhouse so that she can brew up her witch's potions in splendid isolation.'

I thought of those malevolent pebble-wet eyes and the force of Aminah's possessive jealousy, and understood the scullery maid's distress. I had told nothing to Miss Webster of what had been said in Isabel Pritchard's room: it was surely best not to repeat the outpourings of an uneducated and superstitious mind. What Aminah had said had frightened me, though once I had had time to think about it logically, I had been able to laugh at myself. All the same, a tinge of uneasiness remained and it bothered me.

It must have bothered Isabel too, because as the ladies left the gentlemen to their port and cigars, she contrived to walk beside me into the drawing-room.

'I hope you will forget that unfortunate incident this afternoon,' she said. The heavy-lidded eyes stared into mine and there was pleading in them. 'Aminah has been upset by all this moving about and by my illness. She has a natural concern for me which leads her now and again to excessive displays of protection. Normally I would not let her have her head so, but I am afraid that in my exhaustion I allowed her to go too far.'

'Please think no more of it,' I said lightly. 'I have more sense than to believe such superstitious nonsense. Consider that I have forgotten it already.' I must have sounded convincing for she looked relieved.

'Thank you, Morwenna,' she said, adding a little too eagerly: 'You will not mention it to anyone else? They might not understand. If it got to Papa's ears he would be so cross with Aminah and I could not bear that. I rely on her and she is such a faithful servant to me.'

I set her mind at rest. 'It shall be a secret between us,' I whispered conspiratorially so that she smiled and seemed to relax a little.

The rest of the evening passed pleasantly enough. The men soon joined us, and from where Miss Webster and I sat quietly with our embroidery I saw how Isabel became the natural focus of attention. Jessica, almost spellbound by this exquisite bride-to-be of her half-brother, fetched her a footstool and adjusted the cushions behind her head each time she moved. Mr Thurlow and Mr Pritchard pressed refreshments on her and seemed to vie with each other in telling amusing anecdotes and looked pleased when they made her laugh. Maxwell hovered about her in the most protective way, the expression on his thin, bony face both gentle and adoring. They made a handsome couple. He so tall and masculine, with his hard good looks and black curly hair, she so fragile and small, with her copper-coloured hair and her flowerlike face and white skin. A perfect love-match, grown and nurtured over the long sea voyage under tropic skies.

I only wished that once they were married Isabel would demand to be taken back to the Malay States. I should warm to her even more if she took Maxwell away from the Hall and left us all in peace.

Sometimes it is possible to look back and pick out one incident – perhaps something small or of little account at the time – and say: 'There! If that had not happened then all that has followed since might have been very different.' One such incident was when I told Mr Thurlow that I wanted to learn to read. And what happened in the stableyard on the morning after Isabel Pritchard's arrival at Ashridge Hall was, in its way, also a turning point. It sparked off a sequence of events that, like it or not, gave my life a new direction.

I heard their voices, Maxwell's and Isabel's, as I returned from my morning walk. I had stayed out longer than usual with the dogs. The air, cool and as sweet as sparkling wine, had lured me into taking the longer route home through the top park. I remember I was thinking as I came round the back of the stables that the weather looked like holding for the weekend and how glad I was for Jessica's sake. Then I heard them talking and stopped in my tracks. I would have liked to have remained there until they had left the yard, but the dogs had bounded ahead of me and I heard Maxwell say: 'Ah, Morwenna must be around. These are her disreputable charges.' He said it not unkindly but his remark sent the usual prickle of indignation running through me.

I went on reluctantly and there they were.

Tom and Jacob had brought out the horses that were clattering their hooves on the cobbles and blowing through flaring nostrils. Skip was fussing around in his eager way, fronded tail wagging furiously as Maxwell bent to rub his ears. Dancer sniffed condescendingly at Maxwell's boots then backed off, watching Isabel with a suspicious eye.

Isabel looked rested this morning; the feverish, exhausted look was gone though there was still an air of languor about her. I thought that was probably habitual, the product perhaps of a lifetime spent in sultry tropical climates. She wore an immaculate dark green riding habit and carried her gloves and crop in one hand.

'Good morning,' I said. 'You are feeling better?'

'Much better,' she said. 'I slept soundly and woke early as I usually do. We tend to rise early in the tropics to make the most of the coolness of the early hours.' She laughed up at Maxwell. 'It is a habit I am finding it hard to break. Will it be considered unfashionable in England?'

'Unfashionable or not,' Maxwell said, his dark glance gentle, 'it will suit me admirably. This is the finest part of the day and to have your company will make it even more delightful.' And with a gesture, so natural and unaffected, he picked up her ungloved hand and bent his lips to it.

How are the mighty humbled by love, I thought sarcastically to myself. It was an idyllic picture and spoiled only when Skip chose that moment to draw attention to himself. He stood on his hind legs and put his fat paws on Isabel's skirt.

Isabel gave a little cry

'Get down!' she said. 'What a horrid creature! Look at those dirty marks on my skirt.'

Maxwell, with the tolerance of one used to the company of dogs said mildly, 'It is nothing, Isabel; a trace of mud only. See, it rubs off . . . '

'That's not the point,' Isabel said. 'I dislike dogs, flea-ridden things that they are, and I cannot bear an undisciplined animal. Morwenna, call him away this instant!' Her voice had an imperious ring, a voice used to immediate obedience.

I said quietly, 'Skip. Here, boy!' Amiably, Skip bounced to me and pushed his muzzle into my hand.

Dancer, who had been standing alertly near by, growled low in his throat at the tone of her voice. I suppose, in the way animals do, he sensed a threatening atmosphere and his response, as always, was to be aggressive.

Isabel looked round at him. 'He is growling at me. Is he vicious?'

'He will not harm you,' I said, 'provided you keep your distance.' And I added, to be on the safe side: 'Stay, Dancer!'

All would have been well if Isabel had ignored the dog and mounted her horse, but that wilful streak in her was uppermost and it was then she made a mistake.

She took a step towards Dancer, raising the riding crop. Whether she meant actually to strike the dog or whether she was merely making a defiant gesture it did not matter. She said, 'You need a lesson,' just as Tom cried, 'No, miss!' and Maxwell made to pull her back.

It was to no avail. Dancer went for her, as he would any stranger who came into his yard and threatened his authority. He went for the hand with the crop and Isabel screamed. Crop and gloves dropped to the cobbles and Dancer, having demonstrated who was master, trotted back to me and sat at my feet looking pleased with himself.

'Oh, Dancer,' I gasped, 'what have you done!'

He wagged his tail in answer, and when I bundled both dogs into an empty stable and shut them in he looked at me, puzzled.

When I got back to Isabel she was weeping. She cried easily, as a hurt child cries, and Maxwell was mopping her tears with his handkerchief in an almost fatherly way.

'There, there,' he said. 'It is nothing, my love. The skin is not broken and the pain will soon go.'

'It bit me,' she sobbed, 'that horrid dog. It hurts so!'

'You should have ignored him,' Maxwell said. 'He would not have touched you had you not threatened him.'

'How can you defend such a vicious animal?' Isabel wept. 'It should be destroyed.'

'Oh, no!' I cried out. 'It wasn't his fault.'

'Then what was it, do you suppose, that did this?' She held out her hand, her eyes sparkling with anger through the tears. I inspected the injury. There was little to see; Dancer had merely given her a warning and the light imprint of his teeth was already fading. I almost laughed aloud with relief.

Isabel snatched her hand away as Maxwell said consolingly, 'It gave you a fright, that was all. It is hardly a desperate injury, my dear.'

He seemed to take the matter too lightly for Isabel's satisfaction. 'A brute like that should not be allowed to run loose. I am surprised your father does not insist he is chained.'

'Dancer guards the stables,' I explained. 'What use would he be chained up if an intruder bent on mischief sneaked in?'

'And Morwenna warned you not to go near him,' Maxwell added.

She looked from Maxwell to me and suddenly all temper went. She seemed to sag like a marionette with its wires gone slack, leaning heavily on Maxwell's supporting arm.

'I feel quite overcome,' she faltered. 'Will you take me back to the house, Maxwell? I cannot face riding with you this morning.'

Maxwell was then all concern, cursing himself for a thoughtless fool while she stared up at him helplessly.

I watched them walk slowly away, thankful that Dancer had escaped so lightly. I had feared Isabel was going to make a great fuss about the incident. Maxwell knew that Isabel had been bitten because of her own headstrong impulse, but he loved her and would be bound to take her part had she insisted on retribution for Dancer.

My relief was short-lived. Within the hour the house was buzzing with the news, and Mr Thurlow called me to his study where he regarded me with gravity and concern.

'I am most disturbed,' he said. 'It is intolerable that a guest in this house should be attacked by one of our dogs.'

'It was her own fault,' I burst out.

Mr Thurlow raised his hand peremptorily. 'That is no matter,' he said in a voice unaccustomedly harsh. 'Isabel is delicate: her father has admitted to me his worry over her recent health. She has been most upset by the incident and I have insisted that the doctor be called in. I am sorry, Morwenna,' he added more gently, 'I know how fond you are of the animal, but I cannot risk a repetition of this morning's unhappy affair. I have to insist that the dog is destroyed.'

I felt the blood drain from my face. 'No . . . please,' I whispered.

'I am sorry,' he repeated. 'You must console yourself with

the fact that Dancer is an old dog. After all, it was only through your intervention that he was given extra years of life.'

He was trying to be kind, but I could feel only pain like a clenched fist thudding into my midriff. My nails bit deep into the flesh of my palms. My voice sounded unnatural as I strove for control. 'Maxwell saw everything. He will tell you that Dancer was provoked . . . '

Mr Thurlow shook his head and said shortly, 'My mind is made up.'

I saw from his stern face that my pleas would not touch him. Dancer had to die and I could not bear it. Wild ideas stormed through my head as I stood there. I would run away, take Dancer and Skip and rush to the hills. Turn my back on Ashridge Hall and its occupants . . . Then cold reality flooded in. Where would I go? I had no one who would take me in or give me shelter, no money to feed myself or my dogs. But I could not – would not – abandon Dancer to his fate without a struggle. I had begged for his life to be spared once before, now I would do so again.

It was no time for pride and I had no thought for it as I fled from the study. I encountered a startled Hetty with a tray who told me Mr Maxwell was in his room. I picked up my skirts and flew up the stairs. At Maxwell's door I knocked and barely waited for his answer before I was inside the room.

He turned from the small desk by the deep window where he had been writing, unfolding himself from the chair in surprise. 'What the devil – ?'

I said, incoherent with fear, 'You must help me! You must persuade your father. You saw it happen. He will listen to you!'

He took two strides across the room, black brows drawn down. I had interrupted him and he was displeased. 'Take hold of yourself,' he said sharply. 'Have we not had enough drama for one morning? What has happened now?'

I swallowed. I must be calm for Dancer's sake. Maxwell was my only hope. 'It is my dog, Dancer,' I began. I spoke through lips dry as dust, trying not to let the terror that I felt show through. Maxwell listened intently, and did not speak for a moment when I ended on a plea. 'Will you help me? There is no one else.'

An hour ago, ten minutes ago, I would have despised myself for begging anything from this tall, frowning man. Now I waited for his answer, a humble petitioner, and did not care a fig if he would only speak up for Dancer.

His black eyes searched my face and I thought in despair, he will not do it. I was a fool. How could I expect him to intercede on behalf of an old, lame hound of no value to anyone?

He said quietly, 'Very well.' My expression must have changed, for he added quickly: 'Do not expect too much but I will try to persuade my father to let the dog live.' A small wry smile touched his mouth. 'It is only a few days since you accused me of interference, now you beg me to do just that . . . But there, I am being unkind to someone in distress. It is hardly gallant.' The mockery was back but I did not care.

I said, pride gone to dust and ashes, 'I'm sorry I spoke as I did. Thank you for helping me now.' I kept my eyes on the frills of his shirt-front. There was a carved green stone carelessly pinned there, the twin of the stone on the hand that came towards me, touched my shoulder and gently pushed me down into a small chair.

'Stay here,' he ordered, adding drily: 'One female going into a swoon is quite sufficient for one day. I will be back directly with the verdict.'

I was too restless and worried to sit still. After he had gone I strode backwards and forwards across the thick red carpet. It was a large room furnished with dark oak pieces, satiny with years of polish, and the big double windows framed with red velvet curtains overlooked the front park. It was the finest of the guest rooms and normally it wore the air of such places – cared for but characterless. During the short periods it was occupied it took on an impression of its temporary owners before lapsing back into vacant orderliness. Now it had become, subtly, a man's room. There was a pair of plain, silver-backed brushes on the washstand, a leather writing case lay open on the desk covered with a sprawl of papers, a coat flung carelessly on a chair, and on the tallboy the ivory figure of Kuan Yin.

I went over for a closer look. Her smile was serene as she gazed upon the foreign room. There was compassion and sorrow in that smile, a tolerance of human follies and a knowledge that all suffering would pass. As I stood there I found myself silently begging for her aid. No doubt the vicar would have been scandalized at one of his flock praying to a heathen idol. Yet there was something about her that reached out to me, that gave me hope as the dry platitudes of the vicar's preaching had never done. I felt no strangeness, only an odd sort of comfort.

After a moment the focus of my eyes shifted to the mirror on the wall behind the tallboy and I saw why Maxwell had insisted that I remain here. My face was drained and gaunt, my eyes puddles of dark blue above hard white cheekbones. I looked as anguished as I felt and I turned from my ugly mirror image, sorry in an uncomfortable sort of way that Maxwell had seen me so exposed.

I waited in that pleasant room for many long minutes. before he returned. And when he did he was smiling. Dancer was reprieved.

'My father insists that he is to be kept chained during the daytime.' he warned, 'and that you are to be held responsible for any further misdemeanours that he may make.'

That was a light responsibility indeed. I should make very sure that Dancer was kept well away from anyone that he did not know. Foolishly, relief brought a huskiness to my throat as I stood straight before Maxwell and said, 'I cannot thank you enough. Dancer may be only a poor, ugly creature, but to me he is . . . he is . . . ' I wanted to say how I loved the tattered old foxhound but I could not seem to frame the words. I cleared my throat, swallowed and forced my voice to lightness. 'I shall give the good news to Tom.' I said, starting towards the door.

Maxwell caught me by the arm, hesitated as he stared at me, then said, his tone matching mine in lightness: 'I am glad I could be of some help. Give the old dog a friendly word from me.'

'I will,' I said, and made my escape, unaware in my innocence that it is in moments of joy or triumph or happiness that one should be most on guard. That is when fate has a habit of slyly turning and making a mockery of your achievements.

So it was to be. But I did not know it then when I ran so happily to the stables to tell Tom what had happened, and breathed a silent thanks to the little ivory goddess.

We saw nothing of Isabel that day. The doctor came and, after visiting the patient, spoke quietly with Mr Pritchard and Maxwell. Later we learned that Isabel was to rest and have no visitors, and tomorrow she would be able to get up and about again. He had also suggested that if there was no improvement he would arrange for a visit from a specialist physician in Manchester. 'He is an excellent man in his field and especially good with disorders of a nervous nature, which is what your daughter seems to be suffering from.' And he had added heartily: 'This little trouble with the dog had merely jarred her system, a system, I may say, already in an upset state from the travelling and the change of climate. A restful time in these beautiful surroundings will doubtless be all the medicine she requires. But to be on the safe side, a consultation with Dr Fraser will put your mind completely at ease.'

If the good doctor could have seen the house next day he would hardly have considered it a restful place. By mid-afternoon the carriages had all arrived. They contained Mrs Thurlow's three sisters, their husbands and families, two elderly aunts of Mr Thurlow's and several old family friends, all invited for the long weekend.

Jessica glowed like a rose as aunts and cousins kissed her and exclaimed at how she had grown and what a pretty girl she had become. Mrs Thurlow, laced into tight new stays that gave her plump figure a rigid but regal outline, was gracious in the extreme. Her sisters had not married as well as she had. They were all comfortably off, but large growing families had ensured that none of them had become very rich. It pleased Mrs Thurlow greatly that although she had been the last of the sisters to marry, she had been the one to find a husband who had not only inherited wealth but had the wit and intelligence to add to his fortune each year.

The guests were soon settled in. Jessica and the older of her cousins who were considered fit company for adults disposed themselves in a laughing group on the terrace. The old nurseries on the upper floor had been given over to the younger children and their nursemaids. 'We must keep the dear little ones entertained too,' Mrs Thurlow declared gaily to her sisters. She was not overly fond of other people's children and liked to see them organized well out of sight and hearing. I listened stoically as she went on: 'Morwenna is so good with the young ones; she will see that they have plenty to do.'

It was a role I had played before when guests were in the house, and I was resigned to it. I had felt more than once that it was Mrs Thurlow's way of ridding herself usefully of two nuisances – young children underfoot, and me. It meant that, apart from dinner, I ate my meals in the nursery. 'It is so much more convenient for everyone, Morwenna. Then you can see that the nursemaids do not squabble amongst themselves as well as supervising the children's manners.'

In one way I was glad of this arrangement. In the company of the children it did not matter that I looked dowdy: against the prettily gowned cousins I was ashamed of my drab appearance. I was only thankful that my new green muslin dress had been delivered that morning. Mrs Ackroyd must have performed miracles to make it so quickly. At least I should look respectable when I went in to dinner.

Even so, it would have been pleasant to have been part of that bright young gathering on the terrace instead of hurrying upstairs to face a cluster of unfamiliar children, over-excited and over-tired by their long journeys.

I was half-way up the stairs when I met Maxwell coming down with Isabel on his arm, the Malay woman a silent shadow at their heels. I felt a sudden awkwardness but Isabel smiled faintly and smoothed over the moment by informing me that she was going down to meet Maxwell's relatives.

'I am to be thoroughly spoiled,' she said in her soft voice. 'I am to lie in state on the sofa in the small parlour and receive my guests one by one.'

'And if you obey the doctor's instructions and do not over-tire yourself in any way, you will doubtless quite recover your strength.' Maxwell spoke heartily as though through words he could will part of his own strength on the delicate girl leaning on him. Then his black glance fell on me. 'Shall you come down to take tea with us?'

I explained my errand to the nurseries and he said sharply, 'Is it so important that you go? Surely the children have their own nursemaids to attend to them?'

I could see the pressure of Isabel's small white hand on his grey broadcloth sleeve. 'My dear, Morwenna has her duties. It is a busy time.' I felt myself dismissed. Though Isabel's manners were impeccable, it was obvious that she had taken my measure and was fully aware of my standing in the household.

I stood aside for them to pass but Maxwell, for some inexplicable reason, looked truculent and did not move. Then curtly he said, 'I trust we shall see you at dinner?' It was more of a command than a question.

'Yes, of course,' I said quietly, and only then did he move on down the stairs. I noticed that Isabel was limping again. No, it was not quite a limp – a hesitancy, as though her leg dragged slightly. Aminah followed after them, looking more alien than ever in a draped skirt patterned with strange red and green birds and a loose over-garment in gauzy yellow material. There were heavy silver ear-rings in her ears and I could hear the faint jangle of them as she moved. She kept her eyes down and did not look at me, but I could sense her hatred stealing across me like the musky scent of the pomade she wore on her oiled black hair. It was an odd and chilling sensation and I was glad to turn my back on her and hurry away to the more normal, if boisterous, atmosphere of the nurseries.

Miss Webster, as was usual on formal occasions, dined with Mrs Ackroyd in her sitting-room and did not join the guests. I thought wryly that she was the lucky one as I tried to make conversation with a spotty fifteen-year-old cousin of Jessica's and a deaf old friend of Mr Thurlow's. Everyone else at the dinner table seemed full of spirit. The long table sparkled with cut glass and silver and starched white napery: brilliant candlelight fell on powdered white shoulders and peacock silks and the perspiring faces of the maids as they hurried in with dish after laden dish.

I was glad when the meal ended and the remains of the roast meats and fowls, the crimped salmon, the towers of vegetables, the spiced sauces, the tarts, wine jellies and iced puddings were borne away. It had all been very splendid and the talk had grown louder as the wine glasses were replenished. But I was tired after my rumbustious afternoon with the children and bored by the dullness of my table companions.

Time and again my eyes were drawn to the top of the table where Isabel and Maxwell stood out in all that elegant company. I thought again how handsome they were. She was dressed as usual in white; thick, heavy lace this evening, with twists of silver and turquoise at her wrists and throat and a turquoise ornament in her copper hair. She looked composed and serene. And so she might, I thought wearily. Her day – her life – was hardly a tiring one. She did not appear to read, nor embroider, nor sketch, and she had admitted ruefully that her voice was not true enough to sing in company and playing the pianoforte made her wrists ache. Like one of the orchids Mr Thurlow cultivated in his glasshouses, she seemed to exist purely to be decorative. Even Jessica, who had no great intellect, had some skills at her command and when she married, scatterbrain that she was, she would know how to run a household and the way in which servants should be managed. Her mamma had at least ensured that.

I could not imagine Isabel's delicate creamy-skinned shoulders bearing any burden. Her doting papa idolized and protected her as did that sinister Malay woman. I had no doubt that there had always been a dozen servants to see that the little mistress never had to lift a finger, and very soon she would have a strong and rich husband to cosset and cherish her.

Maxwell would doubtless be delighted to have a woman so dependent on him. He had made that clear the first evening of his return when I had piqued him with my independent talk. Yet would it always be so?

I watched him toying with his glass, nodding at some long

tale his elderly aunt was telling. There was a certain austerity and reserve in his manner; a brooding quality of suppressed vitality or impatience well contained. '. . . *A hooded eagle among blinking owls.*' An eagle, to be sure, with that bony nose and sharp dark eyes and the wine-flushed faces round him owlish. I smiled to myself at the aptness of the phrase. But . . . hooded? Surely not. It would be a brave man who would draw a blindfold over that arrogant head. For a woman, though, easier. Isabel had done it; blinded him with her beauty and for a while he would rest content under the hood. But for how long, before he tore aside the blindfold and all that pent-up energy demanded more than mere passivity? Would he then be content with a woman who had been raised in the belief that to be a beautiful ornament was her entire function in life?

Strange thoughts to occupy my mind on this celebration evening and I tried to dismiss them as I followed the ladies into the drawing-room. I did not care two figs if Maxwell Thurlow tangled himself in a marriage superficially pleasing and fundamentally unsound. Yet he had been kind in the matter of Dancer when he had no need to put himself out on my account. For that I owed him my thanks.

So the thought was lodged in a corner of my mind and I could not root it out. I even had a silly dream about them that night. A hodge-podge of nonsense, of course, as dreams usually are. It was all to do with Isabel drowning in the cherub pond. She was sinking into the brown weeds, smiling sleepily, and I was terrified and calling for help. 'She got out of her depth!' I cried. 'I warned her not to!' But Aminah held me back, preventing me from going to her rescue. She hissed in my ear, 'It's all your fault. You will be blamed. You wanted her dead.' Then I, too, was in the water with Isabel, only now it was deep and rough. A ship came beating by with Maxwell in the prow. Isabel was hauled into the ship and Maxwell reached out for me but the currents carried me away. Then another voice, a woman's, said: 'It is all for the best. You are stronger. You can swim ashore . . . '

I awoke to daylight and a frightening feeling of desolation as the ragged edges of the dream swirled in my head. I blinked myself fully awake, my eyes focusing on the sliver of blue morning light slanting between the drawn curtains.

Jessica's birthday.

I forgot the dream as I pushed back the covers. I stuck my head out of the window, disturbing a blackbird who was brooding young ones in the ivy below. She flew off, chattering crossly, over empty, well-kept lawns that by dusk would be full of strolling people. Anticipation caught me and swung my spirits high. It was a day for good things to happen. I would not think about anything melancholy. I would look forward to the ball, to wearing my flame-red dress and holding my head up in all that fashionable company.

Only two things spoiled my resolution to keep cheerful. The first worry was Dancer who was fretting at his confinement to a chain. He had never been tied before and he paced up and down at the extreme end of the tether, tail down and whining mournfully. Skip watched him in a puzzled way, wondering why his grizzled old friend would not come and romp with him.

'I put him in the stable,' Tom told me, his round freckled face troubled, 'but he set up such a howling that Jacob swore he'd get t'master to have him put down before the day were out.'

I rubbed Dancer's ears and he nuzzled against my knee. 'There's nothing else for it, Tom,' I sighed. 'He must be kept tied up.'

'Aye, miss. We knows that but poor Dancer here don't understand.' He lowered his voice. 'I'll take him a bit of a walk when I have me bait. Jacob will be away having his with his missus and he won't be here to laugh at me for being a fool over nobbut a snappish beast.'

I smiled at him. 'You're a good lad, Tom.' He blushed and moved his feet awkwardly. 'I suppose,' I said, 'we *are* fools to make a fuss about him.'

'Aye, there's them that says so.' He ran a black-nailed hand through his shaggy toffee-coloured hair. 'There's only you and me fond of him, like. I expect, miss, it's to do with us having nobody – ' His face went a deeper shade of red as he searched for the right words. 'I mean, you haven't got nobody of your own. Not blood kin. Nor me, neither. We sorta become more attached to animals. Wi' me it's the horses, y'see . . . I gets that fond of 'em it's like having me arm cut off when Master gets rid of one. Wi' you it's these dogs . . . ' He broke off as though he was ashamed of having said so much.

I was touched. I thought I had little enough, but Tom had even less. From Mrs Pike I knew that he had been put out to farmwork after his widowed mother had died when he was seven or eight years old. After a succession of indifferent or hard masters he had come into the employ of Mr Thurlow some four or five years ago. Here at least he had a clean bed in the loft over the stables and plenty to eat. I looked at his slight figure in its faded flannel shirt and patched breeches, sacking tied with string protecting his thin calves above the nobbly boots. I had always known him for a kindly, gentle boy, but now I saw sensitivity in the chiselled curve of his lips and felt ashamed that I had not realized the loneliness he must feel.

I said impulsively, 'Are you happy here, Tom?'

'Happy, miss?' He looked surprised. 'Why, this is a grand place. Master is decent and Jacob talks rough but for all that he's a good heart and has taught me all I know about horses.' He gave a gap-toothed grin. 'I reckon I'm lucky.'

Lucky! I thought of the pampered children I was looking after and compared them with this unkempt lad who was not much older. They would hardly have considered themselves lucky had they been put into his place.

I stood up and dusted straw from my skirt. Half to myself I said, 'It sometimes seems to me that the world is a very unfair place, when some people have far too much than is good for them and others have nothing at all.' At this angry little speech Tom looked bewildered so I said, for reassurance and in a calmer voice, 'I must go now. I cannot dawdle about this morning.'

'Oh, aye, miss,' he said. 'I reckon there's a fair old to-do up at the Big House.'

'Indeed there is and I must rely on you completely to keep your eye on Dancer. I will not have much time to visit the stables.'

'Trust me, miss,' Tom said eagerly, 'and don't you fret none about t'owd dog. He'll maybe settle in a day or two, when he gets used to his new situation like. But I'll see that he doesn't make too much of a nuisance of himself . . . '

I wasn't as sure as Tom that Dancer would soon settle into new ways, but I tried not to worry too much as I took over my charges for the morning. It was too nice to be indoors so I took them into the park, leaving the thankful nursemaids to care for the toddlers in the nursery. There were five children in my care, three of them the daughters of sharp Mrs Thurlow's younger sister, Louie. Louie was a pale woman married to a pompous Liverpool merchant called Rupert Hyde. She had seven children, three still in the nursery and one, Jane, a precocious fifteen-year-old much given to whispering salacious secrets into the ears of the older cousins. All the children had the same ferret-thin faces and pointed noses as their mamma, and they all had the prettiest manners so that the adults were for ever complimenting Louie on the way she had brought up her children. Louie smiled wanly at these pleasing remarks and assured everyone that she believed in keeping the strictest eye on her brood because governesses were so unreliable and she was constantly having to replace them because of slipshod ways.

After two days with the Hyde sisters, I could imagine that dismissal from that worthy Liverpool house would be a great relief to anyone of sensibility. Their pretty ways were pure artifice, covering natures that were sly and devious. They were for ever urging the other children into mischief. One of the boys was already in trouble for throwing stones at the glasshouses and another had been beaten for pinching Grace, the youngest of my charges. I had no doubt whatever that the girls had been the instigators of the stone-throwing incident and that Grace had deserved the pinching she had received. I heard the three sisters sniggering about it, their arms tightly fastened about each other's thin shoulders, when the boy was led away, protesting, by his papa.

'But John is a naughty boy,' Grace had said, all wide-eyed innocence, when I had questioned her sharply. 'I was merely teasing him the littlest bit when he went nasty and pinched my arm.' She held up the arm bearing the red weals. 'If I had not told his papa about it, John might have treated other little girls so. Mamma always says it is better to be punished for a misdeed straight away, then we shall be prevented from doing it again . . . '

After that I kept a very sharp eye on the Hyde girls and when we were in the park that morning ensured that they were always engaged in some game or other. As we walked back to the house for nursery lunch, I was pleased to note that even the energetic Grace was flagging somewhat. Tired, she would perhaps be less inclined to torment the two young boys.

It was as we skirted the cherub pond that we heard the whispering of voices and subdued giggles. Grace perked up at once, her pointed nose turning towards the concealing green skirts of the weeping willow tree as though she scented the furtiveness of the sound.

'There's somebody hiding under the tree,' she declared. 'That's sounded like Jane. I shall go and see what they are doing.'

I said, 'No, Grace!' But she chose to ignore me and ran round the pond to pull aside the fringed branches and reveal the girls crouching there, as I myself had done all those years ago, wanting to hide myself and my misery from everyone. That they, too, were hiding and that the intrusion startled them was obvious. Four guilty faces turned towards us as I ran to Grace and pulled her none too ceremoniously away. She wriggled in my grasp, squealing, 'You are hurting my shoulder. I shall tell Mamma!'

'Then tell,' I said calmly. 'It is time you were getting washed for luncheon and you have no business spying on what the big girls are doing.'

Grace lashed out at me with her hard little heels and showed every sign of setting up a loud wailing. 'You are a nasty bully,' she cried. 'I want to go in there with Jane. I want to know what that ugly foreign woman is doing!'

Aminah? Crouched in there together with the girls? It was my turn to be startled. Grace felt my muscles go loose for a second and slithered from my grasp. But help came from an unexpected quarter. The branches parted and Jane stood there, looking wrathful.

'Go away, Grace, you horrid little beast!' she hissed.

Grace, unperturbed, said pertly: 'You are up to something. I want to know about it.'

'There is nothing to know,' Jane said. 'And if you don't go away this instant I shall most certainly tell Papa who it was who wrote the rude word on the conservatory door *and* who really played that trick on Cook.'

The threat silenced Grace, who backed off sullenly. 'You wouldn't tell,' she mumbled.

'Of course I would.' Jane glared nastily at her sister. 'Go away. Go back to the nursery with the others this instant.'

Grace slouched away and I would have followed: whatever the girls were up to it was no business of mine. But Jessica, too, came through the screen of foliage and caught my sleeve.

'You will say nothing to Mamma, Morwenna?' she begged. Her face was flushed and damp. She managed to look both guilty and excited at the same time. 'We were doing no harm. Jane found out that . . . well, we all thought it would be fun . . . and it has been, hasn't it Jane? But we were all going back to the house now, weren't we – ?' Her voice died at Jane's stare of cold amusement.

'Do not excite yourself, Jessica dear. Grace will not breathe a word now. She knows me too well to go against my wishes. As for Morwenna . . . ' The sharp, ferrety face turned to me. 'She will most certainly say nothing.' Her tone implied that should I speak out of turn, then it would go ill for me. I returned her stare coldly, fighting down the anger I felt at her insolence.

'I have no wish to know what mischief you are hatching,' I said, 'but while you are under your Aunt Winifred's roof it is surely courtesy not to do anything to displease her.'

Jane's lip curled. 'Very proper sentiments, Miss Mealy Mouth,' she sneered. 'But if Cousin Jessica sees no harm in it, then why should we feel worried?'

Ah, yes, I thought grimly, but I would wager my last farthing that Jane, not Jessica, was at the bottom of all this secrecy. Jessica had not a deceitful bone in her body though she was easily led.

'Truly, Morwenna,' Jessica said, 'we were not doing anything wrong. It was just – well, we discovered that Aminah tells fortunes and we thought it would be fun to let her tell ours.' She giggled nervously. 'She told Jane that she would have three husbands and I would go away to a big city to marry and have many sons!'

It sounded harmless enough, but I thought of the disturbing prophecy Aminah had made to me in Isabel's room and a coldness shivered my spine. The other two girls had crept from under the tree and behind them came Aminah. She held back the green branches as though sweeping aside a curtain, and the sunlight fell on her blue-black oiled hair and turned her brown skin a sickly sallow colour. Her eyes glittered as she stared at me.

Jane smiled slyly. 'Why don't you ask Aminah to say what the future holds for you, Morwenna?' Then, as I opened my mouth to protest, she beckoned to Aminah. 'Come here,' she ordered. 'Tell this missy her fortune.' She spoke loudly and slowly, the superior English miss addressing an ignorant foreign servant. Aminah's eyes narrowed at the tone and she did not move. In that moment I felt a certain admiration for the proud way she stood there ignoring Jane's rudeness, like an exotic jungle creature defying those who hounded it.

'It is all nonsense,' I said curtly. 'I must go with the children and you, too, Jessica, would be well advised to leave the woman alone.'

'Why, you are surely not afraid to know what the future has in store for you?' Jane persisted.

'Of course she isn't, silly,' Jessica said, coming to my rescue. Her colour, her voice were almost normal now, as though whatever furtive excitement had been generated in the sultry shelter of the willow tree was dissipating in the sunlight. 'Morwenna is far too sensible to believe such things. But you will say nothing to Mamma?' she added anxiously. 'Oh, I am sure she would be indulgent, today of all days, and she would think it all a prank, but' – she lowered her voice – 'I do not think she would like us to have mixed so closely with the foreign woman.'

Nor I, I thought. But I only said quietly, 'I am no tattle tale,' as I turned to go. It was then that the Malay woman spoke.

They were quiet words in her stilted broken English, and

because of their quietness they seemed to hold a strange intensity.

'Missy go long way,' she droned. 'She running. She not find happiness by that. But must run. Many troubles and happiness always go away. Happiness here and misery here, and the other Missy watch over. Always there. Always watching. She loves. She watches. Missy in blue dress . . .' Her voice slackened and died into a tense little silence. Her eyes were closed, her hands limp at her sides, then she added one more phrase, very clearly: 'He will come to the house by the water. Happiness then.' Her eyelids flickered back. For a second the pupils were filmed, almost milky, then she was herself again.

Haughtily, her face expressionless, her eyes raked us over scornfully. Then she began to walk away across the springy grass.

'Goodness! What – what was all that about?' Jessica faltered. 'She looked – so odd . . . and she said such strange things. Could you understand it, Morwenna?'

'No. It is as I said – a lot of ridiculous nonsense.'

'Yet she looked – she sounded – as though she was truly seeing something we could not.'

'How could she possibly do that?' I said briskly. 'It was all totally incomprehensible, anyway. And now, if you will excuse me . . .'

I hurried after the children before the sharp-nosed Jane could notice my discomposure, for despite my sensible words, I could not help remembering the impression I had had the evening when Maxwell had returned. Lying on Mrs Pike's couch I had seen, or dreamed, of a girl in a blue gown, who had looked at me with love and sadness and had held out her hand to me. It was an impression that had remained clear in my mind and had not blurred as dream memories so often do. Who was she? And how had Aminah known of her?

It is pure coincidence, I told myself sternly. You are

getting as foolish and fanciful as Jessica. Besides, what did all the rest of the 'prophecy' mean? 'He will come to the house by the water.' That has no meaning at all.

And that was the second incident to disturb the tranquillity of the morning.

It had been decided that there would be a small informal family ceremony after luncheon, before the many guests and friends started to arrive for the ball. At the appointed time I escorted the children downstairs to present their gifts to Jessica.

The house had undergone a transformation. An army of gardeners and village people had worked all morning to clear the drawing-room and erect a small dais at one end where the orchestra would play that night. Everywhere there were banks of flowers, mountains of roses and carnations and sweet-peas in every delicate shade of pink and lavender and cream. The air was dizzy with the scent of them, even cloying, and, as we crossed the hall, I thought how warm it was even indoors. Though the sun still shone with a clear brilliance from a sky pale with heat, there was a sultriness in the air. In the small parlour there was not the smallest breeze to move the curtains at the open windows.

I had already given my gift to Jessica – a small bound volume of Lord Byron's poems. He was a favourite of Jessica's, hardly, I felt, for the quality of his work but for the romantic and somewhat scandalous image he had left behind. So I found a chair in a recess, half hidden by a fold of the velvet curtains, and was soon joined by Miss Webster.

There was a dew of perspiration on her upper lip and her normally neat hair was straggling somewhat, but for all that she looked less worried than she had of late.

'The flowers are splendid,' I congratulated her warmly, for she had spent the morning supervising the placing of them.

'Thank you, my dear,' she said, pleased. Then, raising a wry eyebrow: 'I am sorry that you have had the sole responsibility of those rather difficult Hyde children. But I have been so much occupied I could not offer to help you.'

'They have been no trouble,' I said, then admitted with a laugh: 'Well – very little. But I must admit that a few days in their company is as much as I can stomach.'

'They have always been a tiresome family . . . but let us talk of something more pleasant. I heard from Charles this morning. He is feeling so much better that he is preparing to resume his duties in the coming week.'

'That is good news.'

'Of course,' she went on, 'Mr Thurlow, who had been kind enough to call upon him when he was in Manchester a few days ago, had informed me that Charles was much improved.' To anyone else her glance round the room might have seemed casual enough, but I saw the way her eyes sought and found the tall, spare man who was her employer. My heart ached for her, but I knew she would be shocked and distressed if I revealed that I had chanced upon her secret. 'I trust his judgement completely, so much of my anxiety had already been removed.' She discreetly dabbed at her cheeks with her handkerchief. 'I find it has gone unbearably close. I trust we are not to have a storm. It would be so disappointing, for the gardens will look particularly charming after dark. The Chinese lanterns are already hung, and the gardeners are busy creating pretty bowers in the shrubbery for anyone wishing to escape the noise and heat of the ballroom.'

'As Jessica would put it – very romantical.'

'Indeed, yes.' She smiled a little wistfully. 'I expect these young people will make the most of every opportunity for a little flirtation.'

I thought of her upbringing under the stern eye of her righteous and God-fearing father, to whom such frivolities as parties and balls and pretty clothes were instruments of the devil. In the sanctimonious vicarage atmosphere where idle hands were not allowed and any deviation from the rigid rules of conduct punished with severity, how she must have envied the tales of innocent revelries from the girls from less restricted homes, and dreamed her dreams of a lover who would carry her away. Now, when she had found love, it still had to remain a dream, a thing of secrecy and guilt.

I said impulsively, 'Even if we, too, do not have the opportunity to indulge in flirtation, we shall doubtless enjoy ourselves. We shall find a good vantage point and watch everything that goes on.'

'Ah, no,' she said, 'you will not hide yourself away with me, my dear.' She lowered her voice to a conspiratorial whisper. 'You have the beautiful new gown and Mrs Ack-royd did not go to all that trouble so that you could lurk in a corner unobserved . . . Look, dear, the little ones are giving their presents to Jessica. How sweet they are!'

'Little Grace Hyde looks as though butter would not melt in her mouth,' I observed. 'In those white muslin dresses with the pink sashes even the Hyde girls manage to look angelic.'

'It is a charming fashion, certainly,' Miss Webster agreed. 'And I expect all the children are delighted that they are to have a party this afternoon. They will not feel so left out of things and will doubtless go to bed the more easily for that . . . Yes, Hetty, what is it?'

The maid had sidled up to us and now bent close to whisper, 'It's Miss Morwenna. I'm sorry to interrupt, miss, but young Tom says it's urgent.'

'Tom?' I frowned. 'What does he want?'

'He wouldn't say, miss. Just told me to ask you to go to the stables. I said I couldn't call you out of here, but he insisted, miss. Almost rude he was.' Hetty sniffed disdainfully at the thought of being sent on a furtive errand by a scruffy stable lad. 'I've a good mind to complain to Jacob. He'd give him a leathering for his cheek.'

Heads were turning towards us at this whispered conversation, half hidden as we were by the curtain.

'Very well, Hetty,' I cut her short. 'I will come at once.'

I slipped out of the room as quietly as I could. Most eyes were fastened indulgently on the children but Mrs Thurlow saw me go. She frowned and bent towards Maxwell, as though to complain at my singular behaviour in leaving before she had given the signal. I carefully kept my head turned away. I wanted no summons to return until I found out what Tom wanted.

Once out of the house I ran. It was not, as I had been repeatedly told as a child, ladylike to run. But I could not help it. I was impelled by some primitive fear that chilled me, despite the stifling heat that lay now like a pall across the land.

It seemed a long way and I was panting and catching my hand to a stitch in my side when I got to the low clutter of old buildings lying tranquil under their grey slate roofs. The stables looked quiet enough. Not even a horse whickered in that somnolent heat. Nothing moved at all. Not a bird sang. It was all silent. Drowsing.

Then I saw Tom. He was standing in the shadow of the nearest building, knee deep in the nettles that grew there, and he was holding something. A bundle.

I slowed my steps and he began to move towards me. His face was pale and drained, the freckles standing out livid under the white skin.

I saw what he was carrying and stopped.

I said, 'Dancer?'

He came on towards me, holding the dog across his forearms like an offering. He said stonily, 'I found him.'

I put out my hand and touched the smooth fur on one flaccid flank. There was no warmth under my hand and the crippled leg hung down uselessly.

'How did it happen?' My voice had the same stony, controlled quality of Tom's. We might have been having a civil conversation over the price of turnips.

'I took him a walk, like I said. Him and Skip, and when I comes back Jacob calls me to the tack room. Right old temper he was in, swearing and cussing at me because someone had been in there, miss, and turned everything into a muddle. Saddles and brasses and rugs, all piled into a great heap in the middle of the floor. I had to turn to and put it all to rights. Took me best part of an hour. That was when . . .' He stopped, swallowed.

'Go on.'

'I'd tied Dancer where he was this mornin'. Quieter he'd been after you'd gone, miss. I thought he was getting used to being tied. So bein' busy where I was, I didn't take no notice when he stopped howlin'. I kinda heard it with half an ear and took no notice . . .' For the first time a spasm of emotion twitched his lips. 'If I'd have gone an' looked . . .'

'But you didn't,' I said calmly. 'And then?'

'Children, Jacob said it was – them imps of Satan visitin' the Big House. I thought it was, too. Cussin' them – beggin' your pardon – all the time I was working. But I don't think it was them at all. Not now.' He wagged his head from side to side.

'Then who?'

His face was bleak. 'It was done to keep me away from where Dancer was. She done it deliberately, so she could poison him.'

'She?'

'That foreign bitch.' He spat out the words. 'I saw her when I was coming back from walking the dogs, only I didn't reckon nothing to it. Thought she'd been mithering Jacob for some horse liniment she wanted for one of her concoctions. He'd sent her packing once. I saw her go behind the stables.

I thought she was going back to the house, but she must have been coming from the tack room and gone round into that patch of old brambles near the old fallen wall to wait till me and Jacob was both out of the way.'

'You said poison. How do you know?'

'Because of this.' I saw he was carrying something in one grubby fist; part of a bone, succulent and meaty. I took it off him. 'Look at it close to, miss. It was lying half chewed by t'owd dog.'

I could see nothing at first but creamy bone and the pink juicy meat that would be a temptation to any dog. Then I saw what I thought was dust. Not dust. Greenish. A powder lodging in every crevice. I sniffed it warily. Above the meaty smell there was another odour, pungent and sharp. I could not place it.

'It's all over the flags where Dancer had pulled at the bone,' Tom said. 'She must have laid it on all thick. Something that killed him.'

I thought, wearily, I should have known. I should have guessed. The dog had bitten her mistress whom she adored with a possessive and fierce devotion. The dog had escaped punishment, so Aminah had sought her own revenge. What was an old dog's life against a hurt done to her beloved mistress?

I said, 'Give Dancer to me.' Tom hesitated and I went on: 'I'll hold him while you go and get a spade. The least we can do is give him a decent burial. And, Tom, do not feel guilty about this: she would have found a way to get at Dancer, whatever precautions we had taken.'

I found a bit of old sacking to wrap Dancer in, and together Tom and I walked from the stables a little way into the park along the path I usually took in the mornings. Out of nowhere Skip appeared. He kept close to my heels, tail low, until we stopped by a clump of sapling hazels. Then he took himself a little way off and sat watching as Tom cut off the turf and dug down into the soil.

When the hole was refilled and the turf laid back on the top, Skip padded over to me and leaned his head against my leg. I stroked his ears and ran my hand over his rough coat and he whined softly.

'He knows,' Tom said shortly. 'Animals always does. They've a lot more sense than people give 'em credit for.' He picked up his shovel. 'I'll have to be getting along, miss. Jacob'll be after me else. Will you be all right now?'

'I shall stay here a while,' I said. 'And, Tom, I should prefer it if you said nothing of how Dancer died.'

'But she should be punished . . . She'd no right – '

'She will deny it. It will be her word against yours. In any case, Miss Pritchard is very delicate and easily upset and I do not want her distressed today of all days. That would only upset Jessica – Miss Thurlow – too. I would not like to cast such a cloud over her birthday celebrations. Do you understand, Tom?'

'Yes, Miss Morwenna.' The scowl he wore sat ill on his normally cheerful face.

'Later, perhaps, I shall mention it. But in the meanwhile I want no whispers among the servants. It is for the best,' I rushed on and forestalled further protest by saying: 'I want you to know that I am more than grateful for the way you have always looked after Dancer . . . and for being here today. I could have wished for no one else, for besides myself there was only you who cared for him.'

When Tom had trudged back down the path, I stood in the heat and the silence and stared at the rough torn edges of the turf that would slowly, as the summer passed, disappear and blend in with the surrounding grass until there would be nothing at all to show where Dancer lay. I wondered if he had suffered much in dying, then pushed my knuckles against my mouth to stop myself crying. I must not weep. I must not go back into the house with red, swollen eyes so that people would stare and ask questions.

But the tears came all the same, slithering down over my cheeks and dropping on to the sleeve of my dress and staining the faded drab cotton in darker patches.

Then I heard Tom coming back up the path, hurrying. I could not turn to look, blinded as I was by tears. I did not even want him to see me, though he would have understood.

'Please, Tom,' I burst out. 'Leave me alone for just a little while.'

But the steps came on and the hands that took my shoulders and spun me easily round were not Tom's, nor was the voice that said, very gently: 'Tom told me. I am so sorry. I know what it is to lose a well-loved dog.' The tone of his voice and the compassion in his face shattered me completely. I broke down and sobbed, harsh sobs that shuddered my bones, so that he put his arms round me and held me close and tenderly as one would comfort a child. And I did not care any more that it was in Maxwell's arms that I found comfort.

CHAPTER SIX

Presently the tears stopped and I could speak again, though my voice was thick and ugly. 'I am sorry to be so foolish,' I murmured.

'Foolish? Why should it be foolish to grieve over the death of a friend?'

I blew my nose and mopped at my eyes with a sodden handkerchief. 'I have marked your coat. See, there is quite a damp patch.' There was a small dark stain on the dove-grey broadcloth, but I was saying anything, the first words that came into my head, as the realization came that I had leaned against Maxwell without constraint and, what is more, had welcomed the shelter of his arms. Now, as I stood apart from him and tried to regain control of myself, I felt a deep embarrassment, tinged with an emotion I could not name. Contempt? Vexation? It was neither of these, the usual results of any dealings I had with Maxwell.

'How did it happen?' he said. There was still that gentle note in his voice. He stood there, arms folded, the black curly hair tumbling untidily about his forehead above the straight brows. I had seen him stand like that many times, legs apart, head tilted, waiting courteously to be answered by whoever he was talking to. Why did it seem to me that some subtle change had overtaken him? Why did I notice the laughter creases around his eyes and the way his thin-lipped mouth had a humorous twist to it.

Confused, I said: 'I wasn't there . . . Tom saw her – he found the bone . . . ' and instantly realized I had blurted out too much.

'Saw who? What bone?'

I frantically tried to think up a plausible explanation for my faltering phrases, but my brain was numb with weeping. There was nothing to do but tell him the truth and ask for his discretion.

When I had finished the tale he said, 'Where is the bone?'

I looked down the path. 'I dropped it somewhere.'

We searched and found it against a clump of groundsel. He kicked it gingerly with his foot, then bent and took a pinch of powder between his finger and thumb. He examined it, sniffed at it, then remarked without expression, 'It looks very much like a concoction Aminah made up for the cook on the ship we sailed on. The galley was much infested with rats and she got rid of them. There seems little doubt that this is Aminah's handiwork.' His mouth was a thin, hard line and he frowned.

I touched his arm almost timidly. 'You will say nothing? It is for Jessica's sake that I ask.'

'Very well,' he said curtly, 'but when the guests have gone I shall speak to Mr Pritchard quietly. The woman should not go unpunished for such a barbaric act.'

'She is very devoted to Isabel. Her motives were probably of the highest. She did not wish to see her mistress harmed again.'

'Harmed!' he barked. 'It was the merest scratch. In any case, Aminah must learn that she must not bring the ways of the jungle here. If she is to live in England, she must conform to English standards. I shall in future have something to say about these herbal brews she makes, even though Isabel swears that they have healing powers.'

'Aminah is a stranger in a strange land,' I said simply. 'Do not be too hard on her. She will learn our ways in time.'

He stared at me, then after a moment some of the anger went from his face. 'You are a strange girl,' he said softly.

'Why should you defend someone who has been deliberately cruel to you?'

I shook my head. I hardly knew myself. In one way, I hated Aminah for what she had done, yet in some strange way I could feel sympathy for her. She had nobody of her own race here: she was alone. Even the other servants shunned her. Though she had shown only enmity towards me and she frightened me not a little, under all that aggression perhaps she knew loneliness. Besides, Dancer was dead.

'Whatever punishment is given to Aminah,' I said, 'will not bring Dancer back. If I insisted on revenge, that would merely breed more ill-feeling. It is over now. It is better forgotten.'

He said nothing but his eyes lingered on my face for what seemed a long time. I lowered my lashes, uncomfortable under that hard stare, and after a moment I said, 'I should be attending to the children . . . the party – '

'There were enough idle females gushing over the little dears when I left,' he said roughly. 'Let them do something useful for a change, you are in no fit state to act as nursemaid.'

'I must look unsightly,' I faltered, brushing back the damp tendrils of hair that had clung to my cheek. I ventured a halting smile. 'I do not cry at all gracefully.'

'To cry gracefully implies a mere social habit. I hardly think that applies in this case, so do not apologize for giving way to genuine grief. However, it was not your appearance I was concerned about. You need time alone to recover your composure. Do not hurry back to the house: I shall see to it that you are not called upon to mind the children for the rest of the afternoon. As for this,' he indicated the deadly bone, 'I shall see that it is burnt before any other poor brute suffers the same fate as Dancer.'

He strode off down the path, leaving me wondering what tale he would tell to excuse my absence. Mrs Thurlow left me in no doubt when, after a while, I slipped quietly into the house and tried to go unnoticed up to my room. It was unfortunate that I had chosen the normally quiet entrance through the music room and came face to face with Mrs Thurlow, who was casting a critical eye over the arrangement of card tables that had been laid out for those not wishing to dance. I was told in no uncertain terms that a sudden headache and feeling of faintness in no way excused my abrupt departure from the small parlour. However, she did not insist that I proceed immediately to take up my duties with the children, but said that I should go to my room and rest so that I could at least be ready to help Jessica prepare for the ball later on, adding sourly: 'I trust you are sickening for nothing serious. It would be most trying at a time when guests are in the house.'

I assured her it was merely the heat that had upset me and escaped to my room. But I could not rest. Despite the open window the air felt thick and stifling. I tried to read, but sat scanning the same page without making anything sensible of the words. I picked up a stocking to darn but made an even lumpier sight of it than usual, so that I tossed it aside in disgust. I was still upset over Dancer, of course: that was a sorrow that would be with me for many a long day. Even so, standing out there on the quiet green park, with the gentle hills drowsing in the sun, I had achieved a measure of calm. Dancer was at rest, he could suffer no more; that thought had given me comfort. No, this restlessness was something else. It sprang from a deep inner tension that I could not understand. I was like a spring, too tightly wound and taut to the point of snapping.

I went to the wardrobe and took out my gown, carefully unpinning it from its wrappings. I touched the silk and it moved under my hand, glowing like a living fire. I felt excited when I thought of wearing it, of swinging on to the floor into the heady rhythm of the waltz. But even the anticipation of the ball was not the full explanation of my unquiet feelings. There was something else that would not let me lie on my bed and fall into a refreshing sleep, that kept me pacing my room unable to concentrate on any particular task. I could not reason it out and I was glad when, with the lengthening shadows, I heard laughter and excited footsteps floating past my room as Jessica and her cousins came upstairs to begin their preparations for the ball.

Jessica, bubbling with anticipation and chatter, was newly bathed and sitting in her petticoat when I went to her room. Williams, Mrs Thurlow's maid, was busy with curling tongs among Jessica's golden curls. There was a smell of hot hair and discreet carnation-scented toilet water.

'Were not the children quite charming?' Jessica cried. 'Did you see all the presents they gave me? Oh, do be careful, Williams, you are scorching my neck.'

'If you would sit still, miss,' Williams said dourly, 'I could do my work properly.'

Jessica pouted and kept still for fully half a minute before she began again. 'They so enjoyed the games that Maxwell organized for them.'

'Maxwell?' I said, my hands pausing fractionally in their task of folding neatly Jessica's cast-off garments.

'Oh, of course, you were not there. I am sorry you had a headache, Morwenna dear. Maxwell said he had come across you entirely prostrated with it. Mamma was quite put out that you were not at hand to supervise the children's games, but Maxwell insisted – and you know how forceful he can be – that to one accustomed to the many complexities of exporting goods from the East Indies, a handful of children to amuse was scarcely a challenge.' She giggled. 'He really was most entertaining and, do you know, I believe he quite enjoyed himself. The children were much taken with him, especially when he pretended to be a fierce lion who gave wild rides only to the best behaved children. They instantly became models of good behaviour. Dear me, he had the most ferocious roar, though, for any of them who attempted to misbehave . . . Ouch!' She winced as the curling tongs came close to one ear.

'That is all I can do for now, miss,' Williams said, with a glare at me for distracting Jessica at this crucial time. 'I shall return when you are dressed to complete your coiffeur. I must now go and attend to Mrs Thurlow.'

'She is always such a crosspatch,' Jessica complained when Williams had gone. 'I cannot think why Mamma dotes on her so.'

'Because she is devoted and efficient and has a wonderful way with hair. Yours, for example, looks perfectly delightful already.'

Jessica peered happily at her reflection in the dressing-table mirror. 'So it does. I quite forgive Williams for being so churlish.'

She chattered on, leaving me to interpose an occasional remark, while inwardly I contemplated the picture Jessica had given me of Maxwell calmly taking over my duties in the guise of a roaring lion. It was quite incongruous and somehow touching. While I listened to Jessica's prattle and helped her into her gown I wondered with amusement what other skills Maxwell yet had unrevealed. He was certainly a young man of many parts.

'Do I look well?' Jessica demanded when, eventually, she was dressed and Williams had skilfully woven into her golden hair a tiny chain of seed pearls to match those on the neck of her dress.

'Perfect,' I said. 'Every young man in the room will want to dance with you. Lord Easthulme, I think, will have much competition.'

She laughed, her eyes shining, and even surly Williams was moved to make a tight, approving nod at the picture she made. 'Mr and Mrs Thurlow will be very proud, Miss

Jessica. Very proud indeed.'

As I went from Jessica's room across the gallery I could hear the orchestra tuning up in the drawing-room. I went to the rails and leaned over. There was nothing to see but the maids scurrying about at their last-minute tasks, yet the air breathed excitement. The wafts of perfume from the banked flowers below rose like incense: the hushed voices of the maids with the counterpoint of muted squeaks from the violins seemed to scratch at my own nerves, so that my breathing became fast and I felt moisture spring out on my palms. I forced myself to walk decorously to my room, though I wanted to hurry, and once inside I began to get ready with almost feverish haste.

My fingers were shaking when I took my mother's necklace and fastened it round my neck. In the mirror I saw again the transformation that seemed almost a miracle. Gone was the thin, gawky girl in the outgrown print dress. In her place stood this regal, slender figure, richly clothed in rustling silk. My hair was loose. I had brushed it until it had the gloss of a starling's wing, and as I started to coil it behind my head I heard the faint clatter of the first carriage as it came up the drive.

I went very still. My hands released my hair so that it fell again in a shining black cloud around my shoulders. My eyes stared back at me from my handsome reflected image and I saw the sudden fear that sparked in their dark blue depths.

I could not go downstairs like this. I could not go down and mingle with those rich, self-assured people and pretend to be one of them. It was all a mockery. Mrs Ackroyd might have had the kindest of intentions, but no amount of dressing up could disguise the fact that I was a very humble member of the household. The charity child. Bastard daughter of a feckless girl who had run off with a married man and had died in poverty. Oh, it all had a romantic sound to it. A love child, Miss Webster had called me, trying to pretend that it did not matter what my origins were. She had kept up the illusion by insisting that it was what I made of myself that mattered, that character counted more than ancestry. But it did not, not to the elegant assembly downstairs. Fine gowns and proud airs would not deceive them. And Mrs Thurlow, when she saw me dressed as handsomely as her daughter, would be horrified.

There were more carriages now and the first strains of music came to my ears. The orchestra was striking up. The family would be waiting to greet the guests. It was beginning; but it would begin without me, for I could not will myself to move. The anticipation I had felt had gone cold and stale. There could be no glittering evening ahead for the girl brought in from the squalor of a peasant's cottage.

The tap on the door came as I began to struggle with the hooks on my dress. It was Miss Webster and she bustled in, saying: 'I thought to come and help you, Morwenna. I expect Jessica made you late and I could do your hair . . . ' She broke off on a quick intake of breath. She moved more slowly across my room, her eyes fixed on me. 'My dear,' she said softly, 'Mrs Ackroyd told me . . . but I did not think . . . it is quite a shock – ' She stopped again, her hand fluttering to the lace that primly concealed her throat above the grey moiré dress.

'I know,' I said harshly. 'It is too bold a colour altogether: Mrs Thurlow was right. I shall be better in the green muslin. That is simple enough and perfectly suitable for sitting quietly hidden in a corner and watching the ball from a discreet distance.' I could not help the bitterness in my voice. 'It will serve me right for having ideas above my station. Will you unhook me, please?'

She moved quickly behind me and I felt her fingers at my dress. 'Unhook you I will not,' she said. 'And what is all this talk of ideas above your station? There, that is fastened. Now sit down and I shall dress your hair.'

She pushed me down into the chair, and when I tried to rise she held my shoulders.

'But I cannot go like this,' I burst out.

'Why not?'

'Because I am not one of them.' I gestured wildly. 'I shall be out of place. They all know who I am, what I am; it is impossible to pretend even for an evening that I am like them.'

Miss Webster picked up the brush and began to stroke back my hair. 'I think perhaps I shall loop your hair over your ears and take it high on the crown of your head, rather than so severely scraped back as you normally wear it. Where are the pins, dear?'

'You are not listening,' I cried. 'I am not going to the ball.'

'Of course you are going.' She spoke to me as she had spoken when I was younger, commanding me in the nicest possible way but brooking no arguments. 'I will have no more nonsense about being out of place and not being fit to mix with people of a superior class. Remember that your mother came from a good family. In your years here at Ashridge Hall you have learned how to conduct yourself: you have excellent manners and a quick intelligence. What is more, you look so splendid in your new gown.' Her voice softened. 'Go to the ball, Morwenna, and do not be ashamed or frightened. All those people down there, well, that is all they are. People. Human beings with failings and weaknesses and heartaches of their own.' A hint of mischief flashed out. 'Maybe they, too, hide their secrets. Skeletons lurk in many a noble cupboard. The man even now shaking his host by the hand might have made his money by ruthless or cruel means, and the woman Mrs Thurlow greets so fulsomely might have gained her position in society through cunning and deceit. You have a clear conscience, my dear, which is more than can be said of many who have come to the ball tonight. So walk among them with your head high. Enjoy the dancing, for dance you surely will. There will be a few men who will see you without a quickening of the pulse . . . '

I tried to think of that as I stood at the top of the staircase a little later. It all seemed unreal, the laughter and talk in the hall below: the sweet strains of violins, the light from the chandeliers falling on white powdered shoulders and jewelled hair as people milled around the great stands of flowers. At the foot of the stairs stood the Thurlows, and as I looked they were conferring together and beginning to move to the ballroom. The guests were all here, the dancing could begin.

Jessica was on her father's proud arm. Mrs Thurlow walked with Mr Pritchard, and Maxwell crooked his elbow for Isabel to place her small, white hand on his dark sleeve. She was in creamy satin and her coppery hair bore an ornament of blue stones. I tried to summon my courage and I glanced up at Thérèse Thurlow's portrait as though for reassurance. Had she attended occasions like this one? Had she ever felt frightened? Her painted lips smiled, her long eyes seemed sly and amused. I could not imagine her ever being scared, as I could never imagine Maxwell. She had no comfort for me. I must go my way alone and pray for courage.

I took a deep breath and began to descend the stairs. My gown swirled and rustled about me and I held the Chinese shawl loosely over my arm, my fingers tight about its folds. It was too warm to wear it, but it gave me a kind of reassurance to know that perhaps it had been carried by that far-off Chinese princess to greater functions than this.

It was Maxwell who saw me first. He glanced up absently, smiling from some comment Isabel had made. The smile remained: it seemed to freeze on his lips, twisting his face into a mask of polite attentiveness, concealing whatever feelings my appearance had aroused. Only his eyes gave a clue. The fierce intensity of his look in that inscrutable mask of a face almost frightened me. My foot faltered on the stair and I clutched at the banister for support. But I could not take my eyes from his. It seemed for a fraction of time that we were locked in combat, that a kind of invisible force held us in a steely, sharp-nailed grip, willing us to take up arms and fight.

Then it was gone, leaving me shaken and clinging to the banister as a drowning man clutches at a passing straw. I could not understand what had happened. I only knew that my heart was thumping as though I had been running and I was breathing hard and quickly.

Maxwell had turned from me, speaking to Isabel, and now she looked up. Her feelings were not so difficult to read. Surprise was mirrored in the raising of her delicate eyebrows and then, unmistakably, indifference, though she inclined her head graciously in acknowledgement. My transformation was obviously of no particular interest to her. I was not important enough to warrant anything but the most casual attention.

It was this indifference that calmed me, that made me again aware of the noise and the milling throng below and the heavy scent of the flowers; as though for a short space I had been somewhere far away from this brilliant scene into uncharted and unknown country. Now, the moment of madness, of strangeness, had passed. I let go of the banister and descended the last few stairs to where they stood. My courage filtered back and I took care to hold my head proudly. No one should know how unsure I had felt a moment ago.

Maxwell said, 'You dance very well, but you would do far better if you would relax a little. Did my dear stepmamma unnerve you?'

I kept my gaze fixed beyond him, the room blurred into an unfocused swirl of colour. I was torn with confusion. I had not wanted him to ask me to dance, though I had known, once Mrs Thurlow's outrage made itself felt, that in his contrary way he would sweep me on to the floor and so outface her.

'I am used to her censure,' I said shortly. To be honest, her disapproval had not moved me at all, except to add to my sense of exhilaration. When she had first seen me, her studied regal calm had deserted her momentarily. Her jaw had distinctly dropped, her mouth falling open in surprise. Then her cheeks had turned an ugly purple under the dusting of rice powder, contrasting ill with the maroon silk she wore. Her mouth snapped shut as Mr Thurlow, catching sight of me at the same time, beamed and cried, 'Morwenna, how delightful you look.' Then, to Maxwell: 'Why, this does not seem the same sensible creature who spends hours poring over books in my library.' Only then did he catch his wife's eye and hesitate.

Jessica jumped into the breach, with an innocent disregard of her mamma's sensibilities. 'That dress is perfectly gorgeous on you, Morwenna. I had no idea it would look so beautiful.' She laughed. 'Mrs Ackroyd's mistake has turned out to be a benefit after all, has it not, Mamma?'

Behind me Maxwell said lazily, 'Then Mrs Ackroyd must be permitted to make more mistakes.'

'Nonsense!' Mrs Thurlow hissed. 'The dress is indecent and I knew the colour was too bold for any young girl. Morwenna, you must this instant remove yourself to your room and change it.' Her voice sharpened. 'If I had known how badly Mrs Ackroyd had cheated me over this matter, I would have . . . '

'Would have what, my dear Mamma?' Maxwell said, mocking. 'Ordered her to have made a nice drab, unassuming dress for Morwenna so that she would not shine at all?'

'Red is no colour for a young girl! I will thank you not to interrupt me, Maxwell, this is none of your business.' She snapped open her fan, hiding her expression from the guests who, sensing some disagreement, were beginning to look our way.

'But indeed it is my business,' Maxwell said courteously. 'It is my fault that she came to the house in the first place.' His tone was hard. 'I will not allow her to be sent away because she has the temerity to look as fine, if not finer, than any other girl in this room.'

'Please, please,' Mr Thurlow pleaded, 'let us have no quarrelling tonight. It is time to start the dancing. And look, my dear, here is Lord Easthulme, come no doubt to claim a dance from Jessica.'

The ugly moment was over. Oddly enough I was not disturbed by it. Mrs Thurlow's display had proved to me that I truly was well suited by the dress. My spirits began to rise. It had been a long, eventful day but I suddenly felt light and gay. I wanted to forget the day's sorrows; I wanted to dance and to laugh, to be admired and to be sought after.

I did not wait long before a blushing youth sidled up to me and clumsily bundled me into a country dance. As we jigged about I saw the approving eyes of other men upon me. Sidelong, covetous glances some of them were as the older ones danced a slower pace with their stately wives. It gave me a heady feeling I had never known before.

The blushing youth reluctantly gave way to others. I danced a stately measure with Mr Thurlow, who went out of his way to amuse me as though to make up for his wife's hard words. I wanted to laugh and assure him that her disapproval had set the seal of success upon my evening. But he might not have understood. Dancing with him reminded me of Miss Webster. It seemed doubly sad this celebration evening that she should have to be a mere onlooker. I had no doubt that she watched me with envy from her screened seat. How she must long to be in my place! Yet there was no reason why she should not have a taste of excitement too.

I said aloud, 'The evening is turning out delightfully. A

great success, Mr Thurlow, and Jessica is scarcely finding time to breathe before another partner claims her.'

'Indeed, yes,' Mr Thurlow said proudly. 'Though truth to tell,' he added, twinkling, 'I shall breathe a sigh of relief when the weekend is over and we can return to normality.'

'Ah, but for a brief time, you must confess, you have enjoyed all the glitter of the occasion.'

He nodded. 'True. I am glad to see everyone enjoying themselves so well.'

I lowered my lashes to hide the mischief I suddenly felt must show in my eyes. 'It is a pity,' I said gently, 'that Miss Webster cannot join in the frivolities.'

His face clouded and his voice had a stiff note in it when he said, 'Indeed? Is there some reason why she cannot?'

'She would not think it fitting to mingle with your guests. Besides, she does not dance, so she has concealed herself in a corner. See, over there, behind that potted palm there is a little alcove that leads on to the terrace. She is quite hidden there and is happy listening to the music. I look in on her now and again to see if she is comfortable. Next time you pass that spot, peep in and see how cosily she is ensconced.'

More than that I dared not say. I passed quickly to other topics, hoping that the seed I had sown would take root and that some time during the evening Mr Thurlow would seek her out, perhaps pay her a compliment or two or fetch her a glass of wine. I was sure that it would please Miss Webster greatly, and I felt satisfied with my little intrigue.

It was after Mr Thurlow handed me back to my seat that the orchestra struck up a waltz and Maxwell appeared before me. He bowed and held out his hand and all at once my confidence deserted me. I remembered the curious incident on the stairs and would have refused him had it not been ill-mannered to do so. Besides, Mrs Thurlow was close by. Despite her conversation with a group of dowagers perched on gilt chairs, she had not missed Maxwell's approach. Her frosty glance sliced at us through the overheated air, and I had no doubt that Maxwell's formal and somewhat elaborate attention to myself was purely to goad his stepmother. I, too, was not averse to revenging myself on her for the many slights I had suffered, even knowing that the events of this evening would heap wrath upon my head in the coming days. I lifted my chin, smiled agreeably at Maxwell, and allowed myself to be swept into the heady rhythm of the waltz.

I found I could not give myself to the music as I had done in earlier dances. I felt stiff and awkward, and twice I stumbled and would have fallen but for the strong arm that encircled me. I drew attention from my hesitant feet by asking, 'Has Isabel retired? I have not seen her dancing.'

'She finds the noise and the heat a trifle overpowering. I have settled her in the music room to watch her papa play backgammon.'

'She does not mind that you leave her to enjoy the dance?'

'She knows I have my duties.'

'And I am one of them?'

'To dance with you is no duty at all. It is a pleasure.'

'You dance with me merely to spite Mrs Thurlow.'

He threw back his head and laughed. 'My dear girl, you have a low opinion of yourself. I would wager that every man in this room has enquired at some time this evening who is the charming, dark-haired beauty in their midst. Even people who have seen you before and have quite overlooked your quiet, drab presence in the past, now find you worthy of remark.'

'And then scorn me because of what I am?'

'Admire you,' he said gently, 'because of your elegance and grace.'

I was not so unworldly as to believe his comforting words, but I found pleasure in them nevertheless. I was almost sorry when the dance ended.

'Now, alas, I must leave you,' he said. The laughter lines around his eyes sprang into evidence as he smiled. 'I really do have duties to perform. There are spinster aunts and plain cousins to dance with, and I must claim a dance with Jessica even if I have to fight off half the young men here.'

I glanced over to where Jessica stood amid a circle of admirers. 'Lord Easthulme is well to the fore,' I murmured.

He frowned. 'Yes, indeed. However, there are other young men equally persistent at seeking her favours and Jessica is not allowing any particular one to monopolize her time. I give her credit for that.'

After he had left me, supper was announced and I went to see how Miss Webster was faring. She was not in her alcove and I assumed that she had perhaps slipped away to see if Mrs Bradshaw required any assistance. There was a pleasing draught coming through the windows and I made my way out on to the terrace, which had emptied as supper had claimed the hungry dancers.

A yellow moon was caught up in the black branches of distant trees, the velvety darkness glimmered with the firefly glow of the Chinese lanterns. A smell of cool, damp earth wafted from the shrubbery. The threat of a storm seemed to have gone, and I breathed in thankfully of the night air.

Excitement had robbed me of my appetite and I did not wish to join the crowd around the buffet table, even though it was laden with cold beef, salmon, and mountains of strawberries and cream. I was content to enjoy the respite, and I was so absorbed in the pretty scene before me that it was some moments before I realized I was not, as I had supposed, alone on the terrace. From the far end came the murmur of voices. I could not see who it was because the light falling from the drawing-room was too bright, throwing that far corner into deep shadow. Then someone laughed softly and I knew that laugh. I caught the glow of a cigar that lit momentarily the face of the man who smoked it.

I backed away. Let them enjoy their few snatched moments together, I would not intrude. Miss Webster had had little enough romance in her life. It surely could do no harm for two mature people to enjoy a time of privacy and quiet away from all prying eyes – and especially those of Mrs Thurlow.

I silently wished them luck and I retreated into the house. I was feeling quite pleased with my attempt at intrigue, and I decided that perhaps a glass of cold champagne and a bowl of chilled and sugared strawberries would be welcome after all.

When the orchestra struck up again after the supper interval the gathering was much livelier. The noise of talk and laughter swelled up to deafening proportions, so that the older people escaped to the music room and to the peace of the gardens. Perhaps the quantity of champagne drunk had increased the gaiety and certainly one or two of the men had a slightly glazed look, though none could be said to be inebriated. But now that the younger people were left, the orchestra, no doubt well fortified on ale, broke into cheerful country dance tunes. The Roger de Coverley left me quite breathless and a Scottish reel exhausted, but I was soon whirled away into a jig which involved much changing of partners. Just before the dance came to a rousing finale, I found myself opposite Lord Easthulme.

His face was crimson with the exertion of the dance and, I suspected, with an over-indulgence in champagne. His thin hair was ruffled and his cravat somewhat askew. In his red face his little eyes were bright and leery. He did not look at all prepossessing and, as his plump damp hands caught mine, I felt repelled. I hoped with all my heart that Mrs Thurlow would not be blinded by the fact that he was titled and so overlook his faults. To imagine Jessica married to this man so repulsive in his cups was horror indeed.

The last chord sounded. Partners bowed and curtsied amid laughter and gasps for breath. I made my bob to Lord Easthulme, who swept an exaggerated bow and staggered, then shot out an arm.

'Damme, sh'll see you back to your chair,' he muttered. 'Courtesy, y'know.'

I had to take his arm and we made our way to the side of the room.

'Thank you, I will remain here,' I said, removing my hand from his sleeve.

He stood in from of me, his small eyes crawling over my body, his lips pursing wetly.

'Damn fine figure of a woman,' he said. 'Where have you been hiding yourself, sly boots? Eh? Have I seen you before somewhere? I've an eye for a pretty face, but it escapes me where we've met, which is remiss of me.'

He thrust his face close to mine as he spoke. I took a step backwards. I had to keep cool. I could not offend him, or he might cause a scene, but I had no wish to encourage his attentions.

I said calmly, 'We have met before. You joined Mr and Mrs Thurlow and Miss Thurlow on a picnic by the river last week. I was there too.'

Slow puzzlement crept over his features.

'I am merely a companion to Miss Thurlow. Mr Thurlow kindly took me under his roof when I was orphaned.'

I hoped that would cool his ardour. To know that I was poor and scarcely ranked above the servants would surely discourage him. Instead, my revelations seem to fire him with fresh interest. His eyes narrowed to slits: a snake about to strike must look as hypnotically at the rabbit it wants for dinner.

'The devil!' he hissed. 'You are dressed in fine feathers for a poor companion.'

'My benefactor is kind,' I said shortly. 'And now, if you

will excuse me . . . ' I made to move off.

But he blocked my way. 'Not so fast, my pretty one.' He leered at me. 'I gave you no leave to go.'

I tried to retain my poise. I was in an intolerable position. I would have liked to have slapped his silly, leering face and told him exactly what I thought of his attentions, but I must try to think of some way to escape him without creating an unpleasant incident.

Rescue came in the unexpected guise of Mrs Thurlow. She appeared out of the crowd at Lord Easthulme's elbow and I could have kissed her for it; not that she could have known how timely was her intervention. Indeed, she flashed a look upon me that clearly indicated she suspected me of unseemly dalliance. Doubtless she had watched with chagrin and put entirely the wrong interpretation on our conversation. She tapped Lord Easthulme on the shoulder with her fan. He blinked at her in a dazed fashion and seemed about to make some churlish remark when he realized that he was addressing his hostess.

'Lord Easthulme,' Mrs Thurlow cried, 'Jessica has looked for you everywhere. She was quite carried off from you in the last dance.' She simpered at him. 'I hope you will forgive the interruption, but Morwenna has duties to attend to.' Her voice sharpened as she turned to me. 'One of our guests, Miss Thorncroft, has had to retire to her room slightly indisposed. I wish you would go see if she is comfortable. She may need you to sit with her a while.'

As plainly as could be she had put it to Lord Easthulme that I was hardly worthy of his exalted attention. At any other time the slight would have rankled, but I was jubilant at my easy escape and I hurried away before his lordship could protest.

Miss Thorncroft was merely tired. She was an elderly lady who had had a long day and was already asleep when I enquired about her of the attendant maid. Mrs Thurlow's excuse to get rid of me was a weak one. Nevertheless I did not hurry to return to the dancing. I went to my room and poured water into the bowl, then I dipped my hands into it and splashed my face. I combed back the wisps of hair that had straggled around my warm cheeks, and the eyes that stared back at me from the mirror were very bright in the candlelight. I felt full of vigour and ready to dance until dawn.

I had reached the gallery when I came upon Maxwell and Isabel talking to Mr Pritchard. Isabel's face looked small and pale under the weight of her coppery coils of hair and there were faint blue bruises under her eyes. Mr Pritchard was gazing upon her with concern.

'Do not fret, Papa,' she was saying, 'it was only a slight dizziness. I shall go to my room now, and rest. I have explained to Mrs Thurlow and begged to be excused.'

'I think, my love,' Maxwell said somewhat drily, 'that it would have been wiser to have retired when you felt the headache coming on at supper time.'

'Do not scold. I did not wish to miss the fun,' she answered wistfully. 'I thought it would pass. It seems that these days I tire and feel faint so easily. I would have so loved to take part in the dance but even the sound of the orchestra set me trembling.'

'I did not mean to sound cross,' Maxwell said. 'I know how disappointed you felt about the dancing. I was merely thinking of your well-being. You are so lately risen from a sick bed and there has been much recent excitement to overtax your strength. We shall have to ensure that she rests, shall we not, Mr Pritchard, in the coming days?' He took her hand and raised it to his lips. 'Good night, my dearest.'

'Good night, Maxwell.' Her lips moved into a tight smile, but under the heavy white eyelids I saw the glitter of tears. 'Good night, Papa.' She kissed his cheek and turned away, her head bent. She seemed a pathetic little figure and I felt sorry for her, as I had done on the day she arrived.

As though she, too, had been watching the scene, Aminah appeared out of the shadows, moving towards her mistress on silent feet. The dark arm in its gaudy covering moved round Isabel's waist and, almost as though she sighed with relief, Isabel sagged against her and they moved away slowly and disappeared into Isabel's room.

The two men had moved away downstairs, talking in low tones, and after a decent interval I followed them down, thinking of the worry they must be feeling. But pity for Isabel was swept from my mind when a maid approached me at the foot of the stairs.

She was not one of the household staff but a village girl brought in to help out for the evening. She was a slatternly girl with a round red face and wiry brown hair, upon which her white cap sat askew. She grinned broadly, showing a mouthful of decaying teeth, and bobbed a curtsy.

'Miss, I 'ave a message for you.'

'Yes?'

She cleared her throat, obviously aware of the new-found importance of her position.

'It is to say that the master wishes to speak with you in the library, miss.'

'Mr Thurlow?'

She grinned. 'Said it was urgent-like, miss. Said it was important as you went right away.'

I frowned. 'Very well. Thank you.'

She bobbed and scuttled away and I hurried off down the corridor towards the library, wondering whatever had happened to cause Mr Thurlow to send for me. The corridor was deserted and, when I got to it, so was the library. The room was in darkness, and only the glow from the corridor cast a faint illumination over the desk where I had spent so many happy hours and the tall rows of glass-fronted cabinets that housed the books. I went in and stared around, puzzled.

How very odd. The girl had distinctly said the library, but she had seemed rather dull-witted. Perhaps she had meant the small study further on, yet that was mainly used for storing out-of-date papers and hardly ever for interviews.

I moved back to the door and a voice said, 'You're in a fine hurry to leave.' At the same time the door swung to with a solid clunk.

I caught in my breath as the room went black. I recognized the voice and the shadowy figure who had stepped from behind the door and closed it.

'Lord Easthulme!' I gasped. 'What is the meaning of this? I was told that Mr Thurlow wished to speak to me here.'

'So the slut played her part well.' He laughed unpleasantly. 'A handful of silver will turn any peasant into a liar. But not you, I think, my pretty one. You seem a girl of spirit. I like that in any wench.' He had sobered somewhat since I had last seen him and that made him the more frightening. I could see a little now, as my eyes accustomed themselves to the gloom. Moonlight filtered through the tall window, turning everything grey and ghostly. 'Our conversation was interrupted and that seemed such a pity. I always enjoy a pleasant talk with a pretty girl.'

I strove for calm. 'This is quite ridiculous. Will you please open that door and let me out.'

'Oh, yes,' he said softly, 'I will let you out . . . eventually.'

'I wish to go now!'

'But I do *not* wish you to. I have a desire to know you better and I cannot do that with all those gossiping and interfering old women watching every move. Come a little nearer, Morwenna.'

'I will not! And if you do not let me out this instant I shall scream.'

'Dearie me. Who is there to hear? The orchestra plays loudly, the maids are all busy elsewhere; the door is a heavy one, in any case, for the room was built as a quiet retreat.'

His voice was silky soft and slow, but he moved quick as a snake. Two hands fastened about my wrists. 'Do not struggle, dear girl. I shall not hurt you if you are good.'

His hands were soft and clammy. They slid up my arms to my bare shoulders with the slimy tenacity of foraging slugs. It was a nightmare. The close dark room, his breath, sour with wine, against my face as his mouth, open and loose, came relentlessly against mine.

I twisted my head away and forced my arms up, breaking his grip. 'Get away from me!'

He laughed coarsely and pinned my flailing arms to my sides. For all his puffy look his strength was greater than mine, though I struggled with the desperation born of fear. I screamed out as he forced me backwards until my shoulders pressed against the glass of a bookcase. Distantly, uncaringly, the music played on.

'For God's sake,' I gasped, 'leave me alone!'

'Call on God or the Devil, it is all the same to me. Neither will answer. Besides, in a moment or two you will begin to enjoy our little game. It is always the same, my dear. The struggle, the pretence at coyness. Then surrender. Delightful surrender.'

'I will never surrender to you. You are repulsive to me. Vile!'

'Dear me, such names! Well, you will perhaps change your mind soon . . . '

His mouth slithered over my cheek and nuzzled into my neck. His hands were vices on my wrists and all the weight of his body held me pinned against the bookcase. I could hardly take breath enough to speak, but somehow I managed to scream again, though it came out more as a strangled squeal. My struggles seemed only to increase his ardour.

But somebody heard. The door flung open. Light flowed in and with an oath Lord Easthulme spun round. Released from his hold my trembling knees gave way and I sank to the floor.

'Maxwell,' I moaned. 'Thank God!'

He strode across the room and seized my would-be seducer by the lapels of his coat.

'Leave go of me, sir!' Lord Easthulme's voice was outraged. 'How dare you intrude in this manner!'

'I? Intrude? I fancy Miss Tregarth does not consider my presence an intrusion.'

'She came here willingly enough to meet me,' Lord Easthulme sneered. 'Ask the wench who gave her my message.'

I had no doubt that the maid would repeat parrot fashion whatever tale Lord Easthulme had concocted. It was unbearable that anyone should believe I had come here of my own accord.

'It is a lie!' I burst out. 'He sent me a false message to say Mr Thurlow wished to speak to me. Then he trapped me in here.'

'I have no doubt of that.' Maxwell's voice was quiet but there was steel in it. 'It was chance that led me this way in search of somewhere to sit quietly for a few moments away from the noise of the dance. If I had not come . . . ' He broke off, glancing at me as I began to struggle to my feet. His grip tightened on Lord Easthulme's shirt-front as he went on with biting scorn: 'You came as a guest into this house. You have been treated with great courtesy, and you repay courtesy with behaviour that would be despicable in the meanest inhabitant of a city slum.'

Lord Easthulme, caught fast in Maxwell's stranglehold, tried another tactic. 'Come, come' he said, attempting jocularity, 'we are both men of the world. Why cavil at me for being lured by a pair of inviting eyes and an encouraging smile?'

'Miss Tregarth would not lower herself to encourage you,' Maxwell said.

'Why bother to protect her? She is of little account – a girl brought in from the gutter, so I was informed. No better than a peasant, for all her fine airs . . . ' He was cut off as Maxwell's knuckles dug into his windpipe. His hands clawed frantically at his neck, his mouth opened and shut like a stranded fish.

I clutched the desk for support, shocked by the expression on Maxwell's face. It was black with anger, blind anger that was without thought or reason. He was like an avenging angel, magnificent and cruel, and even as I stood there, stunned into helplessness by this sudden switch of events, Lord Easthulme's struggles grew feebler and his face turned an ominous purple colour. Maxwell was killing him.

'Maxwell, no! Please, no! That is enough!' Fear gave me the strength to run to him, to cling to his arm; I felt the muscles hard and relentless as granite under the cloth. 'Please, Maxwell. You are strangling him!'

He let go so suddenly that Lord Easthulme staggered backwards, knocked over the fire-irons with a loud clatter and fell against the marble fireplace, only retaining his balance by clutching at the high mantelshelf. Despite all that had gone before, I felt relief that he was still alive.

The room was silent except for Lord Easthulme's rasping breaths. Some of the murderous light died from Maxwell's face, but he said, dangerously low: 'You were lucky that this girl you would have wronged has a soft heart. I would have seen you dead and carried from this house in your coffin. As it is, you will leave like the gentleman you pretend to be and never set foot here again. Morwenna, ring the bell.'

It was Mrs Bradshaw who answered the ring and if she saw anything unusual in Lord Easthulme's dishevelled and now ghastly pale appearance, or in Maxwell's flushed face, she was far too self-disciplined to show surprise. She went to order Lord Easthulme's carriage to be brought round.

Maxwell said curtly, 'You will kindly accompany me to the door. You will do so discreetly so that people may not be aroused to unseemly interest. If anyone enquires, you are leaving because of a sudden indisposition. I do not wish any hint of scandal to sully the events of this evening, otherwise I would take you by the scruff of the neck and hurl you out of the servants' door. Morwenna, remain here until I return.'

Sullenly, still massaging his bruised neck, Lord Easthulme followed Maxwell out. The room went still and only the fallen fire-irons told of the ugly events of the past few moments. Like an automaton I bent and rearranged them, then, feeling sick and weak, I dropped into Mr Thurlow's big leather armchair.

There was a tear along the seam of my bodice, the silk was torn quite away. Half an hour ago I would have been upset at the spoilage of my lovely gown: now it meant nothing. I should never wear it again after this night.

I should never have allowed myself the luxury of believing Mrs Ackroyd or Miss Webster. Vanity had brought me here, where I had no place. Dressed in my finery, I had believed myself to be the equal of all the other girls who waltzed the night hours away. But it was not so.

What had Lord Easthulme said? A girl from the gutter. I might fool myself for an hour or two, but cold reality was always too close. I leaned back in the chair and closed my eyes. Lord Easthulme had soon seen through my flimsy disguise and had rooted out my little secret. That was how it would always be. There would always be someone to poke and pry and destroy any illusions I wished to build. So it was best not to take the risk. Tomorrow . . . today . . . I would go back to being the sensible, quiet companion, take all the retribution I knew would be forthcoming from Mrs Thurlow, and never again get ideas above my station. My hand went to my throat and the cool touch of the red beads. Such a pitiful gesture of defiance I had made. When I got back to my room I would lock my beads away and never look at them again.

'Morwenna?' His voice was so changed, so soft, that it might have been a different person from the fierce, angry avenger who had left a few moments ago. He had lit the lamp and closed the door and now he stood above me. 'Morwenna,' he repeated. 'How sorry I am that this had to happen, but the blackguard has gone now.'

The sick feeling had passed, but I felt drained, too tired and listless even to rise from the chair and hide myself away in my room.

'I am sorry,' I said in a flat little voice. 'I seem to cause you nothing but trouble. You might have killed him. You *would* have killed him had I not intervened. It makes me ill to think of it. How easily it could have happened and all because of me and my vanity.'

'Your vanity! You are the least vain creature I know.'

I gave a short, harsh laugh. 'I thought I was as good as the others. I wanted to be like them. I wanted to be pretty, for once, in my silk gown and red beads.'

'You wanted to be pretty!' There was a sudden catch in his voice. 'But, Morwenna, you have a beauty that is rare . . . Tonight among all those charming girls you stood out like a flame in a darkened room.'

I shook my head. 'Lord Easthulme knew me for what I am, otherwise he would not dare to have acted as he did. Others must have known, too: known and sniggered at my masquerade.'

'Look at me!' Then again, more roughly when I did not instantly obey. 'Look at me, Morwenna!'

I raised my eyes slowly to his. His eyes burned down into mine. I knew he meant to speak, I knew he meant to say something kind to convince me, to reassure me, but as we stared at each other words suddenly became superfluous. It was like that moment on the stairs when I had felt we were in the grip of some strange magnetic force.

Very gently he lifted my limp hands. Very gently he pulled

me to my feet so that we stood facing each other. Against the warm flesh of my palms I could feel the throb of blood in his fingertips.

We were like two people held in a trance. With infinite slowness he moved his hands to my elbows, to my shoulders, pulling me close. I turned up my face to meet his. Our lips touched, held. My hands seemingly on their own volition went to his shoulders and his were suddenly tight on my back, holding me close and hard, his mouth no longer tender but fierce and demanding.

We stood there a long time in the lamplight. He spoke only once and that to say in a tone of complete bewilderment, 'Dear God in heaven . . . '

I did not speak at all. I could not find words to express the tremendous joy that burned through me. I knew now what the strange emotions were that had troubled me today. This was love. I was in love with the man I thought I hated. A man already betrothed to a girl both beautiful and rich.

With his cheek to my hair and his warm, hard arms holding me close, I wanted these moments to go on for ever. But I knew they could not, for this was an impossible entanglement.

CHAPTER SEVEN

Two days after Jessica's birthday the house resumed its normal air of calm. The guests all left, Mrs Thurlow and Jessica with them. They had been persuaded by the Hydes to return with them to Liverpool for a short visit. Mrs Thurlow had gone in a cloud of suppressed rage and indignation because of the abrupt collapse of her plans for Jessica, and naturally laid the whole blame at my feet.

I had flirted outrageously with Lord Easthulme – she had seen it with her own eyes. No gentleman in his position would have acted so indiscreetly unless he had been encouraged. I had displayed myself wantonly in a gown no decent girl would have chosen to wear. I had disgraced the family who had sheltered and educated me. A fine repayment for years of devotion and care that had been lavished upon me! A scandal had been narrowly averted – though no doubt the gossip would soon be round half of Cheshire . . .

She had been spiteful with rage because Lord Easthulme was now placed for ever beyond the reach of her grasping hands. I fancied that if the affair could have been satisfactorily hushed up she would have been happy to continue her endeavours to win Lord Easthulme for her daughter, but Mr Thurlow had been deeply affected and shocked and would never have allowed it.

Jessica was not so pleased to be dragged off to Liverpool with her disgruntled mamma. 'I find Jane's company pleasing for a little while,' she complained to me, 'but the girls do get rather tiresome. I hope Mamma does not contemplate a long stay.' She was not at all disturbed by Lord Easthulme's sudden exit from her life. 'I did not like him very well. A conceited man, I thought. I have no wonder Maxwell disagreed with him.' It had been considered that the full truth of the matter should not be told to her. Looking at her innocent face, I felt years older. So much seemed to have happened in the last few days: Dancer's death, the events of the ball, the realization – the heady, heartbreaking and exciting realization – that I was in love with Maxwell. I felt that I was living my life on two levels at once: outwardly I was restrained and meek and unchanged, inwardly I churned with the secret knowledge that I shared with Maxwell.

'You will enjoy your visit,' I assured Jessica. 'It will not be for long.' And I felt guilty, because I wanted her to go away so that I should not have her constantly at my heels and I could have time to think out my own affairs.

I was not the only recipient of Mrs Thurlow's scorn, nor, it turned out, the only one to be discovered in a compromising position during the night of the ball. I had noticed the following day how white and stern Mr Thurlow had appeared and had put it down to the Lord Easthulme affair. However, it seemed that I had not been the only one to notice the moments Miss Webster and Mr Thurlow had spent together on the terrace. Mrs Thurlow had seen them slip away and had taxed Mr Thurlow with this. They had had a violent disagreement, so I heard from Tom, who had had it from the kitchen maid on the usual grapevine of servants' gossip. It had been a battle which Mr Thurlow had lost. Poor man, what defence could he offer? Mrs Thurlow had right and virtue on her side. He might well protest the innocence and propriety of his moments with the governess, but without a doubt Mrs Thurlow would have dramatized the event out of all proportion, letting her own brand of poisonous insinuation smear and besmirch something that was unspoken and pure.

The result was immediate dismissal for Miss Webster.

'But that is unfair,' I burst out, when Miss Webster came ashen-faced to my room to tell me what had happened. 'How can she dismiss you for something so trivial!'

'It was not only that,' Miss Webster said. 'It appears that she has been thinking for some time of giving me notice to leave. Jessica no longer needs my services.'

I was silent, recollecting that this was true enough. I wished now that I had hinted to her of what I had known. I could only take her hands in mine and hold them tightly.

'Oh, I shall miss you so.'

She smiled painfully. 'As I shall miss you, my dear. And this house . . . and the . . .the family.'

'Mr Thurlow should not allow you to be sent away like this! Such haste is indecent. Surely his regard for you is such that he can insist you remain until you find another position.'

Two spots of colour flared in her cheeks. She averted her eyes and gently withdrew her hands from mine. 'Mr Thurlow is under no obligation to me, Morwenna. Whatever Mrs Thurlow imagined, our relationship has been purely that of employer and employee. I have always had the highest regard for his opinions and for his courtesy, and I think he has been pleased with my abilities as a teacher to Jessica and to you.' So she was not going to admit her feelings, even now when she would soon be gone. She even allowed herself to sound faintly amused as she said, 'Mrs Thurlow has branded me the scarlet woman. It is quite laughable. She wants me out of the house before she leaves for Liverpool for fear I might lure her husband in her absence.'

'She does it, too, to spite me. She knows we are fond of each other.'

She sighed. 'We are both in disgrace. And I cannot feel that we are much at fault, either of us.'

'What will you do?'

'I shall return to Charles. I can make myself useful there. Mr Thurlow has given me a fine reference and a generous portion of my salary. It will enable me to be quite independent until I find another post in Manchester.' She kissed my cheek. 'We will write to each other often.'

'Of course we will.' My throat was tight: I was going to miss her more than I could say.

'And you must remember this, my dear,' she said gently. 'You have no family of your own, but I have always looked upon you as a very dear younger sister. You must never hesitate to turn to me if you ever need help. Who knows what tribulations lie ahead? With Mrs Thurlow in this mood, your future may be as uncertain as mine.'

I could not speak. She smiled, her own eyes brilliant with unshed tears, and went quietly from the room.

The carriage bearing Miss Webster to the station had rumbled down the drive before the storm broke over the countryside. It had threatened all day: departing guests had tilted anxious eyes at the purple clouds moving relentlessly from the south, gradually blotting out all the blue sky. Mrs Thurlow had contemplated delaying her journey for another day. 'You know how nervous I am in storms,' she had declared. 'And I cannot but think that travelling in a railway coach will be highly dangerous. We shall be at the mercy of the elements.' But in the end she had been persuaded to go, well prepared with smelling salts and a dark veil to cover her eyes should the lightning get too fierce.

I stood in the empty drawing-room and gazed through the window over the formal flower-beds. The roses stood motionless in the eerie, brooding light. Not a leaf nor a blade of grass moved. The whole world seemed to hold its breath, waiting for the tempest. Then an invisible hand brushed across the lawns, bending branches, bearing down on the heavy flower heads, bowling fallen petals along the terrace, and with an explosion of sound the rain came. The spell of fine weather was over.

There was something about the play of lightning and the fierce cannonades of thunder that suited my mood. It was a release just to stand there in the storm-darkened room and let my thoughts wander as they would. Alone here, I had no longer to worry about keeping my feelings on a tight rein. I could think of Maxwell, think of those stolen moments in his arms, feel again the bruising strength of his mouth against mine, and the gentleness of his fingers twining themselves in my hair. I could remember the desolation I had felt as he had broken away from me. 'This is madness,' he had said.

'If this is madness,' I had whispered, 'then I dread the return to sanity.'

'I am engaged to be married to a woman I love and admire.' He spoke the words carefully, as though for reassurance. 'And yet I am tempted by a slip of a girl with eyes that have haunted me for years. Ever since I saw her, a child, defying me over the body of her father.'

'I hated you then. I carried on hating you as I grew up. I do not know when that hate changed and became . . . something else.'

'Do not imagine yourself to be in love with me,' he said harshly. 'This is not love, but some attraction soon aroused and soon over. Tomorrow we will have forgotten it.'

'You perhaps. Not I.'

His skin seemed tightly drawn over the bones of his face, so that the healthy sun-flush was sallow. His black eyes lingered on mine as though they could not bear to tear themselves away. 'You must forget, Morwenna,' he said, but there was no conviction in his voice. Then he turned away abruptly and went soft-footed from the library, back to the music and the dancing.

We had met since only in the company of others. He had been cool with me, controlled, speaking to me briefly when courtesy demanded it. I could have believed that he had spoken the truth, that it was a brief madness that had possessed him, to die away with the dawn, but I caught him looking at me when he thought I was occupied. I saw the sudden flare of his nostrils, the light that smouldered in his eyes, and I knew that his emotions were merely banked down like a smothered fire.

The drawing-room door opened, making me jump.

'Did I startle you?' Mr Pritchard came into the room. 'I am sorry. I thought to find Mr Thurlow here.'

'He and Maxwell rode out to visit one of the tenant farmers who was concerned about the condition of his roof. That was before the storm started. I dare say they have taken shelter.'

'Not under the farmer's leaky roof, I hope,' Mr Pritchard said. 'Not in this weather.'

I smiled politely at his small joke. I did not welcome his company, but he was a pleasant little man and I had no wish to offend him.

'Isabel is feeling better?' I asked.

'She is sleeping.' He shook his head as he joined me at the window and we both stared out through the streaming glass. 'I shall be glad when the good doctor brings his colleague from the city to look at her. It seems an odd sort of illness, one that has no visible form. One day she is well, another she can hardly drag herself from her bed.'

'I am sure it will pass soon,' I comforted him. 'Has the noise of the storm bothered her?'

'Not at all. Living in the tropics all her life has conditioned her to violent storms. There the weather is all extremes – fierce heat, torrential rain, intense storms.' He gave a shiver. 'But it never gets as cold as this. The room seems positively chilly now.'

'Would you care to have the fire lit?'

'Bless you, no,' he said.

'Then I shall ring for tea,' I said. 'It would not do for you to catch a chill with the sudden drop in temperature.'

An apprehensive Emmy brought in tea, though she almost dropped the tray when a sudden crash of thunder sent its echoes round the house.

'Oh, miss,' she wavered, all her pertness quenched, 'it's awful close. It sounds louder here than in the kitchen.'

'Then hurry back,' I said, and when she'd gone I laughed and said to Mr Pritchard: 'It will be like a siege in the kitchens. Every blind will be drawn, every spoon and fork and knife hidden away, and the mirror covered over in case the lightning is attracted. And most likely Cook will be hiding in the pantry. It is a very primitive thing, this fear of thunder.'

'But you are not afraid.' His eyes twinkled at me. 'You do not cower in a cupboard. You are a strong-minded young lady, I think.'

I poured tea and handed him a cup. 'I have my weaknesses,' I assured him. 'For many years I had a great fear of horses and, even now I have learned to ride, I still shrink from a horse with any spirit.'

'Ah, yes,' he said, 'but that is understandable.' He paused, then said kindly: 'I have heard a little of your story from Mr Thurlow.'

I sipped the hot tea. 'I owe Mr Thurlow a great deal. Without his generosity my life would be very different.'

'He is indeed a fine gentleman. I am more than happy that Isabel should be marrying into such a secure and comfortable family. The time will come when I shall have to return to the East Indies. I shall go with a much easier mind if I know that my dear daughter is in such good hands.' He smiled complacently. 'She adores Maxwell and he is devoted to her. No father ever wants to lose his daughter in marriage, but if I could have chosen anyone for her life partner, then I think it would have been Maxwell.'

The pain was swift and sharp. It knifed into me so that my hand shook and the cup rattled as I replaced it on the saucer. Since that moment when Maxwell had taken me into his arms my mind had shied from acknowledging that his future lay with another woman. I had cocooned myself in the warmth of my new-found love. It was enough to live for the moment: the future was blurred, unreal. Mr Pritchard's words brought it into focus, flooding my mind with bleak despair.

'When will they marry?' I heard my voice calm and polite.

'Maxwell was eager for an early marriage; they had spoken of July. This illness of Isabel's has rather altered things, though. We should both like to see her fully recovered before she is swept up in the excitement of wedding preparations.'

So soon! The knife twisted and for the first time in my life I felt the cruel pangs of jealousy. To imagine them living here as man and wife, sharing the same bed, raising children . . .

'I think the storm is abating a little,' I said, wrenching my thoughts away.

'They will be pleased in the kitchen, then,' Mr Pritchard said. He regarded me over the rim of his cup, his bright eyes sharp with curiosity. 'Forgive me for asking – and please tell me if the subject is a painful one – but I understand your parents were born in Cornwall and you certainly have a truly Cornish name. Have you any relatives still living in that part of the world?'

'None, as far as I know,' I answered briskly, glad to turn the conversation from Maxwell and Isabel.

'I ask because I am expecting to pay a visit to Truro shortly. My sister Clara married a Cornishman. Her husband's family is a large one and spread over much of the county. I should be happy to make enquiries on your behalf, if you thought there might be some kin of your late mother and father still living there.'

Perhaps my father's deserted wife, I thought bitterly, or even some half brothers and sisters. How glad they would be to know of my existence! Aloud I said, 'My parents eloped, as you may have been told.' He nodded, somewhat embarrassed at my frankness. 'Of my father's family I know nothing. I have reason to believe that my mother came from a respectable family. Her father was strict and when she disobeyed him and ran away with the man she loved, he would have nothing more to do with her.'

'Did she ever try for a reconciliation?'

'I understand she did write to my grandfather before I was born, but he never replied. He was also informed of her death. He never sent any acknowledgement of that, either.'

'And you have never tried to communicate with him since?'

'I had no reason to think he would acknowledge me any more than he did my poor mother.'

'Time has a mellowing influence,' Mr Pritchard said gently. 'He may have changed.'

I lifted my chin. 'I have managed well enough for eighteen years without his assistance. I would not trouble a man who allowed his daughter to die in poverty and disgrace, and if you ever come across Oliver Pendine in Cornwall you may tell him that.'

'Pendine, eh? And where might he live, this Oliver Pendine?'

'It is called Treroc, but whether that is the name of the town or the name of the house I do not know. It is written down in a prayer book that belonged to my mother.'

Mr Pritchard leaned back in the chair tugging thoughtfully at his sandy side whiskers. 'It is beyond my comprehension how any father could deny his own child. Perhaps I am the exception, but whatever crime Isabel committed and however hurt or offended I was by it, I should be bound still to love her and to find it in my heart to forgive her.'

'Then she is a lucky girl,' I said, smiling at him.

'You are not offended that I asked about your family?'

I shook my head. 'You had a kind thought and I appreciate it. But you really must not bother about trying to discover my long-lost relatives . . . More tea?'

'Thank you, no.' He stared at me a little pityingly as though he had been moved by my explanation, and as we began to chat of other matters I wondered unhappily if he would have been quite so sympathetic if he could have looked into my heart. He would have seen there that I represented a threat to his beloved daughter. I loved the same man. I had reason to believe he was attracted to me.

It was a horrid situation and one that was only likely to worsen. I had fallen in love almost against my will, and all the strength of my reason could not make me fall out of love again.

It was an ironic twist of fate that the following day Isabel sent for me. She was tired of her own company and there was no scatter-brain Jessica to bring her titbits of gossip.

'I am so bored, lying here,' she fretted. 'Maxwell is busy with his father and it is only right that he should be. He must learn everything about the running of the estate and his father's mills, for one day it will all be his. He comes to see me as often as he can, and Papa too. But one cannot expect men to be always hovering about a sick room; they are not suited to it. Oh, if only I could regain my strength!' There was a feverish brightness to her eyes, but she looked more beautiful, more like a china doll than ever, propped among the banked pillows, her coppery hair threaded with white ribbons and a fine lace shawl about her shoulders. 'Aminah made me a splendid posset, but for some reason Papa has forbidden me to take any more of it. I am quite sure it was doing me more good than the dreadful medicine the doctor left, but he is quite adamant and I haven't the strength to argue.'

'It is better to take the advice of a qualified medical man,' I said calmly. Mr Pritchard had been quietly told of Aminah's part in Dancer's death. He had reprimanded her and barred her from making any more of her weird concoctions. 'Now, what would you like me to do? Read to you or talk?'

I stayed with her most of the day, though from Aminah's scowls and mutterings my presence was not welcome. I read to her, but her concentration wavered after a few paragraphs. I started up discussions on several topics, but she seemed apathetic. I began to realize why she enjoyed Jessica's company so much. An endless supply of bright, inconsequential chatter was what she liked, chit-chat that did not tax her in any way. I tried my best but I was no Jessica, and I was soon casting around frantically for fragments of gossip or little anecdotes to amuse her.

The only time she really became animated was when Maxwell came to sit with her after lunch. I answered his knock and admitted him, then tried to make myself as insignificant as possible in a corner. Aminah had disappeared somewhere and I wished fervently that she would return so that I could relinquish my unlooked for position of chaperon. I tried to occupy myself with the glove I was mending, but in spite of my resolution I could not help glancing across to where Maxwell sat by the bed.

Beyond a curt nod, he had barely acknowledged me. Towards Isabel he was gentle and courteous, teasing her mildly once or twice so that she laughed. He told her about the farm he had visited the day before. 'As soon as you are feeling stronger, we shall ride there together. It is a pleasant, easy jog along the river bank. The farmer and his wife are a kindly pair. They enquired most solicitously about you and made me bring away a crock of fresh butter and a fat jar of honey from their own bees. Mrs Williams insisted that it is good fresh English food you are in need of after all that spicey foreign stuff.'

'Ah, but she would change her views if she could have tasted *rijsttafel* or a scalding Madras curry.' Isabel sighed nostalgically.

'Or *satay* dipped in steaming sauces! I am afraid our palates have become accustomed to richer, tastier food than good, plain English fare.'

They fell into a discussion over food they had eaten, which drifted on to a reminiscence of places they had visited. I jabbed my needle fiercely into the cotton so that I pricked my finger. They had so much common ground between them. Their sojourn in a tropical land, their easy acceptance of wealth and privilege. How could I ever have imagined Maxwell would view me other than someone with whom to have a casual affair? I had believed those snatched moments in the library to have been the results of some real, deep emotion. I had so much wanted to believe that I had imagined his cool behaviour since was a mask to cover his true feelings. The possibility that the attraction I had held for him was superficial and his response, in its way, merely a shadow of that which had inflamed Lord Easthulme, wounded me to the quick.

I could not see the needle or the glove for a sudden blinding of tears. It was humiliating that I, who hardly ever wept, who presented a stoic face to the world, should be swept by such weakness, such longing for Maxwell that I was reduced to tears.

I moved my chair slightly so that I should not face the bed and kept my head bent over my sewing, though I wanted more than anything to look at Maxwell. I was beginning to realize how vulnerable a woman in love was and to understand a little of the anguish Miss Webster must have felt.

After Maxwell had left, Isabel fell back into apathy. She allowed me to straighten her bed and plump her pillows in silence. Her face wore a look of brooding and sadness, the long gold-tipped lashes shadowed the expression in her eyes, but she said in a low, small voice as she pulled the shawl slowly about her thin shoulders, 'I feel so helpless.'

'It will pass,' I said. 'You will recover your energy if you do as the doctor says and take your medicine.'

She sighed. 'I hope so, and I hope it will not be too late when I do.'

'Too late?'

Her eyelids slid shut. 'I should be with him now. I should be his constant companion as I was on the ship, instead of lying here.' She spoke half to herself. 'If I continue like this he will grow tired of me.'

'Nonsense! You must not have such foolish fancies,' I said with hypocritical briskness. 'He loves you. How could your illness make him care any the less for you?'

She shook her head, her fingers twining and untwining in the fringe of her shawl. 'You are right, I am imagining possibilities that may never happen. I have too much time to think, lying here through the long night hours when sleep will not come.' Her eyes opened wide, fixing me with a distressed, pleading stare. 'I cannot help it, though. I love him so. If he left me now I think . . . ' Her voice dropped to a whisper and she turned her head on the pillow and closed her eyes. I had to lean over to catch her words. 'I think . . . I should die . . . '

She seemed to drift asleep. I looked down at her with mingled pity and jealousy. I was glad when Aminah glided into the room and I could leave. I felt suffocated by the cloying atmosphere of the sickroom, weighted with guilt. I went out into the blustery afternoon, heedless of the chill wind. I walked Skip a long way, treading the gorsey hillsides until my feet and the skirts of my dress were soaked from the rain-wet grasses. I hoped to find peace of mind out there under the sweeping clouds. But I came back to the house as troubled as I had left it.

Now that the weather had broken it was hard to believe that it had ever been hot and dry. The sky was a brooding grey and showers raced across the gardens with squal peevishness. Each day dawned cool and gloomy, matching my mood.

I kept myself busy. I visited Isabel, I darned and patched every threadbare item in my scanty wardrobe, I wrote to Miss Webster, I spent hours reading quietly in the small parlour. And I avoided Maxwell, as though by keeping myself aloof I might cure myself of loving him.

It was inevitable, though, that we met at mealtimes. I grew to dread the ordeal. It was hard to sit there making polite conversation, attending to what Mr Pritchard and Mr Thurlow said, and trying not to let my eyes wander too often or too long in Maxwell's direction. I felt tense and nervous. My appetite, usually robust, deserted me so that Mr Thurlow enquired if I was quite well. I assured him, overbrightly, that I had eaten far too much during the birthday celebrations and now I felt obliged to curb my appetite or I should never fit into my dresses. Mr Thurlow laughed. 'Why, child, an extra pound or two would never be noticed on your slender frame. What do you say, Maxwell?'

Maxwell's eyes flicked coolly at me. 'I agree with you.' he said shortly, immediately returning to the discussion on the prices of imported silks he was engaged in with Mr Pritchard, as though the brief interruption had been distasteful. It was humiliating. I longed to burst out. 'You did not look at me so coldly on the night of the ball!' Instead, I forced down the remainder of the meal and excused myself as soon as I could.

I went up to my room and took out the crumpled red dress that I had flung to the bottom of the cupboard. I pressed my burning face into the crushed silk, but after a moment I took a hard grip on it and ripped it viciously across from bodice to hem. It gave me a certain bitter satisfaction to hear the material rending, to see the threads of torn silk float down to cling to the rug at my feet. Had I not worn the wretched gown to the ball I might never have realized my love for Maxwell. But even as I thought that I knew that I was wrong. The incident with Lord Easthulme and Maxwell's rescue of me had only confirmed what my heart had known earlier. When he had comforted me after Dancer's death I had felt the first stirrings of love. If Aminah could have foreseen that, she would hardly have been so eager to lay poison for the old dog, for by her act of vengeance she had brought Maxwell and I together. Her possessive love for Isabel had led her blindly astray. She had foreseen in her uncanny way that I presented a threat to her mistress and had taken the first opportunity at hand to strike out at me. But the plan had misfired; she had succeeded only in making matters worse. Time would allow me to forgive her for Dancer's death, but for her part in bringing me to this state of confusion and misery I could only hate her.

I made a bundle of the dress and hid it under my cloak as I went out into the chill afternoon wind. I walked briskly from the house. Once through the lodge gates and in the empty lane I flung my dress into a ditch. It sank down into the muddy water and I hurled branches and stones on top of it until it was quite hidden. Soon the full summer's growth of grass and cow parsley and brambles would smother the ditch and, when it dried out, the mice and the shrews and the small hedgerow creatures would be the only ones to know that my hopes and dreams were buried there.

Two letters arrived for me. Jessica wrote: '. . . *It is much more pleasant here than I had anticipated. At a soirée I was introduced to the most devastatingly handsome gentleman. He has shown the most flattering attention towards me and Mamma is much impressed. His family owns one of the larger shipping lines and is quite one of the most influential in the city . . . We are to go to the theatre tomorrow where Mr Salter has reserved a box . . . We are so enjoying ourselves that Mamma has decided to extend our stay to which decision Aunt Louie is most agreeable . . .'*

I smiled as I read the untidy writing, glad that Mrs Thurlow was appeased for the loss of Lord Easthulme. She would perhaps return in a better temper.

Miss Webster's letter was longer and less exuberant. She wrote of her journey and of the kind way her brother and his young sons had welcomed her. *'I have no wish to be a burden, so I make myself as useful as I can. The children adore the fuss I make of them – without spoiling them, of course. They have sadly missed the attention of a mother these past years. I help in the school Charles has started and have been fortunate enough to obtain a post in the household of a banking acquaintance of Charles. I go to the house on three mornings each week to converse in French with the banker's wife and his two daughters, as they plan to tour the continent next summer. I am hopeful that if I make a success of this, I may be recommended to other persons. The house I visit is very fine. Alas, I cannot say the same of the district where Charles lives. The houses there are much decayed and there is a great deal of poverty and disease. It grieves me to see poor, thin, pale-faced children clustered in damp cellars, playing in narrow courts and entries that scarcely admit any daylight. Some of them are lucky enough to find work that will bring in a shilling or two, to supplement the wages their parents receive in the mills or the tannery. Others, I fear, turn to crime as a means of employment, and once they are set on this course it is a short step to prison. If only we could catch these little mites, take them from the streets and educate them, how much happier a future they might have. Charles's efforts in this direction seem almost futile against this great tide of ignorance and poverty, but I shall do my best to support him in any way I can . . .'*

She mentioned only briefly how she missed Ashridge Hall. I felt sad for her because she loved the country and disliked the smoky confines of the city where she was now forced to live. Even so, I knew she had the willpower to overcome her feelings. She would doubtless throw herself wholeheartedly into helping those children who came into her care. She would do so with kindness and firmness, perhaps finding in her work some compensation for the cruel change in her fortunes.

I had taken the letters out of doors to read. Now I refolded them and put them into my basket. The morning had turned unexpectedly warm and I was glad that Mr Thurlow had not opposed my plan to take a picnic lunch into the park.

'I shall gather wild flowers suitable for pressing,' I had explained. 'I am thinking of making a dried-flower picture. Jessica does them so beautifully but all my efforts have gone sadly awry. I shall make a great effort this time, and if my picture is a success I shall send it to Miss Webster as a keepsake.'

His eyes clouded at mention of the governess, but he said in his usual calm way, 'Well, do not stray too far. Would you like one of the maids to go with you? I tend to forget how lonely it must be for you with Jessica away and Isabel confined to bed.'

The last thing I wanted was an escort. 'Skip will be company enough,' I assured him, 'And I shall not go beyond the upper park. I shall return in good time to spend an hour with Isabel after tea.'

My flower gathering was a desultory occupation. I strolled over the grass, making the slow ascent of the land that rose behind the house. At the highest point I spread my cloak in the lee of the wall and ate my sandwiches, while Skip frisked about the grass tufts. After I had eaten I lay back on my cloak and gave myself sensuously to the warm sunshine. How good it was to be out of the house! Never had it seemed so dull and gloomy, as though the sickroom atmosphere had crept from Isabel's room and invaded all its corners. The doctor had looked in most days to deliver a cheerful little homily and leave more medicine, but his ministrations did not seem to help Isabel at all. Perhaps when the physician from Manchester made his visit at the end of the week he would recommend some form of treatment that would be effective. I hoped so. I had little cause to like Isabel but I could not wish her to remain permanently in an ailing state.

I narrowed my eyes at the glare of the sun. Puffs of white cloud chased across the blue sky like ships running before the breeze. Thinking of Isabel inevitably led me to thoughts of Maxwell. I allowed my mind to stray into forbidden territory. I slipped into the luxury of a daydream . . . a luxury I had sternly prohibited myself since I had faced the stark truth that Maxwell's attraction for me had been only a passing fancy.

Lulled by the warmth, by the whisper of the breeze through the grass, by the distant, soporific calls of sheep, I imagined how it would be if Isabel was not here. Suppose she decided that she did not want to marry Maxwell, after all, and left the house with her papa. Maxwell would be desolate at first, but I should be here. I should be ready to listen to his problems, to take an interest in the affairs of the estate . . . I should even put on a bold show and ride with him to visit the tenants. He would learn that I could converse intelligently and that I was a far more interesting person than the beautiful, languid, china-doll Miss Pritchard. Perhaps on one of our rides we would pause in some wooded glade and dismount. We would feel that magical attraction, he would take me in his arms and declare, passionately, that it was I whom he had always loved. We would marry . . . we would be madly, wonderfully happy . . . we should call our first son Maxwell . . .

I slept. My recent nights had not been restful, I had slept fitfully. But now I went into a deep, heavy sleep and it was only the first drops of rain that roused me.

I was stiff and cramped. I had no idea how long I had

slept, but I guessed, blearily, that it had been some considerable time. The sun had gone. The sky was a uniform grey with scuds of fretted black cloud sweeping across, and Skip was whining and shaking himself as the rain suddenly descended in earnest.

I gathered my wits and my belongings and sought shelter under the wall, huddling down into my cloak. It was only a shower, surely, I told myself. It might ease soon, and I could hurry back to the house without getting too wet. But the rain came down heavier and the sky darkened. I heard the faint, ominous sound of thunder.

The wall was little protection against the downpour. I was getting steadily wetter and I was cross with myself for sleeping so soundly. 'It's no use, Skip,' I said aloud, 'we shall have to make a run for it. Come along, boy.'

He bounced on ahead with an excited yelp as I started to pick my way as quickly as I could over the slippery tussocks of grass. He trotted back to me once or twice, but soon he galloped off into the sweeping veils of rain heading for the warmth of the stables. I wished I had his speed and sureness of foot. I slithered and tripped and could not see for the rain streaming into my eyes. My cloak did not have a hood and my sodden hair began to loosen in the wind and flap about my cheeks. I was wearing light slippers which had soaked through when I first started to walk, and now, to my exasperation, one got stuck in a muddy patch and I stepped out of it. I decided it was hardly worth putting it on again as my stockings were soaked, so I tore off the other slipper and dumped them both into my basket.

It was surprising how sharp every stalk and stone seemed. I remembered, wryly, the barefoot child who had run over stubble fields and rutted lanes as though they had been soft carpets. I would have given much for a pair of calloused soles. My poor tender feet slowed me down as I picked my way gingerly around thistles I had hardly known were there before and over stones with razor edges. I had just caught my toe on one and uttered a most unladylike word when a voice said sarcastically, 'Do you usually go for walks in your stockinged feet?'

I looked up from the inspection of my bruised toe to find Maxwell walking his horse towards me. He was as wet as I, his riding coat dark with rain, his black curly hair plastered to his skull.

I said tartly, 'No, I do not. I was caught out in the storm and lost my slipper.'

He looked as bad-tempered as I felt. 'Tom was worried because the dog had returned without you,' he said. 'I was returning from the farm as he was preparing to come and look for you. As I was already wet, I said I would instigate the search.' His cold black glance swept over me as he edged the horse nearer. 'Come here,' he ordered, 'and I will lift you up in front of me.'

I straightened my shoulders and took a step backwards.

'I am quite capable of walking back to the house,' I said in my frostiest manner. 'I am already so wet I will not harm for an extra few minutes.'

'Do as I say,' he said harshly. 'This is no time to be having an argument.'

'I am not arguing,' I said sweetly, aware of the ludicrousness of my stand. A bedraggled, soaked sight I must look, standing in a downpour and trying to look dignified. 'I wish to walk back to the house and walk I shall.'

I began to step out, but he was determined that I should do his bidding. He moved the horse past me and leaned from the saddle, grasping me round the waist and scooping me upwards as he went.

It was then that the lightning came. It dazzled down out of the blackness, followed instantly by a mighty crack of thunder. The horse whinnied and reared, and Maxwell, unbalanced, was flung to the ground and I with him. For a few seconds I lay there, the breath driven from me. The horse with a great snort galloped off down the slope towards the stables, stirrups flying wildly.

'You see,' I cried furiously, when I could catch my breath. 'This is what happens when you try to have your own way. You are insufferable! A bully and a cheat! I hate you, and don't you dare try to touch me again!'

I was scrambling to my feet as I spoke, picking up my spilled basket and uselessly trying to brush mud from my skirts. I turned towards him to fire the last salvo.

'I hate you! Do you hear that, you . . . you wretch! I never want to hear the name Maxwell Thurlow again . . .!' My voice faded into the roar of the wind. 'Oh, God,' I breathed. 'Oh, dear God. He is dead! Maxwell! Oh, Maxwell!'

He lay on the grass, unmoving. He was on his back, his arms spread wide, the rain falling on his upturned face and his closed eyes.

I fell to my knees beside him, all my fury gone and only a terrible, soul-shaking fear remaining. I lifted his head and cradled it in my lap, leaning over him in a vain effort to shield him from the storm. I stroked the hair back from his brow, letting my fingers run tenderly across the hard bones of his cheek and jaw.

'I didn't mean it,' I whispered. 'I spoke in temper. Oh, Maxwell, please wake up. Please speak to me. Oh, my dearest, my dear love. I cannot bear it. It was all my fault, I am so stubborn.' His face was white and still under my hand. 'Come back to me, my love,' I pleaded. 'I will never be so stupid again, I promise. I love you, my darling. I would not have you hurt for the world.'

There was a movement, an indrawing of breath. His eyelids flickered.

'Oh, thank God,' I breathed. 'Thank God.'

'Morwenna?' His voice was faint. 'Morwenna? Is that you? What happened?'

'I am here,' I said, relief flooding every part of me like a warm tide. 'You fell from your horse and knocked yourself unconscious. Can you move your arms? Your legs? . . . Yes, you can. You do not appear to be badly hurt. Oh, that is such a relief! I thought for an awful moment . . . ' I broke off, turning my head so that he should not see my face. But his hand came up, forcing my head round so that I was looking down at him once more. He was staring at me as he had done that evening in the library. Gone was the haughty, remote unfeeling stranger who had addressed me so curtly. His eyes were warm, his expression a mingling of wonderment and tenderness. I felt again that stirring of the heart, that frightening, exciting sense of two people being drawn together by an unknown force that was too powerful to resist.

His hand moved to my shoulder. He caught the soaked, limp tresses of my hair and gently pulled me down. Somehow I found myself lying beside him and there, in the wet grass, with the storm rumbling and pounding around us he held me and kissed me. Rain was in our mouths, in our eyes. The wildness of the day was in our kisses, in the desperate way we clung to each other.

'Morwenna,' he said, 'Morwenna. How I have longed to hold you.'

'I thought you did not care for me.' I was laughing and crying and kissing him all at once.

'I tried not to care. I tried like hell. But it has been a losing battle.'

'Then why fight at all?'

'Because I had to. Because my life was settled, my path pleasantly clear. I had found a woman suitable in every way to be my wife. I admired her and loved her . . . at least I thought . . . I was convinced I did.'

'And now?' I said softly.

'Now – now I still feel the same for her. A gentle affection.' He groaned and buried his face in my neck. 'It is nothing against the feelings I have for you. This is a fever that burns in my blood – seemingly incurable. And, God help me, I do not wish to be cured.'

'Nor I,' I murmured, then added shakily: 'We cannot stay here like this. Tom will come looking for us.' I tore myself from his embrace and got to my feet, making a feeble attempt to smooth my hair 'It would be most . . . indiscreet to be caught.'

'Who cares about discretion?' he said, standing and pulling me close again. I sighed and leaned my head against his shoulder.

'Not I,' I whispered. 'I would run away with you to the ends of the earth. But other people would be shocked to see us. Shocked and hurt.'

His arms tightened about me. 'Isabel,' he said harshly. 'She must not find out from gossip and tittle-tattle. She will be hurt enough and the least I can do is to be totally honest with her.' He pushed me away from him, gripping my shoulders, so that he could look into my eyes. 'But I can say nothing yet, she is too sick. It will be best to wait until she is well again. We must live a deception until that day. Is it too much to ask you, Morwenna?'

I shook my head, remembering the face on the pillow and the sad words – " . . . if he left me . . . I should die . . . " I shivered and it was not entirely due to the wetness of my clothes that clung soddenly about me. 'As long as I know that you love me,' I said, 'anything is bearable. I will wait a week – a year – a lifetime. But I wish – I wish that there was some way of avoiding pain to Isabel. She loves you so much. Her father will be distressed too . . . and Mr Thurlow. As for your stepmother, I can hardly bear to think what she will say . . . '

He pressed his fingers to my lips. 'My dearest girl,' he said, 'we will face them in good time and it will not be easy for anyone. There will be acrimony and bitter words and heartbreak. But for the moment, all that I know is that I love you and want you. I would not,' he added with a touch of the old irony, 'ask you to be my mistress, so it appears I needs must marry you.' Then he smiled to take the sting from his words. 'Indeed, I would not have it any other way. I respect you far too much.'

'To wait and guard our secret will doubtless be good for us. As Miss Webster would say. "Self denial makes for strong character." But it will be hard, Maxwell.'

'I know that too well. These days since the ball have been an agony. Each time I have seen you looking so downcast and forlorn it has taken all my strength not to snatch you into my arms and comfort you. Instead, I schooled myself to be cold and unapproachable. Can you ever forgive me for that?'

'You are already forgiven,' I said.

'I thought I was doing the right thing, the honourable thing, by ignoring my deepest feelings. Now I think it is surely better to be honest and make a clean break, however unpleasant the immediate consequences may be, than to spend the rest of my life living a lie; making one woman my wife but loving another.' He sighed and under my hand I could feel the thudding of his heartbeat. 'It is strange,' he went on after a moment, 'but with you I feel a sense of rightness – of recognition, as though I had been searching for a long time and now found what I had been looking for. It was like that when you walked into the drawing-room that first evening: you, in your skimpy dress, with tugged-back hair and your unquenchable, touching dignity. And those eyes – so wide and so vivid a blue; like the sea under a brilliant sky. I felt I was drowning in their depths. As I do now.'

I laughed aloud for happiness. 'Oh, but we surely both shall drown, my dear, if we stand here much longer. The rain is coming down harder than ever.'

We began to walk back to the house, my hand in his, wet

palm to wet palm. Only in my stockinged feet, I still could not walk easily so presently he swung me up into his arms and carried me to the stables to where a harassed Tom, an old sack about his shoulders for protection, was about to come and search for us.

'Eh, master, I thought there'd been an accident,' Tom cried when he saw us.

'No accident,' Maxwell said evenly. 'Miss Tregarth lost her shoe and the horse bolted and unseated me when the thunder came too close. We will shelter in the barn until the storm has passed.'

So we went into the barn and sat on a bale of straw out of the wind and rain. It was warm and dry and sweet-smelling, and beyond the rattle of the rain on the roof and the whickering of the horses in the stables and Tom's cheery whistle, there was nothing to disturb us. We sat and held hands and whispered to each other and made plans and did not care a jot for the storm. So little we had. So very little. And yet it seemed so very much.

I had never been so happy in my life. The two days that followed stand out in my memory as golden ones. Whether there was sunshine or not I cannot remember; I only know there should have been and that I had come alive in some mysterious way, like a flower blossoming on a summer's day.

I went about my tasks quietly. I visited Isabel and should have been burdened with guilt, yet even the sight of her lying in her bed did not trouble me. I was cushioned by my own inner happiness. I felt strong and proud and vibrant with well-being.

We were careful, Maxwell and I. Nobody had any inkling of what had happened. Certainly neither Mr Thurlow nor Mr Pritchard noticed anything untoward in our behaviour to each other. Of course, we were scrupulously correct, especially in front of the servants. But if I chanced upon

Maxwell in the park as I walked with Skip, or if we both decided that a stroll along the Yew Walk would be pleasant before dinner, who was there to say it was not mere coincidence?

Our embraces were brief, our endearments spoken hurriedly and in whispers, but the snatched moments together were doubly precious for that.

The only person I avoided was Aminah. I disliked the implacable stare of her wet-pebble eyes: they seemed to bore into my head as though they would search out and seek my innermost secrets. She had always looked at me like that, with scarcely veiled malevolence but, now that I had something to hide, I was suddenly afraid of her; afraid that she would, with her uncanny senses, guess how I had betrayed her mistress. It seemed that whenever I was in Isabel's room now she hardly left the side of the bed. She was for ever patting the bedclothes or the pillows, or smoothing Isabel's hair or stroking the limp hand that lay on the covers, crooning softly to herself in her strange language. It was as though she said, 'I am here. I shall protect her. You are not wanted. You only mean my mistress harm.'

It is imagination, I told myself severely. You have buried your guilt but you know that you are acting in a hypocritical manner, so you make up these strange ideas about Aminah.

All the same, I was always glad to escape from that implacable black stare.

I longed for Isabel to show some improvement. I prayed for it. If only she were better! If only she were strong and healthy as I was! She would be able to face up to Maxwell's decision . . . his cruelty. For cruel it was: I acknowledged that in my quieter moments. I wished it could be otherwise, but the feelings Maxwell and I had for each other were overpowering, swamping body and soul and mind alike. When I was in his arms I forgot everything. Even when our eyes met across a room and he smiled, I felt that delicious sense of communication . . . of a link between us, an awareness so strong that I was sure other people must realize it too, so that I was forced to lower my lids and try desperately to think of something else until my flushed cheeks cooled.

But the doctor would come. The clever doctor from Manchester would recommend some excellent form of treatment. Isabel would recover in time. I only needed patience. Patience and understanding . . .

He came on the Friday, a bony, dour man in a sombre frock coat and tall hat. He was ushered upstairs into Isabel's room and remained there, locked in consultation for the best part of an hour.

I waited in my bedroom. I thought it best not to be in the way. I would stay until the great man had drunk his glass of Madeira and departed in the doctor's trap. Then I should go downstairs and presently Maxwell would find me and tell me what happened. We could start to make plans then, tentative ones perhaps, if it looked as though Isabel was to be sick for a little longer. But plans for the future.

I stood by my window, leaning my forehead on the glass. The blackbird's nest in the ivy below was empty. The raucous fledgelings were scattered now about the shrubbery and the parents were worn thin bringing them worms and grubs. Soon the young birds would be able to find their own food and the parents would leave them. Then there would be winter to get through, there would be another spring, and the cycle of courting and mating and breeding would begin again. How easy it was for birds, creatures of instinct, blindly following the seasons, untroubled by emotions.

I sighed and paced about my rug, and was glad when at long last I saw the doctor's trap going down the drive.

There was no one in the drawing-room when I went downstairs. Emmy was crossing the hall with a tray of empty glasses.

'Mr Thurlow and Mr Pritchard are in the library,' she

informed me. 'I believe Mr Maxwell went out into the gardens in the direction of the Yew Walk. And, miss,' she called after me as I began to walk away, 'there is a letter come for you.'

I picked it up from the table as I went, barely glancing at the handwriting. I could not stop to read it now. Maxwell was waiting for me by the cherub pond. How sensible of him to go out there, where we could talk freely without fear of eavesdroppers.

I ran along the velvety grass of the Walk, the dark yews like sombre sentinels on either side. Beyond them, in the sunlight, Maxwell stood. He had his back to me, staring down into the water of the pond. Something in his stance made me falter in my headlong flight, made me catch my breath. I waited for a moment in the shadow of the yews before I could bring myself to cross that stretch of lawn to where he was waiting.

I said, 'Maxwell?' and my voice was not steady.

He did not speak, or move: he was as still as the stone cherubs. We seemed trapped in a web of stillness and silence and, suddenly, I was afraid. Afraid to hear what he had to say . . . afraid to know.

'Why, Maxwell,' I cried, 'I wondered where you were. It was so clever of you to come out here so that we could talk privately. I trust all went well this morning. I saw the doctor leave . . . ' I was pouring out the words, anything to fill the silence, to prevent him from speaking. ' . . . Did he suggest some medicine for Isabel? I hope he was able to recommend something helpful – '

He turned slowly to face me and my voice died. He was ashy-white, his eyes black hollows above gaunt cheekbones. He looked old and haggard.

He said harshly, 'He could recommend nothing.'

'Nothing at all? But he was supposed to be a clever man. Is he a charlatan, do you think?'

'I wish to God he were.'

'I don't understand.'

'Nor do I,' he rasped out. The words seemed to drag from him painfully. 'It was all to have been so straightforward, wasn't it? Isabel would get better soon. I would tell her that I no longer wished to marry her, that the engagement was better broken, that it was foolish to marry when one partner loved another. Now . . . now everything is changed.'

'Why? Tell me, Maxwell. Why?'

'Isabel,' he said, 'will never get better.'

My hand went involuntarily to my lips as though to stifle a cry. But I did not cry out. I waited for him to go on.

'She has some ailment . . . "a palsy of the nervous system", the doctor called it. He told us at great length the consequences: a general feebleness interposed with periods of normalcy when she will be a little better, but a gradual decline. A slow creeping paralysis will overtake her. He informed us that there are signs that it has already begun.'

'Poor Isabel,' I whispered. 'Is there nothing that can be done for her?'

'The doctor suggested that the best way to help her was to keep her in good spirits. He said in cases of this kind there was a tendency to morbidity and a lowering depression. He said a loving family about her and freedom from all worry was the best medicine. He thought that our forthcoming marriage would do much to retard the development of the symptoms as it would keep her mind occupied. He suggested that we do not delay our wedding plans, but bring the date forward and perhaps take our honeymoon at some spa such as Malvern, where the waters might be of some help to her.'

I knew my face must now be as white as his, for I felt the colour drain away.

'She does not know any of this?'

He shook his head. 'She must on no account find out that she is suffering from an incurable illness. Apart from my father and hers, you and I are the only ones who know. For fear someone should accidentally let the secret out, we think it best not to tell the rest of the family. She will live out the life she has left in happy ignorance.'

'Will it . . . how long . . . ?' I could not frame the words.

'The doctor says some cases degenerate rapidly, a matter of a year or two. Others linger on for a long time, only gradually succumbing to the palsy.'

We stood close together, but the distance between us might have been measured in miles. It seemed that a chasm had opened at our feet, a chasm that was widening by the minute, forcing us further and further away from each other. I longed to hold out my arms and feel his strong hands pull me close and hold me safely. But I did nothing but stand there, stricken and cold.

Presently I said in a small, strange voice, 'Then this means that all is finished between us.'

He stared at me hopelessly. His eyes burned in his white face, his mouth was a tight line of pain.

'How can I leave her now?' he said. 'She is ill and weak and she needs me.'

'And I do not?'

'Oh, God, Morwenna, do not make it harder for either of us. I want you more than words can say, but my duty lies elsewhere.'

'Duty!' I exclaimed bitterly. 'So you will marry her from duty?'

'And suppose I do not?' Anger sparked in his eyes. 'Suppose we tell her that we love each other and we wish to marry? And suppose our revelations lead to a worsening in her condition or even her death? Do you think we could live on happily with that knowledge like a dead weight about our necks?' His voice softened. 'You would not want that any more than I should.'

I closed my eyes against the hurt. I said, 'Go away,

Maxwell. Leave me now. I must have time to think, to be alone.'

I felt him take my hand and uncurl the tight fingers. I felt his breath upon my palm, then the pressure of his lips. He said softly, 'You are my other half, Morwenna. My dear love. We may be parted by circumstances but I shall never forget you.' Then he dropped my hand and went away.

I did not open my eyes until I was sure he was out of sight. Then my knees sagged and I sank down to the stone rim of the pond. I was shaking as though I had an ague, and though I stared down into the weedy waters where the goldfish swam so serenely, I did not see them. All I could see was Maxwell's face. Maxwell's eyes. All I could remember was the warmth of his body next to mine, the fire in my veins as we kissed.

And now he was gone.

After a while I realized I was still holding the letter I had picked up in the house. It was crumpled from my grip and I smoothed it open and read it through once without comprehension. Then a sentence leapt out at me, and gathering myself together I read it again.

It was from Mrs Thurlow, short and to the point.

'*. . . my sister Louie, Mrs Hyde, has urgent need of a governess for her younger children, as she has had to dismiss her current one due to suspicion of thieving. I have suggested that you would be suitable to fill the post. The time has come when you should be thinking of taking some useful employment, and by taking this position you would be repaying in some small part the many kindnesses shown to you in my house. I am sure you will be grateful for the opportunity of living in such a respectable household and looking after such well-behaved children. I am writing to Mr Thurlow separately so that he may make arrangements for your journey here.*'

I sat there for a long time before I decided exactly what I must do.

CHAPTER EIGHT

I left the sleeping house well before dawn. I had waited until I was sure everyone must be asleep before I rose from my bed and dressed and gathered my few belongings into a bundle. I slipped like a ghost through the dark corridors, leaving the note I had written for Mr Thurlow on the table in the hall. I felt badly about him. He had shown me nothing but generosity and kindness and now I was running from his house like a thief in the night. But I could see no other way. I could not stay here keeping a guard on my feelings as Miss Webster had done. Each time I saw Maxwell I would be reminded of all that might have been. Each time he saw me would be bound to make him aware of his divided loyalties. Now that I was calmer I could see that he had made the honourable decision, but at such a price! As for the idea of becoming a governess to the Hyde children, I was appalled by it. Those sly creatures would batten on to me like leeches. With their tricky ways they would find every means to torment me and there would be nobody to turn to for help. Their mamma would hear no wrong of them and I would be the whipping boy for every mischief they committed.

No, it was best that I leave the Thurlow family completely. Rid myself of every reminder of Maxwell. I hope Mr Thurlow would accept at face value my excuse that I did not want to be a governess and did not wish to be a burden to him any longer. I had apologized for my abrupt departure and told him I should never be able to repay his generosity to me. He would be saddened, I knew, and Mrs Thurlow would reproach him for having taken me under his roof in the first place. I could just imagine her: 'Breeding will out. A girl of that class will never alter. She may put on a show of being a gentlewoman, but she remains at heart a guttersnipe. The ungrateful hussy!'

I went out through the music room window into the moonless night. The air was damp and fresh against my face as I hurried across to the stables. There was one goodbye I had to say before I left.

I heard Skip's growl as he came silent-footed from his bed in the stable. I spoke to him and the growl changed to a yip of welcome. I shushed him and stroked his shaggy head, then I crept up the ladder to the stable loft when Tom slept.

He lay on his straw pallet somewhere in the dark loft. I could hear his breathing as my head poked through the trap-door. I called his name several times before a startled voice cried, 'Who's there?'

I told him and there was the scrabbling sound of bare feet and then a flame flickered to life as he lit the candle. He looked at me blearily.

'What's up, miss? What are you doing here? It's the middle of the night.' He listened in silence, his eyes getting rounder as I explained. 'Eh, it's a shame, miss,' he said when I'd finished. 'Fancy them wanting to send you to Liverpool, and you part of the family, like . . . '

I cut him short. 'No matter now, Tom. I want to be well away before sun-up. I shall go to Manchester and find work there. I intend to seek Miss Webster's help, but nobody else but you must know that.'

'I'll not tell.'

I smiled at him in the dim flicker of the candle. 'I leave Skip in your care, Tom. I would like to take him with me but I do not think he would take kindly to the city streets. Here, give me your hand.' I pressed into his palm a precious half sovereign, one of my small hoard, saved from birthday and

Christmas gifts from Mr Thurlow. He began to protest when he saw what I had given him.

'Please, Tom,' I insisted. 'Keep it in case you ever are in need. If you like, think of it as a guardian's fee for looking after Skip, for some day I shall perhaps be able to take him back. The money will be a little security for you. A nest egg. Remember, those who are alone in the world must help each other. You have helped me and now I help you.'

He seized my hand and shook it vigorously, pumping up and down, his face broken into a wide beam. It was the remembrance of his honest, freckled face that I took with me into the cold night and into the darkness.

There was not much in my bundle but it was a dragging weight after a mile or so. All the same I made steady progress. I was well beyond Macclesfield by dawn, and then I was lucky enough to get a ride in a farm wagon as far as the village of Hazel Grove. I was tired by then, feeling the effects of my sleepless night, and my head nodded as I dozed to the jolting of the cart. I rested a while when the wagon had trundled off down a lane, sitting under a clump of hawthorn while I munched on an apple and a slice of cold meat I had sneaked from last night's dinner table. It tasted good out there in the fresh air, and afterwards I could have lain down in the grass and slept. But I knew I must move on; it was still a long way to the city and then I would have to find where Miss Webster's brother lived.

I plodded on, and now, tormented by fatigue, the certainty that I was doing the right thing had fled. I felt alone and lost. I had left Maxwell – Mr Thurlow – Jessica – all those whom I loved and respected. I had even spurned the offer of a respectable post as governess, and all to throw myself into an unknown situation. Of course Miss Webster would be kind to me, but what of her brother? He might not like the idea of a young woman turning up on his doorstep without so much as a by your leave. A position might be hard to find; I could not impose on Miss Webster's charity and my money would not last for long.

The thoughts went round and round in my head like mice in a cage. And above all else was the one overpowering realization: I had left forever the man I loved, the man who was dearer to me than life itself. I felt sick with the weight of grief, and the nearer I got to the pall of smoke that lay over the city, the lower my spirits sank.

I had been to Manchester twice before on visits to friends of Mrs Thurlow but the city seemed very different today. Then we had ridden in a carriage from the fine country house at Higher Broughton where Mrs Thurlow's friends lived. We had visited only the best silk mercers or jewellers or milliners and taken tea and pastries at an elegant teashop. It was one thing to be driven in and out of the city in a private carriage and to promenade only the fashionable pavements of St. Ann's Square, it was quite another to find oneself alone, exhausted and bewildered in the middle of a seething, unheeding crowd.

All around me people hurried. A fine drizzle had set in and everyone, it seemed, was bent on getting out of it. Over the greasy cobbles carriages rattled and shook and the great flat wagons – the lurries – piled with bales of cloth lumbered after straining horses. The air smelled of soot and everything looked grey, each building grimed with a black sooty patina. Even the pigeons and sparrows that pecked at blown chaff in the gutters had grubby feathers. I had no idea which direction I should take, and there seemed no one in this faceless throng that I dared stop and ask.

I wandered along Market Street and presently I plucked up courage to ask an old flower-seller with a kind face if she could direct me to St. Clement's Street. She looked at me from bright eyes buried in a network of wrinkles.

'What's a respectable lass like you wanting wi' an address like that, might I ask?'

My heart sank still further, but I said calmly, 'It is the house of a clergyman I am seeking.'

'Are you now?' She looked at me with suspicion, but she gave me clear directions and called after me: 'Mind how you go, miss. Don't linger anywhere – 'tis a rough place for a young lass to be alone.'

The streets grew meaner once I had left the main thoroughfares. Shops and commercials buildings gave way to rows of dilapidated houses, once obviously of some stature but now fallen into decay. I caught glimpses of dark courts down covered entries, and I quickened my steps past the clusters of half-drunk men and women round the doors of the numerous public houses. There were fewer people about here, but each one seemed to me to wear a furtive air. Women, huddled under black shawls, slid like beetles down cellar steps, where ragged children squalled and squabbled; idlers watched me slyly from street corners; even the hurdy-gurdy man with his sad-faced monkey looked greedily in my direction and scowled when I did not stop to give him a coin.

I found the church first, its squat red-brick tower rising above the houses, a church not new enough to be handsome nor old enough to be picturesque; built probably fifty years before, at the turn of the century, when the district was fashionable, and soon neglected when the hordes of people swarmed to find homes and work in the spreading city. The people with money had moved to the smart new suburbs and now the slums lapped at the churchyard walls.

St. Clement's Street, I saw with relief, was a little better than some of the dingy ones I had travelled through. And though the far end was blocked by the looming walls of a mill building, the vicarage and its neighbours opposite the church were respectable enough, with whitestoned steps and polished brass knockers.

I was so weary that I hardly cared what my reception might be, but the plain little maid who answered my knock had a sweet smile. 'Please to come in, miss,' she said. 'Miss Webster is out but Mr Webster is in his study. If you will wait, miss, I'll tell him you're here.'

She showed me into a high-ceilinged room, much burdened with heavy furniture. Long plush curtains, half-drawn blinds and an enormous green fern in a heavy pot cut off the view of the street and served to make the room dim and cold.

But Mr Webster's greeting was warm.

He could have been Miss Webster's twin, he was so like her. The same plain, thin-nosed face, with its high forehead and intelligent hazel eyes: yet a gentler one than his sister's with the somewhat dreamy expression of a visionary rather than a man of action.

He said, holding out his hand, 'Miss Tregarth. Ellen has told me so much of you. This is an unexpected pleasure.'

I took his hand. His clasp was warm and dry.

'And what has brought you here?' he asked after a moment, when I did not explain myself. Then when I still did not speak, he went on easily: 'May I offer you some tea? Please do sit down, you look very tired. Have you had a difficult journey?'

I did not speak because I could not for the sudden welling of anguish deep inside. He went on talking in the same kind, fatherly way, the tone of his voice reaching out and touching the tight knot of my misery.

The maid brought in a tray and as she set it on a lace-draped bamboo table I, to my intense shame, burst into tears. I saw her look of surprise and I saw Mr Webster shoo her away, and after that I could not see at all. The dam burst and nothing could stop the flood.

I cried for a long time in that cluttered, dim room. Great racking sobs shook me from head to foot. I cried for all that I had lost, for the hopes shattered so soon; I cried for Isabel whose fate was so ghastly, I cried for Maxwell, who must care for her and who must watch her die by inches. I cried for myself.

Charles Webster sat with me all the time, neither speaking not attempting to comfort me. And when it was all over he asked me nothing. It was his gentle, unquestioning kindness that made me realize that I had indeed found the perfect shelter. And when I came to myself again, I was glad that I had come to this grimy house in the run-down street.

They were grey days that followed. The passion of weeping had drained me of all emotion, I was calmed into a state of total passivity. I moved into a limbo. I talked, I moved, I listened, I even smiled, but it was all mechanical. Inside I was dead: nothing mattered any more. Maxwell was taken from me and there was no longer any point to my existence.

They had given me a small room next to the one in which Charles Webster's two small boys slept. It was at the back of the house with a view over slate-tiled roofs and smoking chimneys. They were dear little boys; Andrew was nine and Victor seven. They were quiet and well-mannered and I hardly knew when they were in the house.

I had meant to make myself useful, but the strange lethargy of mind now took over my body. I could summon up no energy. I sat for hours in the dim front parlour or at the window of my room staring out over the chimney pots. I could not seem to rouse myself until I was fetched for meals, and then I only sat at the table and barely touched the food set before me.

'I am so worried about her,' I overhead Miss Webster say to her brother one day. 'It is unnatural for her to be like this. I feel we should be doing more to help her.'

'Leave her be,' her brother said. 'Whatever hurt she has suffered will mend in its own good time. These wounds of the mind often take longer to heal than those that are visible.'

'I would give much to know what really happened at

Ashridge Hall before she left,' Miss Webster said tartly. 'This tale of being sent to Liverpool . . . why, that is merely an excuse. There is something else involved, I am sure.'

They moved away then and I heard no more. I was vaguely bothered by their concern, but I lapsed back into apathy almost as soon as they moved out of earshot.

Miss Webster tried, tactfully, to probe a little.

'It was cruel of Mrs Thurlow to order you to leave so abruptly. But surely Mr Thurlow would have taken your part had you appealed to him?'

I shrugged. 'Perhaps.'

'And now he must be worried to know where you are. Do you not think you should write to him?'

'I do not wish to.'

'Then would you like me to?'

'No. Please. I do not want to discuss it.'

'But, Morwenna dear, the mill Mr Thurlow is to buy is at the end of the street. It is quite possible that you may meet him by accident. He may even call here to see Charles, though it would be somewhat embarrassing to everyone after the unpleasantness Mrs Thurlow caused by her ridiculous suspicions. I am sure he would respect your confidence if you wished your whereabouts kept secret from . . . other people.'

I said, rising to my feet, 'I have a headache. If you will excuse me, I shall retire to my room.'

I heard her sigh of exasperation as I left her. She asked no more direct questions after that, but tried to shake me from my lethargy by initiating a programme of outings.

I was taken to visit one or two elderly parishioners, hand-picked by Miss Webster, no doubt, because they were cheerful, chatty old souls who might be expected to draw me out of myself. I was shown round the school Charles Webster had started in a converted store-room alongside the church. The room was filled with undersized, ragged children scratching at squeaky slates. It smelled unpleasantly of unwashed clothes and bodies and I wondered, vaguely, how Miss Webster could bear coming here day after day. We went to a concert one evening at the Mechanics Institute in Cooper Street. Listening to the Italian tenor straining for his top notes brought my all-too-constant headache back. I was glad when we returned to the vicarage. I felt that I didn't want to leave its sheltering walls again, so I declined any further trips.

'Please do not bother about keeping me entertained,' I told Miss Webster. 'I should like to rest for a day or two and then perhaps I might look around for some suitable work . . . '

But as the days passed, I spent more and more time shut in my bedroom and Miss Webster's worried look deepened.

It was a surprising incident that jolted me back from my strange, numb existence, something of so little consequence that it seems to me now that I must have been ready to face the world again; that my bruised emotions had begun to mend and Mary's little sisters were only the means whereby I renewed my interest in what was happening about me.

Mary was the maid-of-all-work. She was a scraggy little creature, scarcely more than thirteen, with work-reddened hands and a smile that lifted her face from plainness. I had noticed her absently, noticed her anxiety to please and her energy. Beyond that she had hardly impinged upon my consciousness.

I remember feeling mildly annoyed with her that afternoon. It had gone very warm. My room, catching the sun, was airless and I woke from a troubled doze, feeling hot and thirsty, and the water glass under its bead-fringed dust-cover had not been refilled from yesterday.

I picked it up and wandered downstairs with the intention of giving Mary a gentle scolding. The house was unusually silent. Everyone was out and there was no petitioner, as there so often was, cap in hand, waiting patiently to see 'The Reverend'.

I listened and could hear no sound from the kitchen. I wondered if Mary was taking advantage of the quiet to have a nap. If so, I had no wish to disturb her, her day was long and wearying. All the same, I needed that cool drink, so I tiptoed along the hall and quietly opened the kitchen door.

The whispers and giggles I had heard as I opened it were cut off in an instant. I stopped in surprise and stared at the startled faces turned towards me. It was Mary who recovered first.

'Oh, miss,' she cried, 'how you frightened me.' Then she glanced nervously from me to the open-mouthed children seated at the kitchen table, each with a piece of bread in its hand. 'It's all right, really, miss,' she assured me. 'Mr Webster knows. He says that I'm always to give them a bite to eat when they come for the tea leaves. An' I don't give them much. That's yesterday's bread they're eating and it's only a scrape of dripping on it . . . ' Her voice trailed off, then she added as though remembering her duties: 'Was there something you was wanting, miss?'

'Yes,' I said. 'A glass of water, if you please, Mary.'

She took the glass, apologizing profusely, and went into the scullery with it. I shut the kitchen door behind me and walked slowly across to the table. Four pairs of round eyes blinked up at me, four pairs of jaws continued to munch.

I said, 'Tea leaves, Mary?' when she returned with the water.

'The used ones, miss. I saves them all. Mr Webster said I could. There's a brew or two left in them and our mam's glad of them.' She turned and hissed fiercely at the wide-eyed munchers. 'Now hurry yourselves and get off home.'

'No. Please,' I said. I perched myself on the edge of a stool, watching in fascination as the last pieces of bread were hurriedly chewed and swallowed. 'Don't send them away on my account. These are your sisters, are they?'

Mary nodded, uneasy at my presence in the kitchen. 'Yes, miss. The littlest one, she's Lizzie and just on four. Then there's Cissie and Nellie and Florrie; she's eleven and looks after them while Mam's at the Dora.'

'The Dora?'

'The mill down the street.'

'And your father?'

'Dead, miss.' Her plain face sagged for a moment. 'Died two year ago along with the new baby. It was the cholera took 'em. We was in a nice house then. Me dad was a mechanic and working regular. But after he died we couldn't pay the rent so we had to move. It was right bad for a bit because all we could afford was a cellar that was damp all the time. Anyway, Mam was lucky and got took on at the Dora, even though they call it a bad mill and say it isn't safe to work in. But there's to be a new master there who's going to have it all put in order. Then I got this place here and Mr Webster's that kind and generous.' Her bright smile flashed out. 'Mam and me sisters have a nice room now and our Florrie earns some coppers running errands for a woman as keeps a stall in the market. So we're doing all right.'

I looked at the four little girls in their patched dresses covered by spotlessly clean pinafores, and it was like a blurred picture suddenly coming into focus. One minute I felt cushioned, dulled by the woolly grey feeling in my head, the next everything was sharp-edged and colourful and brilliant. Even the pain was back and that was sharp-edged, too. Gingerly I tested it. I thought of Maxwell, remembered our last awful meeting. The sense of loss was as keen as ever, but bearable. In some odd way I could look at what had happened objectively. I could accept it and know that it was possible to go on living, go on facing up to whatever pain and sorrow or laughter and joy that lay in the future.

'Are you all right, miss?' Mary's voice was anxious. 'You

look a bit flushed.'

'It's nothing,' I said. 'Only the heat . . . and the funny smell.' It seemed that all my senses had come alive at once. I had been aware of the odd aroma all day, but now I really caught its sick taint in full measure.

'Oh, that!' Mary giggled. 'You get so's you don't notice it. That's the tannery. It's always bad in hot weather when the wind's blowing from there.'

'Then I certainly must get used to it if I'm to stay here.'

'You are staying on here, then? Miss Webster didn't say . . . ' She broke off, biting her lip in embarrassment. 'I'm sorry, miss. It isn't my place to ask.'

'You are perfectly entitled to ask, Mary,' I said calmly. 'And Miss Webster couldn't tell you definitely because she was not at all sure what my plans were. Nor was I, to tell the truth.' I smiled at her: really smiled for the first time since I had arrived at the vicarage, because suddenly I knew just what I wanted to do. 'I hope,' I said, 'I shall be allowed to work with the children in the school. I should like that very much.'

'Eh, miss, some of them are a rough lot. Some of them lads as go have been in prison,' Mary said solemnly. 'Our Florrie would like to learn her letters, but me mam won't let her go to that school, and she can't afford to pay for her at a proper place.'

'Well, we shall have to see what we can do for Florrie,' I said, 'and the others.' I could have hugged the four little girls regarding me so uncertainly from the other side of the scrubbed white table. They had unconsciously brought me back to reality; made me aware that there were things to be done and I could not go on for ever nurturing my grief as though it was a hothouse flower, nor could I go on escaping from the world. 'Now,' I said, 'I think I shall put on my bonnet and go for a little stroll. I have some catching up to do.'

I went for a long walk that afternoon.

I walked through the foetid streets and alleys, where the houses pressed together in narrow sweltering ranks. For the first time since the day I had arrived I really looked at my surroundings. Miss Webster had taken me to one or two places, but I had observed very little in my dumb, numb state.

It was every bit as bad as I feared.

I saw the ancient tannery. I smelled the stench of overflowing privies from the dark holes of back courts. I stood close to the Dora Mill and heard the endless thud and clatter or machinery within its forbidding walls. I smiled grimly to myself as I looked through the sleazy windows of the houses at the lower end of St. Clement's Street and realized why the flower-seller had looked at me strangely when I told her the address. The harlots there were rousing from their slumbers and emerging to flaunt their painted faces and garish finery in open doorways.

Everywhere there were children. They played in the gutters and the entries and the cellar steps. The cleanly-dressed ones with freshly-ironed pinafores from homes where the struggle for respectability had not been entirely abandoned, the filthy, ragged, diseased ones staring at me with hopeless eyes. The spectre of poverty stalked them all.

By the time I returned to the vicarage I was hot and tired and burning with anger.

Miss Webster met me anxiously in the hall. 'Morwenna! I was worried! Mary said you had left without saying where you were going. You really should not go wandering about on your own. Anything can happen . . . '

'I am perfectly all right,' I said, undoing my bonnet ribbons and peeling off my gloves. Something in my tone of voice startled her. 'I just decided to see for myself exactly what sort of parish your brother has to cope with.'

'And now that you have seen?'

'I realize that his work must be hard and unrewarding.

And, like you, I want to help him. I want to help the children.'

'Then . . . you are feeling better.' It was a statement not a question. Relief flooded into her face. We smiled at each other like friends long parted and reunited and she held out her hands to me. 'Come along inside, my dear. Charles is already home. He will be as pleased as I am that you are recovered.'

She was right. He was. We sat in his study and discussed what I should do.

'I have been a burden to you ever since I came,' I said. 'I am sorry about that and grateful that you have been so understanding. Now I should like to repay you in some way.'

'Your recovery is reward enough,' Charles Webster said gently. 'I should not like you to rush into work for which you may be totally unsuited, out of a sense of mistaken gratitude. You have been gently raised, Morwenna. Perhaps it would be better if you found employment with some good family who would offer you a home in a better neighbourhood.'

'No,' I said firmly, 'that is not at all what I wish to do. You forget that I was brought up in a cottage as poor as many I have seen today. The only advantage I had was that it was in the country and not in some stinking alley. At least the air was clean and sweet and I had fields and commons to run wild in. But poor and ignorant I should have remained had not Mr Thurlow rescued me. Now I, in my turn, should like to help the unfortunate souls I have seen today in the streets.' I willed him to believe in what I said. 'I am no weakling, I am strong and will work hard and will not shirk unpleasant tasks. But please let me stay and help to teach these little ones.'

He did not speak for a moment, then he raised his eyes from contemplation of the blotter on his desk. His hazel eyes were tired. There was a puffiness under them and a hollowness in his cheeks that spoke of someone who did not sleep well and who worked and worried too much. He ran his hand through his thin brown hair, stifled a sigh, then said with resignation, 'I see you have quite made up your mind. Very well. I shall not dissuade you further. And it may be that your offer comes at a convenient time.'

'You have heard, then, Charles?' Miss Webster broke in.

He nodded, then explained. 'I wrote to an acquaintance who has interested himself in relieving some of the sufferings of the poor in London. He is a man of some means and I told him of our difficulties here. The result is he has sent a generous donation. There is enough to pay a modest salary to a full-time teacher for a year, as well as to buy equipment for our school.'

'It is like providence,' Miss Webster said quietly. 'For you see, Morwenna, the French classes I have been giving have proved so popular that my employer has encouraged two of her friends to take up the language. It would be impossible for me to take on these extra duties as well as teaching all day in the school.'

'So I shall offer you the post instead,' Charles said. 'Let us say for a month's trial period. Will that suit you?'

'Very well,' I said. 'I'll start tomorrow.'

I began my teaching career with enthusiasm and optimism. I needed every ounce of both.

Many of the children, especially the boys, were rough and wild, their language was that of the gutter. Some were like half-starved wolves, who came to the school only in order to qualify for the cup of milk and the piece of bread every child was given in the lunch break. There were those who were swarming with fleas and lice, those who came on legs bowed with rickets. Some of them had parents locked away in prison, some had parents who worked in the mills or the tannery, some had no parents at all.

After a few bewildered days I began to find my feet. Charles Webster helped me greatly and Miss Webster too, when she was not at her own work, but there were many occasions when I was left on my own. But I coped: and I learned as the children learned.

I picked one or two of the older girls who could read and write with some skill, and set them to drilling the tiniest ones in the alphabet and simple numbers. The rest I taught myself, separating them into groups of ability, and going round each in turn. It was an arbitrary method but it seemed to work. My only problem was with the big boys, the ten-and eleven-year-olds, who did not want to learn but saw the schoolroom as a kind of shelter when the weather was wet or when the odd jobs they had were not available. Charles Webster solved that problem for me by getting them to help in the redecoration of the dingy room. When they had finished the job, the boys were so proud of their work and I praised them so lavishly that they began to take a pride in our little school. I had no more cheek or gutter talk after that.

I had other pupils, too. Each evening when I returned from the school I went into the kitchen and there at the kitchen table I initiated Mary's four sisters into the intricacies of reading and writing.

'Eh, it's that kind of you,' Mary said. 'Our mam's ever so grateful.'

'It's a pleasure,' I said, and I meant it. They were sweet little girls, especially Florrie, who had the sturdy independence of one accustomed to responsibility from the cradle. She mothered the three younger ones. She cleaned their little home, she did the meagre shopping, she cooked for the whole family. She was as bright as a button, and the more I saw of her the more I wished that there was more I could do for her and her sisters.

I could teach them, I could help them to make marks that made sense on pieces of paper, but when I had finished my tasks, what lay ahead of them? Drudgery in some factory or mill, or in the kitchens of some house where they would not be so lucky with a generous employer as Mary was.

I worked very hard and I had no time for brooding thoughts when I went to bed, for I fell instantly to sleep, exhausted by the long day. My routine was set. For five days I taught at the school. On Saturdays I helped Mary to bake for the weekend, then I generally took Oliver and Andrew under my wing and read to them or took them on a little outing. On Sundays I went to the church services, where I heard Charles Webster give his gentle, scholarly sermons that I fear were far above the heads of most of his flock. Even so, his church was always full.

It was a useful, orderly life. I liked my work in the school. I was content in the vicarage; I had a measure of independence now that I was earning and I was glad that I could pay for my board and lodging. Money was always short in that household as so much of it went to helping people in need. I never knew anyone who was desperate turned away empty-handed by Charles Webster, and the more I got to know him the more I respected him. It was sad that his wife had died. He needed someone to look to his needs, for he was a man who forgot to eat unless he was reminded, and would have gone round with his clothes in an unpressed, disorderly state. It was as well that Miss Webster had come to live with him when she did, or he would have grown more and more neglectful of himself.

So the summer days slipped away into autumn, days marked by the sounding of the hooter from the Dora Mill and the clattering of clogs on cobbles as the workers hurried back and forth from its shuddering walls; by the noisome smells from the tannery when the days were hot, and by the outbreaks of dysentery and measles and whooping cough that swept through the slums like plagues of old. It was then that Charles Webster was at his busiest; visiting the sick and the dying, burying the wasted bodies in the simple graves, comforting stricken families. It was then that he looked so worn, his eyes puffy from sleeplessness and his slight frame stooping in his rusty frock coat.

'He drives himself too hard,' Miss Webster worried. 'He takes everyone's burdens upon himself. It is more than flesh and blood can stand.'

'There is no way to stop him,' I said simply. 'He is a dedicated man. Physical weariness is nothing to him because his mind and spirit are strong.'

And when Andrew and Oliver demanded to know why Papa never came to bid them good night or read to them, as he usually did for half an hour after dinner in the evenings, we had to explain that Papa had gone to visit a poor sick person. They would go off to bed meekly enough, but Oliver sometimes cried and Andrew sometimes grew argumentative and I thought that to be so dedicated was hard on one's family.

The days shortened. The leaves on the few stunted bushes in the strip of back garden fell to the soot-black earth and the autumn winds began to whistle in the gables of the vicarage. The epidemics faded away with the colder weather, and Charles had more time to spare. He came to the schoolroom more often and I was pleased when he took over the instruction of the boys for an hour or two. He fell into the habit of walking back with me to the vicarage during the dinner hour.

It was during one of these brief journeys that he asked me to marry him.

It was cold that day, with a fierce wind gusting across the churchyard. I was holding my cloak tightly about me, concentrating on keeping my balance in the gale. When he spoke, I thought I had misheard him for the noise the wind was making. But he repeated it. He said: 'Morwenna, would you consider becoming the wife of a poor parson? Would you marry me?'

My grip loosened my cloak so that it billowed out behind me, almost sweeping me off my feet. He caught at my arm.

'Forgive me. I have shocked you. Let us talk of this inside,' and he hurried me into the quiet vicarage. The boys were at school, Miss Webster out giving her French lessons. For a wild moment I wanted to run from the quietness, but I was quickly ushered into the study, where we stood and faced each other.

There was colour in his face from the wind and a brightness in his eyes I had not seen before, and as I looked at him I tried to think if in any way I had brought this upon myself. I could not think of anything. We had treated each other politely, like the friends we had become. I consulted him over matters pertaining to the school, we discussed books we had read; it had all been most casual. Now this! He was right – I was shocked.

'This is no sudden impulse,' he said. 'I have considered it very carefully and I would never have spoken had I not been sure in my mind that you would at least give some thought to my proposal.'

'I . . . I do not know what to say.'

'Then say nothing.' He smiled shyly. 'I have no wish to rush you. Marriage is a solemn affair and not to be taken lightly.'

'I am flattered, naturally,' I said, recovering my speech. 'But I had no idea – no inkling . . . '

He sighed. 'I have been too impulsive. I should not have sprung it upon you like I did. I should have waited for a more suitable occasion.' Again the shy, boyish smile that made him seem younger. 'You see, Morwenna, I have come to regard you with the greatest admiration. You have tackled an unsavoury job with such spirit. I see how the children in the school are devoted to you . . . as I am.' He paused, then rushed on as though his courage might desert him before he had finished: 'There is a difference in our ages, but that is not an insurmountable barrier. I am twenty years your senior and not, I fear, a man of a romantical disposition. But I would care for you, Morwenna, and I have no doubt that Andrew and Oliver, who are already fond of you, would be delighted to have you as their new mamma.'

I could find no words. I could not look at him. I turned my back and went to the window, staring out unseeingly. I did not want to hurt him; I could not do that to someone who had been so very kind. But how could I refuse him without hurting him? And how, then, should I go on living in this house?

'Morwenna,' he said tentatively, after the silence had lengthened into minutes. 'Morwenna, please do not give me your answer straight away. Give yourself time. A week – a month . . . '

I could have given him the answer there and then. I did not love him. I had never once thought of him as a man I might one day marry. He was a person whose friendship I valued and for whom I had the greatest respect.

But he was not Maxwell.

The longing for him, then, was so intense that my bones seemed to melt to water. I clutched at a chair back for support, remembering as clearly as though it was etched before my eyes that day when we had lain in the wet grass and our kisses had been as wild as the storm about our ears. It was as though the months between had never existed, as though this ordered life I had carved for myself had vanished.

I forced myself to calmness. I said, 'I am honoured that you have thought of me as suitable to be your wife . . . '

'Oh, my dear, you make it sound so cold. I am very . . . fond of you.'

'I realize that,' I said, still keeping my gaze fixed out of the window. 'But it is all too sudden. I cannot think that I should make a good wife for a vicar . . . '

'Perhaps I am a better judge of that,' he said gently. 'But I shall not press you now. I shall ask you again in a little while – say a month from now?'

I said breathlessly, 'Yes, yes! I shall give you my answer then . . . ' And I made my escape from the study, hoping that he would take my anxious flight as pure nervousness on the part of a young girl receiving her first proposal of marriage.

That night, for the first time in a long while, I lay awake through the slow hours. And when I did sleep it was to troubled images and restlessness. It seemed that my newfound peace of mind had once more fled.

Now that I knew how Charles felt towards me I became aware of much that I had overlooked previously. How blind I must have been not to have seen the affectionate glances, the deference to my opinions, the small considerations he showed me. Had it been Maxwell I would have been made ecstatically happy by these attentions. Because it was Charles Webster I only felt embarrassed.

I was glad of an excuse to leave the house, though I could have wished it to be for more pleasant reasons.

Mary had whispered to me one morning after breakfast, 'Me sisters won't be able to come for their lessons tonight. Our Florrie's took bad.'

'Have you had the doctor? Is it serious?'

She shook her head. 'Not yet. It was only a cold and cough, but she's gone proper chesty and feverish, so she's to stay indoors until she's better.'

As soon as I'd finished school I went round to the 'nice room' Mary had so glowingly described. It was on the second floor of a seedy old house. As I went up the crumbling stairs, bearing my basket of mixtures from the druggist and tasty items from the larder, I felt rather than saw eyes peeping at me from other doors. I could hear a child crying somewhere and a voice raised in argument. The whole place smelled of rotting wood and stale food, and small scampering things scuttled into the dark corners as I moved.

But the room was clean. The sparse furniture was well scrubbed and Florrie lay on the one large bed on clean sheets that she had wriggled into a sordid tangle. The other children were playing some game on the rag rug before a stick fire and shrieked with joy at my surprising appearance.

I soon had Florrie's bed straight and a hot drink made for her. She was wheezing and coughing, and her little flushed face looked small and pathetic. I sat with her until Mrs Clegg returned from the mill. She was a small, faded woman, scarcely taller than her daughters. She was perhaps thirty-five, but looked fifty. She plucked at the skirts of her dress with her roughened hands as she talked to me. 'Eh, miss, it's right good of you to come and see our Florrie. I slipped home in me dinner break, and it fair mithered me to have to leave her like this. But I think she's a bit better tonight, not quite as hot as she was this morning.'

Florrie did begin to mend but she was listless and wan. I went to see her each day after school and watched her slowly revive. I should have liked then to have taken her far away from these sordid back streets; taken her into the good country air, let her run wild for a week or two until the colour came back to her cheeks and the sparkle to her eyes. But that was not possible. Now that she was almost recovered, Florrie must turn to and keep house once more and bear all the responsibility of her three sisters.

There was no excuse now to slip away from the vicarage. I walked back that last evening from the Cleggs' place and wondered how else I could avoid seeing so much of Charles Webster. The evenings were dark and I could not take myself off for a walk without some purpose in view. Indeed, I thought, as I went quickly through streets puddled patchily with lamplight, past houses bolted against the night and picked my way over the pitfalls of broken flagstones, I should not want to. The streets were no place to be alone after dark.

The slivers of light arrowing between the shutters of the vicarage windows were welcoming. I let myself in and closed the door. There were voices coming from the front parlour. Charles Webster must have a visitor in there; Miss Webster was there, too. I could hear her laughing. It must be a friend, for Charles usually interviewed everyone else in his study.

I made to creep quietly past the door. I did not wish to intrude, but it flung open as I went up the hall and Miss Webster looked out. I had only time to notice the unusual colour in her cheeks and a certain liveliness in her manner, instead of her normal careful calm, before she cried: 'I thought I heard someone come in. Morwenna, take off your cloak and bonnet and join us in the parlour. We have an unexpected visitor.'

I did as I was bid, feeling an odd sense of reluctance. As well I might. The man who rose from the chair to greet me was Mr Thurlow.

I might have expected reproaches or stern looks, but Mr Thurlow merely held out his hands. 'Morwenna, I am delighted to find you safe and well,' he said simply.

I took his hands. It was difficult to find words to say how I felt. Remorse took hold of me. How unkind I had been to run off and leave him with only a curt note! I should have had the common decency to have let him know that I was settled with friends, even if I had not explained where I was staying.

Something of how I felt must have shown on my face because he shook his head and drew me down on to the stiffly padded sofa.

'Miss Webster has told me how deeply upset you were when you came here,' he said. 'How sorry I am that you felt forced to leave as you did. But believe me, my dear, I should not have let you be pushed into taking a situation against your wishes. If only you had come to me!'

'I – I did not stop to think. And I did not wish to cause any . . . ill feeling.' I could scarcely meet his eyes.

'You have been sadly missed, Morwenna,' he went on gently. 'Jessica fretted for you, and as for me, well, my library is gradually slipping back into its old state of disorderliness.' He smiled. 'Should you ever wish to return and complete your cataloguing I should be honoured.'

'But then she would be sadly missed by her pupils at our little school,' Charles said, glancing at me with pride. 'As I have told you, Morwenna has proved herself to be an efficient and dedicated teacher.'

'If I am,' I said quickly, 'it is because I myself was taught so well.' Then, to change the subject, I said: 'And how is Jessica? And Mrs Thurlow?' I dared not mention the one name I longed to speak.

'My wife is in good health,' he said. 'As for Jessica, she grows prettier by the hour. I think a certain Mr Salter from Liverpool has much to do with it.'

'Indeed?' Miss Webster said with some interest. 'Then am I to take it that there is another wedding in the offing?'

Another wedding! The words were like daggers penetrating me to the heart.

'Ah, not yet awhile,' Mr Thurlow said. 'At least, I hope not. The house is quiet enough, now Maxwell and Isabel and Mr Pritchard have left.'

'She . . . Isabel . . . is recovered?' I was surprised how calm my voice was, when I could feel the blood pounding thick and slow in my veins.

His eyes clouded, though he smiled. 'Very much better,' he said. 'In view of her health the wedding was a quiet one, and Maxwell took her to Malvern and then on to Bath where they are at present. The waters do seem to have had a most beneficial effect. Maxwell writes that she is quite her old self again and we will see a great change when he returns with her to Ashridge Hall next week . . . Mr Pritchard is in

Cornwall at present and I shall have to let him know that I have been in touch with you. I had a most interesting letter from him recently.'

He was looking at me as though expecting me to be curious. I tried to form a suitable expression of interest on my face and, seemingly satisfied, he went on: 'Apparently his sister knows of a certain Mr Pendine, though her knowledge of him is somewhat hazy as he is an elderly gentleman with a reputation, I am afraid to say, of being a somewhat eccentric recluse. Naturally, Mr Pritchard did not wish to proceed any further with his enquiries unless you could be contacted. But now I shall be able to write and tell him where you are.'

He sounded so pleased that I held back the harsh words I wanted to say. What did I care about a hateful old man who had cut himself away from human society, just as he had cut himself off from his own flesh and blood? Besides, what did it matter when my heart was like a leaden stone inside my chest and the world had gone grey and bleak? I said quietly, 'Pray tell Mr Pritchard not to trouble on my account.'

'I do not think it is any trouble to him,' Mr Thurlow assured me. 'He took quite a liking to you, you know, and he really enjoys investigating the little mystery. And,' he added confidentially, 'I think it keeps his mind occupied now that he no longer has Isabel to look after. Gives him an interest, so to speak.' He did not add that it kept him from brooding on his daughter's terrible illness, but I realized that was what he really meant.

'Ashridge Hall must be very quiet,' Miss Webster said, a trifle wistfully, 'with Maxwell and his bride gone.'

'Indeed, yes,' Mr Thurlow said. 'I am glad to have my business interests to keep me occupied.'

'Are your negotiations with Mr Chorlton over the purchase of the Dora complete?' Charles asked.

Mr Thurlow made a wry face. 'He is a stubborn old gentleman,' he said. 'He fights for every last penny. I have already increased my original offer twice and he will not get a better, but still he hesitates.'

'And in the meantime,' Charles said drily, 'my parishioners continue to work in an unsafe and dangerous building. It will be a blessing when you persuade Mr Chorlton to sell out.'

'When that happens,' Mr Thurlow said, 'the first thing I shall do is to get surveyors in and have the building thoroughly examined. Though old Chorlton assures me that his own surveyors have declared the building quite safe, and I have seen the documents to prove it.'

Charles shook his head doubtfully. 'I hope he is right. But the vibration in there with all the looms going is astounding.'

'Well, it has stood many years,' Mr Thurlow said reassuringly, 'it would no doubt stand a good many more. But I shall make quite certain all is well when I take the mill over.' He pulled out his pocket watch. 'Dear me, look at the time. I have an appointment at my club in under an hour.'

He rose to his feet, shaking us one by one by the hand.

'I am glad I came,' he said, as he took his hat and silver-topped cane from Mary. 'I was somewhat reluctant to do so . . . in the circumstances . . . ' He broke off and cleared his throat in some embarrassment, his eyes resting on Miss Webster. 'However, I see no reason why past unpleasantness should come between friends.' He smiled at me. 'And of course if I had not had the impulse to come, I should not have discovered where Morwenna had so hidden herself. So I am doubly thankful I came. I should be honoured if you would allow me to call upon you again.'

'We should be delighted,' Charles said warmly. 'Come to supper next time.'

He did so a fortnight later. And this time Charles was able to give news of a wedding, for the morning following Mr Thurlow's initial visit I went soberly into Charles's study and told him I would marry him.

CHAPTER NINE

My wedding day was a day snatched from another season. Instead of the grey, low skies of early December I awoke to sunshine and a faint, still mist that hazed the distant chimneys to a blur of amethyst.

'On such a morning even the view from here has a certain beauty,' Miss Webster said, as she handed me my breakfast tray. 'It looks settled enough. A lovely day for a lovely bride.' She bent and kissed my cheek warmly. 'Now do not hurry to get up. Take your time over your breakfast and I shall come up to help you dress in a little while.'

'You are spoiling me,' I protested.

'Nonsense! When cannot a girl be spoiled unless on her wedding day.'

I looked at the crisp toast, the egg under its cover, the matching china cup and teapot with the pattern of roses, the tiny silver butter-dish. 'How prettily you have arranged it all,' I said. I knew I could not eat a morsel.

After she had gone, declaring that there were a hundred and one things to attend to, I poured the tea and sipped at its scalding sweetness, my eyes fixed on the square of opalescent blue sky between the curtains. They said it was lucky for the sun to shine on one's wedding day. Perhaps it was an omen to signify that my decision had been the right one; that by choosing to marry Charles Webster I had been sensible and prudent. After all, as I had told myself over and over again, I was gaining some security for myself, something I had never really had, for in all my years at Ashridge Hall Mrs Thurlow had never allowed me to forget that I was penniless, that I was there merely because of Mr Thurlow's charitable impulse. Now, today, I should become the wife of a minister of the church. A humble church in a more than humble district, it was true, but nevertheless I should have a status and dignity as Mrs Charles Webster that had never been mine as Morwenna Tregarth.

I put down the tray and slid down under the covers, pulling the sheets up to my ears. I felt a tremor in my stomach; not the nervous, excited flutter of a bride-to-be but a sick sense of loss and hopelessness: loss because Maxwell was gone from me forever, hopelessness because I did not love Charles and the fear had grown in me in the past few weeks that I should never make Charles a good wife.

I had been honest with him that morning in the study.

'I have a great respect for you,' I had said quietly, 'but I do not love you. However, I will do my best to care for you and I feel deeply about the work you are doing. If you are willing to take me on those terms, then I will marry you.'

'But, Morwenna,' Charles said, interrupting my halting sentences, 'I quite realize that I am no young handsome suitor to sweep a girl from her feet. Indeed,' he said, taking my hand, 'I think there is too much nonsense talked amongst young ladies.' His eyes twinkled. 'Too much reading of novels in which the handsome hero sweeps the swooning heroine off to his castle and a life of eternal romance. True life is not like that. True life is full of troubles and sadnesses and difficulties, and if two people can gain strength from the affection of each other then happiness can be found. Of a gentler and less dramatic kind than the heroine of fiction, but I am sure I can make you happy, Morwenna: otherwise I should never have dared to ask you to be my wife.'

He raised my hand and kissed it. Unexpectedly I had felt a pang of tenderness. He was so unworldly, so good . . . and he would be kind. I felt then that we might achieve some quiet degree of happiness, but that assurance had gradually faded. Doubts had crept in, probing my thoughts with slimy fingers. I was tying myself for life to a man I did not love. Perhaps in the long run it would be a union we should both regret.

The house was full of homely, bustling sounds – the light, quick sound of Mary's feet on the stairs, Oliver and Andrew laughing and chattering in their room next door, the faint clattering of crockery. I felt apart from them: cut off and remote. Frightened of what lay ahead. I gripped the sheets. Frightened of seeing Maxwell again.

That possibility had racked me for days.

The wedding was to be very quiet. Only a few close members of Charles's family were to be present, though one or two friends had been invited to luncheon afterwards. Mr Thurlow had promised to look in for a few moments. He was exceedingly busy, having recently completed his purchase of the Dora Mill. He and Maxwell were at the mill constantly and, though Maxwell had never accompanied him, Mr Thurlow had dropped in at the vicarage once or twice, looking tired.

'There is much work to be done there,' he admitted. 'I am so glad to have Maxwell's assistance. He has a fine head for business and has done a great deal to help me.'

'I should very much like to meet him,' Charles had said in his usual friendly way. I had felt my heart quicken its beating as he spoke and had to keep my face bent over my needlework. 'Do bring him to see us.'

'I tried to persuade him tonight,' Mr Thurlow said, 'but he has his nose buried in the account books and I fear he will be poring over them until the small hours.'

No, I thought frantically, he would not want to visit me here any more than I wanted him to come.

'Then you must tell him he is invited to take a glass of wine with us on our wedding day,' Charles said. 'Morwenna and I would be so pleased if you would both join us at luncheon.' He threw a proud glance in my direction.

'Why, yes,' I said faintly, seeing that I was expected to speak. 'That would be . . . delightful.'

'I am sure that will be an invitation he cannot refuse,' Mr Thurlow said. 'However, I fear we shall not be able to stay for long as that is the day we have arranged to have a full survey of the mill. We both wish to go over every stick and stone of the place, together with the engineers and surveyors. But we shall be sure to join you before you leave. For Alderley Edge, did you say?'

'My uncle, who is at present away in London, has offered us the use of his country residence,' Charles said. 'But we shall be able to spare only a few days away from the parish . . . '

I had not heard any more of the conversation. I was awash with horror. It was a bitter twist of fate, indeed, that would bring the man I loved so helplessly to my wedding to a man I loved not at all. I should never be able to bear it.

But bear it I must.

I climbed from the bed and went to the window. I lifted it and slipped the crumbled toast on to the scullery roof below, where a flock of sooty sparrows immediately began to quarrel over it.

It was too late to go back now. I had made my decision and must face up to it: face up to a future that would be useful and hard-working – and emotionally barren.

'Oh, you did not eat your egg,' Miss Webster scolded when she came to help me dress. I called her Ellen now, but somehow I still thought of her as Miss Webster. It seemed strange that this woman, who had always been my mentor and guide, was now to become my sister-in-law. Sad, too, that we were both fated to fall in love with the wrong man. 'Still, I suppose we must expect a little nervousness today and doubtless you will eat well at luncheon with the ceremony over.' She drew my dress from its white cotton wrapper. 'The old lace that was your mother's has come up very well,' she said approvingly. 'It was quite an inspiration of yours to get it out.'

I had wanted something of my mother's to wear. Miss Webster had suggested the red beads. 'They looked so pretty at Jessica's ball.'

'But too gaudy, I think,' I had said quickly. 'They are not suitable for a wedding.' I wanted no reminders of that fatal night. 'But this old lace might be cleaned satisfactorily.'

So we had stitched it to the collar of the plain blue dress I would wear to the altar, and now I slipped it on and Miss Webster fastened the row of tiny buttons at the back.

'You look charming,' she said. 'Charles will be so proud.'

'Is he returned yet?' I asked, going to the mirror.

'I heard him come in as I came upstairs,' she answered. She shook her head, smiling. 'He had hoped to have no calls this morning, but he was sent for by an old lady who wanted comfort in her last hours. He could not begrudge her that.'

'Of course not,' I said. I looked at my reflection, at the dark-haired girl in the rather prim blue dress with its collar of old lace. My face was white, my eyes seemed to have lost the sparkle they once had. I looked very different from the glowing girl who had swung from partner to partner in her scarlet dress and seen admiration flare in the eyes of men. But I should never again dance like that, or feel like that. My path was set. It was well that I looked the part I was called upon to play – a sober, solemn girl who would become a docile, earnest wife.

'Are you pleased with the dress?' Miss Webster asked.

'It looks very well,' I said. 'Now, if you will hand me my bonnet I will put it on. It is a little early, but I should like to see the full effect . . . '

I broke off, because in that moment two odd things happened. I took the bonnet Miss Webster held out to me and turned back to the mirror to put it on. I found myself staring into another face in the glass.

I knew – at least the logical part of my mind knew – that I was gazing at my own reflection. Yet it was not me. In some weird way the girl in the blue dress with the lace collar was transformed – overlaid – become someone else. My face and yet not my face; the features smaller, the eyes a steady grey, the mouth fuller, more wilful. A face out of a dream: the girl who had come to me that day Maxwell had ridden into my life on his horse. I had laid on Mrs Pike's sofa and dreamed of her and thought that she was standing by me and trying to speak. And in the same, haunted way, I knew without question that she was trying to speak to me now.

I stood there unable to move, the bonnet motionless in my fingers. Then . . . Snap! In the space of half a breath the hallucination – the vision – whatever, whoever she was, had gone and I saw again my white, startled face, just as Miss Webster flung out her hand and clutched my arm.

I turned to her, expecting her to say that she, too, had seen what I had seen. But she was not looking at me, she was looking at the china bowl and jug on the marble-topped washstand. I followed her glance. The bowl and jug were dancing, trembling on the cold surface with a faint, hollow chattering sound.

Then the thunder came; a great rumbling, reverberating peal that went on for a long time. I felt the boards quiver under my feet as though the whole house was shaking. Somewhere a door banged shut and I heard a voice cry out.

Into the silence that followed, Miss Webster whispered, 'Whatever was that?' She was still clinging to my arm, and I put my hand on hers, glad to feel the warmth of another living being, somebody who was real flesh and blood and not being conjured up by my overstrung nerves. For that, surely, was what that strange vision had been.

'A thunderbolt?' I said. 'But the sky is quiet clear; there

are no clouds any where.'

The unnatural silence seemed to enfold us, then we heard the children crying out and the noise broke our frozen attitude. Miss Webster flew to the door, where a frightened Oliver flung himself into her arms. I went to the window. Nothing had changed, the roof-tops and chimney pots still dreamed in the sunshine. The sparrows that had wheeled away at the noise were fluttering down again on to the guttering of the scullery.

It was then we heard Mary scream. She screamed in her thin, high child's voice, on and on, a single piercing note.

'Whatever is the matter with the girl!' I cried, seeing Andrew turn pale and Oliver, whose tears had dried, starting to sob again.

I hurried on to the landing and peered over. Down in the hall were two strangers. I learned later that they were Charles's aunt and a cousin whom Mary had just admitted when the bang came. Now they stared in confusion at the little maid who, head back, stood at the front door emitting the dreadful screams.

I ran down the stairs as Charles came out of the study and I realized that Mary's screams were not the only ones. There were other voices in the street: yells, screams of pain or fright, I could not tell. The clattering of clogs as people ran past the door, all going in one direction – to the Dora Mill.

I caught up with Charles at the door. Together we stared down the street. 'Oh, no!' I cried. 'Oh, no!'

Charles's arm went tight round my shoulder.

'God help them,' he murmured. 'God have mercy on the poor souls.'

The end of the street was no longer barred by the walls of the mill. Instead there was a great pall of dust, through which could be seen the jagged teeth of ruined masonry. From the corner where the engine house had stood an ominous tongue of flame licked up towards the sky. A throng of people milled about in the fog of dust: little scampering figures like ants pouring from a disturbed nest.

Charles recovered first. 'I must go,' he said. 'I must go and help.'

'I shall come too . . . '

'No.' He steered me gently back into the hall. 'There will be many injured. We shall need beds, bandages, hot drinks. We can bring some of them here. You and Ellen must look after them – see that everything is ready . . . '

'Take care,' I said. I had never admired him so much as in that moment. He was calm, resolute, but I could see from the anguish in his eyes that, despite his steady manner, he was inwardly preparing himself for the sights he must see.

'I shall take care,' he assured me. He smiled, then bent to kiss my cheek. 'Alas, we shall have to postpone our wedding for a few hours. I am sorry, Morwenna.'

'I am sorry too,' I whispered. 'But for all those poor men and women at the mill . . . '

Maxwell! The knowledge struck me like a fist thudding into my midriff. Maxwell was in there and Mr Thurlow. Today was the day when they were to have surveyed the mill. I swayed a little and, if my face paled, Charles only took it as a natural reaction to the disaster.

'Be calm, my dear,' he said. 'You must be strong for the sake of the injured.'

'Yes,' I said. 'Yes, I will.'

Calm, I thought. Calm! How was it possible when fear pounded through my body with every beat of my heart? I hardly saw Charles go and it was an automatic reaction that made me turn to the now silent Mary and take her in my arms. Her small frame shuddered and she began suddenly to sob, crumpling up against me.

'There, hush now,' I said. 'Come to the kitchen and make tea for us all.'

'I want to go!' she said, pulling back. 'I want to see if our mam's all right.'

'You will know soon enough,' I said. 'We need you here. There is work to do.' I spoke almost sharply. For both our sakes it was best not to be too sympathetic and gentle.

They started to bring the injured to us within half an hour. By that time every sheet and blanket had been looked out of storage and rough beds made up in every space. Mostly, the ones who came to us were dazed and suffering from cuts and bruises. They carried the seriously injured carefully on doors up to the church and laid them in the aisles until they could be conveyed on carts to the infirmary.

Charles returned once. He was covered with thick grey dust, from his hair to his boots. He ran his hand wearily across his forehead, leaving a dirty smear there.

'Is it – is it – very bad?' I whispered.

'The top two floors have collapsed in upon themselves,' he said wearily. 'There are many dead. Many mutilated.'

We were in the front parlour, which we had set up as a bandaging station before passing on our patients to the care of Charles's relatives – the guests who had arrived for a wedding and found themselves running a makeshift hospital. But there had been no demurs. They had all turned to and worked as hard as we had, covering their best clothes in large aprons we had found for them.

Miss Webster, who was gently sponging blood from the arm of a dazed young girl, caught her breath. Then she asked the question I dared not.

'The . . . Thurlows . . . Maxwell and Mr Thurlow . . . is there . . . have they – ?'

Charles shook his head. 'There is no word of them. I heard they were on the second floor when the accident occurred. There are people trapped up there, but the building that remains is in such a parlous state that it could fall again any time. The rescuers are having to work very carefully and slowly towards them.'

'And . . . the fire?' I asked.

'It did not gain a good hold. The fire tenders were most efficient and controlled it before it reached the main building.'

'Then that is something at least to be thankful for.' Miss Webster was white to the lips. I knew I must be the same. I said, 'Mrs Clegg, Mary's mother, what of her?'

'Nothing. I did discover that she works on the topmost floor. I am afraid that there are few survivors from the top storeys. But say nothing to Mary yet. While there is no news there is always hope.'

Hope. I clung on to hope as the crying, stunned, bleeding mill workers passed before me to be comforted and soothed and bandaged. Then, when the vicarage was full to capacity, it seemed that the wave of victims became a trickle.

'They are using other houses in the street,' Miss Webster said. 'Everyone has thrown open their doors, even' – she lowered her voice – 'the unfortunate fallen women at the other end. How a catastrophe such as this brings out the best in people!'

Now that there was less to do, I could not wait any longer to have news secondhand. I put a shawl over my head and pulled it close round my shoulders as the mill-girls did. It hardly protected my dress, my wedding dress, but that was already spotted with blood along the cuffs and much crumpled. But I did not care about it. I wanted to hurry to the mill, concealed under my shawl so that Charles would not recognize me and send me back to the vicarage. I must find out what had happened to Maxwell.

I went down the street. The dust had settled now and the ruined walls of the mill poked up into the serene blue sky. As I drew nearer I had to fight my way through crowds of people. Huddles of men and women with drawn faces waiting for news of loved ones; children darting about, loving the excitement and hardly realizing the tragedy; sightseers come to 'ooh' and 'aah' as each fresh victim was borne out on planks.

As I pushed through the press, two burly constables blocked my way. 'You mustn't go near, missus,' one of them said, 'it's dangerous. T'owd mill's likely to fall again any minute.'

I looked round him into the mill yard where men crawled about the blocks of tumbled masonry, then I looked up to the gaping front wall. What was left of the upper storeys was hung about with great machines, all tossed at crazy angles and hanging from the lips of torn floors like black, broken teeth. I imagined the weight of all the machinery dropping on to the floors below. Nobody who was directly underneath could have survived. There must be many bodies lying under the wreckage: it might be days before they were dug out. Maxwell might be there: his black curly hair matted with blood, his black eyes empty and staring, his bones crushed and the arms that had held me close shattered. Oh, God, how could I bear the pain!

The constable said sharply, 'If you feel faint, missus, get along out of here. I'm sorry if there's someone you know in there, but we've enough to do without dealing with swooning females.'

'No,' I said quietly. 'No. I shall not faint.' I groped around for some excuse to get past him. 'I – I have a message for the vicar, Mr Webster. Can you direct me to where he is?'

'T'vicar? Now I did see a reverend gentleman down by the side door.' He lowered his voice. 'Where they've laid those beyond help, missus.'

'Then I must see him. It is urgent.'

With some reluctance and with admonitions to make haste and get away from the building as soon as my message was delivered, he let me through. But I did not go to the side of the mill where the dead were laid, I went among the rescuers, the men and boys who were moving timbers and chunks of masonry, frantic in their efforts to seek out the living before the machinery slipped again. I asked over and over if anyone had seen the new master, Mr Thurlow, or his son before the disaster. They had been seen earlier in the day on the lower floors with the engineers, but no one seemed to know where they had been in those last minutes. As I stumbled over the pitted ground and climbed the ruined walls I began to feel hope slipping from me. No one living had seen them. The only people who knew where they were buried under the ruins.

Despairing as I was, it came as a shock when I suddenly found myself confronting Mr Thurlow. He was sitting on a block of stone, surrounded by a group of men. His face was grey and a trickle of blood had dried on one cheek. His eyes as his glance took me in, were dull and blank

'Mr Thurlow!' I cried, going up to him. 'You are here and alive. This is a miracle.'

He stared at me dully. 'Morwenna? Is that you?' He rubbed his hand across his face with the gesture of a tired child. 'I fear I am acting stupidly. My mind is unclear . . . '

'Never mind, sir,' one of the rough working men said. Then to me: 'We have only just got him out. He was trapped on the back staircase. He cannot seem to take in what's happened.'

Through tight lips I asked, 'And what of his son? Mr Maxwell Thurlow?'

The man shook his head. 'The staircase is half torn down. Above where t'master was we dared not go or we'd all have been killed else. If the young master's up there, there's no way of reaching him.'

'Are there no ladders? No ropes?' I heard my voice rise hysterically. 'There must be some way of getting to him.'

'If there is, then we shall find it,' the man said. 'But it could be he's up in the angle of the stairs where there are no windows to put a ladder or a rope. There was some as was trapped on the other side of t'mill.' He shrugged expressively. 'The stairs collapsed under them before we even knew they were there.'

It was hopeless, as I had known. Perhaps that was what the girl in the mirror had tried to tell me, as she tried to warn me that day when Maxwell rode into my life. I shivered and huddled into my shawl, aware as though for the first time of the noise around me. The groans and creaks of straining timbers, the calls and gasps of the men as they struggled with crowbars to move weights of metal and stone, the murmurings of the crowd.

I stood there beside Mr Thurlow, keeping my hand upon his shoulder; whether it was to reassure him or myself I did not know. Together we watched the rescue work; together we must have prayed that the building would not crumble further and that soon Maxwell would be found.

'Morwenna, what are you doing here?' Charles was by my side and I had not heard or seen him approach.

'I had to come. I could not stay in the house, not knowing . . . '

Charles looked at my face and whatever severe words he was about to say died on his lips. He cleared his throat, then said gently, 'You have found Mr Thurlow, then.'

'He has injured his head, but he will not go and seek aid from a doctor. He is waiting to see if . . . if Maxwell is found.'

'Quite so.' Charles murmured. 'That is understandable. But you, my dear, you should not be here.'

'I must stay,' I said flatly. 'I must stay until I know.'

There was a small pause, then Charles said quietly, 'About Maxwell Thurlow?'

'Yes. About Maxwell.'

We stared at each other and I knew he read in my face all there was of my heart. Pain flared in his eyes, and he said softly, 'I see.'

'Charles,' I began haltingly, but I got no further. There

was a great cry and men started to run away from the corner of the mill. Mr Thurlow rose to his feet as the men began to urge us backwards. I could not take my eyes from the wall as, with infinite slowness, it began to sag. It bulged in the centre, cracked open, and the stone began to tumble down like the toy bricks a baby knocks over with his fist. With a diminishing rumble the stone crashed to the ground, thankfully injuring no one.

The dust cleared and when it did we saw that the staircase, zig-zagging from floor to floor of the mill, was peeled bare. Parts of it were missing, parts hung askew. It was as though the front of a battered old doll's house had been removed, showing the broken interior with the doll inhabitants still remaining.

'Maxwell!' Mr Thurlow cried. 'That is Maxwell.' He pointed with a shaking hand to where three figures, two women and a man clung precariously to what remained of an iron banister on a narrow ledge.

I heard the crowd behind us gasp, and someone shouted, 'Fetch the ladders.' But ladders were pitifully small, and even as one was leaned against the lower steps, the stair buckled and the man had to leap back for safety.

'A rope would do it,' Mr Thurlow cried. 'Cannot someone get a rope to them?'

'Up those stairs?' a man asked. 'It would be suicidal.'

'There must be some way,' I whispered. 'We cannot just stand here and wait for the building to fall. We must try.' I looked round wildly. 'I will go. Find me the rope and I will try to reach them.'

Strong hands held me and I fought against them. I had to go to Maxwell! I had to try to reach him! I did not care for my life; I would not wish to live it if he were dead.

'No, missus. Nobody can go up there!'

I struggled against the restraining hands but I was no match for two burly men. Tears of frustration poured down my cheeks.

'Let me go. Please let me go!' I sobbed.

'I will try,' said a quiet voice. 'Give the ropes to me.'

'But it's madness, sir. Forgive me, but the steps will crumble away . . . '

'Give me the rope,' Charles said.

Reluctantly the man passed him the heavy coil. Charles put it over his shoulders.

'Charles, it should not be you,' I said. 'I beg you, let me go.'

He looked at me with tenderness and love and pity. 'No, Morwenna,' he said with finality. Then he began to pick his way over the rubble towards the gaping staircase.

'God go with you,' I whispered, pushing my fist against my mouth, and something that was like a prayer borne on a long, drawn-out sigh went up from the crowd.

There was little noise as Charles began the long, slow ascent of the tattered staircase. Foot by foot, inch by inch he moved. Where the steps were fallen away, he miraculously found holds. His reaching hands clung to infinitesimal protrusions in the wall and his feet disturbed little puffs of dust and stone that drifted downwards like smoke trails. Only once did he falter, when, crossing a gap, the brick his foot rested on slithered out of the wall, taking a great gouge of plaster that clattered down to the rubble below. He hung perilously by his hands for a few strangled seconds. My heart thumped like an imprisoned bird in the cage of my ribs as I watched his flailing legs seek out another foothold. Then he found it and slowly the slight, almost frail, figure continued to climb upwards.

It was almost an anti-climax when he reached the last gap, the one that could not be crossed, the one that made Maxwell and the two women prisoners on the little ledge. Carefully, because the step he stood on was narrow and broken away, Charles took the rope from his shoulders and recoiled it ready to throw. I prayed he would not lose his balance, that his aim would be true, but having got so far Charles was taking no risks. He motioned Maxwell to the edge of the ledge, took careful aim, and with incredible strength for one of such a scholarly stature, he hurled the rope upwards.

A cheer went up from the crowd. Maxwell had caught it! Cautiously he fastened it to one of the iron railings, tested it and flung it over. It was about ten feet short of the ground, but there were many willing hands to help the girls as they slithered terror stricken to safety, fear giving them the courage to swing down the rope over the sickening drop. As the second girl came down, the railings above bent out ominously. And still Maxwell was to come! But there was nothing for it but to risk the descent.

Cautiously he let himself over the side and gripped the rope with his feet. The railings groaned and buckled outwards even further as they took the weight. I held my breath as he slid steadily downwards. Only when he dropped to the ground, to the steadying hands of the men below, did I breathe freely again.

Then I ran. Blindly I ran to him, stumbling over timbers and fallen masonry. He came out of the press of men: his coat was torn, his hair and face grey with dust, and he was limping. But he was alive. His eyes, black and brilliant, focused on me. From incomprehension his expression sharpened to disbelief. Then, suddenly, his face was avid with hunger, the same hunger that possessed me.

I flung myself forward and his arms went about me, holding me so tightly I could scarcely breathe.

We neither of us spoke. Words were useless, unnecessary things against the overwhelming knowledge that nothing had changed. We clung together, wanting nothing more than this: this meeting of two bodies of flesh and blood, two hearts and two minds. I felt as though I had been dead these past months and now I was alive, all my senses, my emotions sharp and clear.

Presently he released me, pushing me backwards gently. 'You must get away from here,' he said. 'It is not safe.'

'I do not care. If you stay here, so shall I.'

'There is work to do and I must help,' he said. 'Please go, Morwenna. I do not wish to think of you in any danger.'

Danger! For a few moments I had forgotten where we were. I had felt such relief that we could have been beyond time itself, out in some lonely place where we were two people alone. Now I saw we were still standing amid the ruined walls of the mill, still surrounded by grimy, sweating men.

'And I must thank my rescuer,' Maxwell said. 'He is a brave man indeed to have attempted such a climb. Do you know who he is?'

I looked beyond Maxwell to the zig-zag of the stairway. It was empty. Charles had made his way down and I had not even noticed.

I said faintly, 'Oh, yes, I know him. He is the man I should have married today.'

'Charles Webster?' Maxwell's face was suddenly bleak.

'An irony, is it not?' I said. 'It seems our love is a fated thing; something destined to bring hurt to other people as well as ourselves.'

'He knows?'

I nodded. 'I have tried to forget you, Maxwell, tried to build a secure new life for myself. Today I found that it was impossible to hide my feelings. When you were trapped up there and there seemed no way out . . . ' I broke off and turned my head away, feeling the scalding tears sear my eyes.

'Oh, my dearest love.' He spoke softly. 'Do you know what I was thinking up there on that ledge? My one regret was that I was to die without seeing you again.' He gave a short, harsh laugh. 'They say that one's whole life flashes through a person's mind before death. In my case I could think only of you.'

'Thoughts are all we have, all we can have,' I said bitterly. 'Thoughts and memories . . . '

I heard the noise then. We both did. Maxwell looked up.

'Look out! Run for it!' a voice called.

Maxwell grabbed me by the waist, swung me upwards. His long legs strode forward over the obstacles of piled masonry. Everyone was surging away from the mill as, with a groan, the corner that had held the stairs collapsed.

I buried my face in Maxwell's neck, not wanting to look. I had seen enough damage and disaster for one day. But presently I had to lift my eyes when I heard someone say, with relief, 'I think everyone was clear.'

But he was wrong. One person was caught in what proved to be the last piece of the mill to fall away. The rest of the old building stood firm enough to allow the people trapped within to be rescued.

But it was too late for Charles. A block of stone felled him as he moved to safety. And while he lay there mortally injured I, God forgive me, was held close in another man's arms.

They carried Charles back to the vicarage on part of an old broken door. The harassed doctor came, shook his head and departed. Miss Webster and I sat with him in the square front bedroom. He lay on the big double bed that I would have shared with him on our return to the vicarage as man and wife. I sat there in my torn and stained blue dress. I would never walk to the altar in it now.

Late in the afternoon he opened his eyes and looked at us both. I pressed his hand and he returned the pressure. He half-smiled and in his eyes was the same gentle expression of kindness and understanding. Then his breathing eased and he slipped away from us.

I was beyond tears, beyond all feeling. I left Miss Webster weeping by the bed and went downstairs. The house bore the traces of the day's events. Tumbled blankets lay about, furniture was moved, cups and mugs that had contained refreshment for the sick were abandoned on every surface. But now all the injured had gone, assisted to their own homes by willing helpers. Poor little Mary had gone too, back to her own small home to see to the four little ones who were now motherless. Later she would bring them all here until we could decide what was to be done for them . . . and for the other orphans and widows left in the parish.

A kind neighbour had taken Andrew and Oliver for a few hours and only one person was left in the house. Mr Thurlow. He sat by the window in the dim parlour; we had not been able to persuade him to move any further away. 'I shall remain here,' he insisted, 'and Maxwell will bring me news of how the rescue work is going.'

I went in to him, and thought sadly that he seemed to have aged by twenty years in the day. He looked an old man bent over in the chair.

I said, 'Would you like tea, Mr Thurlow?'

He shook his head. 'No, thank you, Morwenna.'

'A glass of wine then? You should have something.'

'You are kind, but no.'

I went to him and touched his shoulder. 'Charles is dead,' I said softly. 'I do not think he was in any pain towards the end.'

Mr Thurlow buried his face in his hands.

'It is all my fault – all my fault. I should have closed the mill until I had had it properly surveyed. I should not have trusted Chorlton – a man who thought only of money.'

'You could not know and you must not blame yourself.'

'It is not only those who have died. It is the other lives I have ruined; the broken families, the ones who will be crippled. Whatever money I give them, it will never compensate for the damage that has been done.' He raised his head and looked at me with anguish. 'I have spoilt your life,' he said. 'Today you should have been married and now . . . ' The unfinished sentence hung in the air.

I thought, vaguely, what shall I do? I had made up my mind that I was to be a vicar's wife, concerned with good works, living here in this house a steady, devoted life. But now what was left? Another incumbent would be moved to the parish. Doubtless there would be provision for Charles's boys to be educated but there would be nothing for Miss Webster – or me. We should have no home, and the new vicar might have different ideas about the school Charles had so hopefully started . . .

'There is always a home for you at Ashridge Hall,' Mr Thurlow said, as though reading my thoughts.

'Thank you,' I said. I could not hurt his feelings now, but that was one place to which I should never go back.

He sighed. 'I thought I was to be the bearer of good tidings today. A most suitable wedding gift, I had thought. Instead . . . ' He waved his hand vaguely.

'Tidings?' I said.

'From Mr Pritchard. He has been in touch with your grandfather.'

'My grandfather?' I repeated stupidly. It seemed an age ago when we had talked of Mr Pritchard's visit to Cornwall.

'Would you not like to find you have living relatives after all these orphaned years?' Mr Thurlow said, with a feeble attempt at his old jocularity. 'Apparently your grandfather is alive, though sick. He is anxious, it seems, to contact you. You may hear from him any day.'

'My grandfather!' I said bitterly. 'I have no grandfather. When he disowned my mother all those years ago, he disowned me. Perhaps he only wishes to ease his conscience.'

'Do not be too harsh on him if he does write,' Mr Thurlow said. 'Mr Pritchard told me that he was devoted to his daughter, your mother, and it broke his heart when she defied him and ran away. He refused even to have her name mentioned in his house and cut himself off from all society. It was his way of protecting himself from further hurt, I suppose. Tribulation takes us all in different ways.'

We were silent, each thinking of our own private troubles. Eventually I said wearily, 'Perhaps he will not write, but if he does I shall not snub him.'

Mr Thurlow managed a smile. It sat ill on his lined, tired face, but it was the first time I had seen him smile that day. 'I am glad, my dear. You will not regret it.'

It was quite dark when Maxwell returned. His limp was more pronounced and he looked ready to drop with tiredness. I longed to comfort him, to smooth away the weariness from his face. But that could not be. The impassioned moments, when we had cared for nothing but being together and alive, were gone and could not be repeated now.

I watched him as he talked to his father, telling him that everyone who had been in the mill was now accounted for and the number of dead was not as great as had at first been feared. Mr Thurlow nodded: the blank look was back in his eyes as though the details were too much to encompass. I knew then that Mr Thurlow was a broken man; the tragedy had overwhelmed him as much as it had overwhelmed the broken bodies in the infirmary. He would never again gain satisfaction from his businesses. It would be up to Maxwell to take the reins, to take over the smooth running of the house and the family fortunes.

He was strong, and for his sake and for the sake of Isabel and the Thurlows I must be strong, too.

I had felt back there in the ruins of the mill that it would not have taken much persuasion to bring Maxwell to my side. It was such a small step for both of us that would plunge us into the agonies and ecstasies of an illicit love affair. But I could not . . . would not . . . do it.

I spoke once to Maxwell before he left with his father. In the dimness of the hall we said goodbye.

'Shall I not see you again?' There was pleading in his voice.

'It is best not to.'

'But I shall make provision for you. My father would like that, I know. You have been part of the family for so long, we could not see you penniless. And there is no one else.' He paused and then went on quickly: 'Oh God, Morwenna, I cannot leave you again.'

'You must,' I said quietly. 'There are too many people who rely on you, people who are defenceless and weak. And I am not weak, my darling. I am strong; strong because I know that you love me and because I know one day we shall be together.'

'How can you be so sure?'

I shook my head. 'I feel it in my heart, in my bones. You must go now and carry that knowledge close to your heart, as I shall.' I smiled to myself. 'Perhaps my blue lady will tell me when that time is come.'

'Blue lady?' he said, puzzled.

'No matter, my love. A figment of my imagination merely.' I reached up to him and we kissed for the last time. A long, gentle kiss.

Then he went out into the street and I closed the door softly behind him.

CHAPTER TEN

It is very beautiful in Treroc. The house stands snug against the side of a low hill and in front of it the ground dips away into a wooded valley that leads to the sea. For ten years I have glanced through the windows as season followed season and seen the dark green tufts of the summer trees ripen to gold with the advance of autumn, then stand stark like grey-green bones against the dead winter fields. I have watched the house martins build their nests under the eaves, raise their young into strong fledgelings and leave for sunnier climates as the autumn rains sweep in from the west. And with each spring they return as the daffodils bend to the warm breeze that bears the salty scent of the sea.

My grandfather did not live to see me. I had two letters from him and sent two in return before I began to make arrangements for my visit to Cornwall. By then the vicarage was stripped of its furniture and waiting for the new incumbent. Miss Webster had found a position with a charity that was organizing relief for the destitute and Andrew and Oliver were in boarding school.

But I got here too late after all and was in time only to be a mourner at the funeral. In his will he left everything to me; everything that should have been inherited by my mother whose portrait hangs here in the room where I work. I am sorry that we did not meet, my grandfather and I, but still I am not lonely in this big old house.

I have the children. Mary is my right hand and has grown into a good, gentle young woman and I value her more as each day passes. She helps with the young ones and sees to their welfare in a practical way. They never have holes in their stockings or torn pinafores, things which I tend to overlook. Yet I like to think it is to me they turn for love and comfort when they have taken a tumble or been in trouble for some misdeed. I dread the day when she must leave, as leave she must. Already I see her blushing when young Tregaskis from the nearby farm calls. He lingers far longer than necessary over the delivery of eggs and milk. But I will be very happy for her. She deserves happiness, and very soon Mrs Pike will be here to help me.

Dear Mrs Pike. Her husband died recently and I offered her a place here. She will love having the children around her, and now old age is creeping upon her I can offer her a pleasant home in which to end her days. Young Tom, the stable boy from Ashridge Hall, has been with me almost from the beginning. I sent to see if Mr Thurlow could spare him as soon as I was settled, and he travelled to Cornwall with only Skip for company and thought it a grand adventure. He is married now to a local dark-eyed lass who has borne him two sturdy sons.

As for Skip, he lies under the desk as I write. He is ancient and grey-whiskered and stiff in his limbs, but he clings to me like a shadow as I move around the house and gardens and even occasionally tries to scamper like he did over the tussocky grass of Cheshire.

Though three of Mary's sisters are here, Florrie went back to the Manchester slums as soon as she was of an age to want her independence. She now works with Miss Webster and I hear that she devotes herself heart and soul to those who are as poor and defenceless as she once was.

Miss Webster has been to visit me twice, which was a great joy, but she was anxious to be back at her work. She has sent to me over the years a regular flock of city sparrows; orphans who will be with me until they leave to gain employment or to marry; sometimes sick little souls whom I keep until they are fit enough to return to the drudgery of their lives in Manchester factories. It breaks my heart to see them return. Yet I think that the future is looking brighter for these little waifs, as thinking people begin to realize the destitution and misery that lies like a sore in the heart of our industrial cities.

I have never since that last, fatal day seen Maxwell, nor have we communicated in any way. I know it is for the best, though sometimes it is hard to restrain my longing for some direct word.

I have news of him, of course. Jessica writes and tells me the family news when she can spare time from her own family in Liverpool. Isabel remains childless and he spends much time taking her to doctors and spas and on long vacations in Italy. But the disease that wastes her is slow and merciless and ugly. I believe she has lost all her looks and has become as dependent as a baby. I weep for her sometimes and at others I hate her for hanging like a dead weight about Maxwell's neck. But I am glad all the same that Maxwell is kind to her.

Not long after I arrived here a parcel was delivered. There was no note, but the box contained the little ivory figure of the Kuan Yin. She stands now on the edge of my desk smiling her compassionate smile. It is my one link with Maxwell; that and the cream and red shawl which belonged to a Chinese princess. I wear it often: I wear it now close around my shoulders. As for the red beads, it is a strange thing to know that all those years I could have sold them and made myself independent of Mr Thurlow. They are not beads but tiny matched rubies worth several hundred pounds, for my grandfather was a wealthy man and did not stint his daughter.

His daughter. My mother. I look at her portrait, the girl in the old-fashioned blue dress. It is an odd thing but last night

I dreamed of her. I dreamed that she came to me and smiled and I woke this morning feeling strangely lighthearted.

Some impulse has made me move my desk to the window so that I can glance out as I write. It is a day of sweeping clouds and brilliant skies. As the clouds race across the heavens like ships in full sail before the wild March wind, their shadows fly before them, casting the valley first into darkness and then into light.

I watch the road that threads along the valley bottom and climbs the hill to Treroc. I remember the words of the Malay woman, so empty of meaning when she spoke them to me, so full of meaning now. "He will come to the house by the water."

The road is empty now, but one spring day I shall see Maxwell riding to me along its rutted surface.

One day soon.

THE FLAME OF THE BORGIAS

Jean Briggs

The torchlight flickered and shone over the figures moving to the swaying rhythms of the dance. Two people met and held each other's burning gaze across the crowded room.

She was Lucrezia Borgia, Duchess of Ferrara, wife to Duke Alfonso, part of a world of intrigue, corruption and violence. He was Pietro Bembo, a nobleman of Venice. Between them blazed a love that if discovered would spell death for them both. A love that burned from the crenellated walls of the palaces of Ferrara, to the bustling canals of Venice: from glittering formal evenings spent dancing under the malevolent eye of Cardinal Ippolito to nights in each other's arms. A love doomed to destruction.

FLAME AND THE FLOWER

Kathleen Woodiwiss

The Tempestuous epic of America's deep south at the end of the eighteenth century.

Heather Simmons escaped from the drudgery of her aunt's farm to what she imagined would be the magnificence of London high society. Instead she fell into a far more degrading captivity which took her from a squalid London dockside to the splendour of a Carolina plantation, as the unwilling companion of arrogant and devil-may-care Captain Brandon Birmingham. A man who had abducted her, robbed her of her virtue, and sworn never to let her go.

THE WOLF AND THE DOVE

Kathleen Woodiwiss

A novel of stirring passion and adventure set in Anglo-Saxon England.

The Normans swept across England, ravaging, pillaging, murdering, and at last they came to Darkenwald. When the massacre was over, only lovely Lady Aislinn survived to protect her vanquished people from the conqueror, but the price was servitude to Ragnor, one of the most hated knights in William's army

Then Wulfgar, the Iron Wolf of Normandy, came to claim Darkenwald as his prize of war, and Aislinn faced a more terrible bondage still, as she grew to love the enemy warrior who had destroyed her family, degraded her people, and despised her as a slave.

VOTE FOR A SILK GOWN

Jay Allerton

Three men wanted her: Max, ironic, witty, tied to a woman he despised, Guy who had loved her from the first moment he saw her, John with the quiet smile . . .

Janet Semple was blonde, intelligent, beautiful and she wanted perfection. When John Robson, the managing director promoted her to be his secretary, she was overjoyed. But the new job became a nightmare, for John Robson, a married man with three children, fell deeply in love with her, and Janet found herself see-sawing between happiness and despair as she realised that she would never be able to face life without him . . .

Winner of the Romantic Novelists Association Major Award for 1974

FALLS THE SHADOW

Regina Ross

Beautiful Nicola Beaufort is spirited, stubborn, and determined. Top British Intelligence agent Charles Forsyth is tough, resourceful, sardonic and experienced. Their initial encounter at Heathrow Airport is violent and explosive, setting a pattern that is to be repeated in the days ahead in distant Rumania, where both are seeking, for different reasons, Tony Rothman, fellow operative of Forsyth, and former lover of Nicola.

Plunged into a whirlpool of intrigue and violence, Nicola and Forsyth are drawn together against their will in a desperate race to reach the missing agent, as they realize that the key to their search lies in the discovery of the 1,000-year-old Crown of St Stephen, symbol of the Hungarian monarchy, buried somewhere in the heart of the mountains.

POLMARRAN TOWER

Charlotte Massey

Polmarran Tower stood high above the Cornish cliffs, a landmark for wreckers and smugglers, frowning over the sea.

Katherine Ainsley came to Polmarran as a governess to Adelaide Northwood, but found herself drawn into a vortex of terror. For over the house brooded the spirit of a woman who had once lived there, a woman whose very name drew a chilling silence from the Northwoods of Polmarran, and over Katherine's charge hung the shadow of a mystery that threatened the lives of both pupil and governess.

THE SEVENTEENTH STAIR

Barbara Paul

The velvet silence of the tower hung like a pall around her . . . she lay, drenched in a chill sweat of terror, straining to hear the sound that had woken her . . . then it came again . . . a low sobbing cry echoing through the lonely chateau.

Rosella Eastwood was summoned to Paris by her guardian, but when she arrived she found no one to greet her, only a will bequeathing her the Chateau de Louismont in the Loire Valley: a place of hated childhood memories, where she had to face the hatred of the Louismont family, the agony of loving a man who could never be free, and the evil secret of the west tower.